"Protect yourself from me, Victoria.

"That's important," Brandon whispered.

Victoria kept looking at him, though. It wasn't right to leave him like this—so vulnerable.

She *did* want to hold him. She wanted to be there for him when the lights turned down and his dreams grew harsh. She wanted to stroke his cheek and tell him it would be all right, because when he said her name, she felt pretty. And last night, he'd put his arm around her when she had really needed to be held.

He gave her things he probably didn't even realize, and now, when he was wounded and raw, she was going to walk away. They both knew it was the only choice she had.

But God

D0827224

Dear Reader,

They say all good things must end someday, and this month we bid a reluctant farewell to Nora Roberts' STARS OF MITHRA trilogy. *Secret Star* is a fitting windup to one of this *New York Times* bestselling author's most captivating miniseries ever. I don't want to give anything away, but I will say this: You're in for the ride of your life—and that's after one of the best openings ever. Enjoy!

Marilyn Pappano also wraps up a trilogy this month. *Knight Errant* is the last of her SOUTHERN KNIGHTS miniseries, the story of Nick Carlucci and the bodyguard he reluctantly accepts, then falls for—hook, line and sinker. Then say goodbye to MAXIMILLIAN'S CHILDREN, as reader favorite Alicia Scott offers *Brandon's Bride,* the book in which secrets are revealed and the last of the Ferringers finds love. Award-winning Maggie Price is back with her second book, *The Man She Almost Married,* and Christa Conan checks in with *One Night at a Time,* a sequel to *All I Need.* Finally, welcome new author Lauren Nichols, whose *Accidental Heiress* is a wonderful debut.

And then come back next month for more of the best romantic reading around—right here at Silhouette Intimate Moments.

Yours,

Leslie Wainger
Senior Editor and Editorial Coordinator

Please address questions and book requests to:
Silhouette Reader Service
U.S.: 3010 Walden Ave., P.O. Box 1325, Buffalo, NY 14269
Canadian: P.O. Box 609, Fort Erie, Ont. L2A 5X3

BRANDON'S BRIDE

ALICIA SCOTT

Published by Silhouette Books
America's Publisher of Contemporary Romance

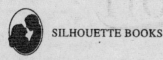

SILHOUETTE BOOKS

ISBN 0-373-07837-4

BRANDON'S BRIDE

Copyright © 1998 by Lisa Baumgartner

This edition published by arrangement with Harlequin Books S.A.

® and TM are trademarks of Harlequin Books S.A., used under license.
Trademarks indicated with ® are registered in the United States Patent
and Trademark Office, the Canadian Trade Marks Office and in other
countries.

Printed in U.S.A.

Books by Alicia Scott

Silhouette Intimate Moments

Walking After Midnight #466
Shadow's Flame #546
Waking Nightmare #586
At the Midnight Hour #658
Hiding Jessica #668
The Quiet One #701
The One Worth Waiting For #713
The One Who Almost Got Away #723
†*Maggie's Man* #776
†*MacNamara's Woman* #813
†*Brandon's Bride* #837

*The Guiness Gang
†Maximillian's Children

ALICIA SCOTT

recently escaped the corporate world to pursue her writing full-time. According to the former consultant, "I've always been a writer. It's the perfect job, and you just can't beat the dress code." Born in Hawaii, she grew up in Oregon before moving to New England. Recent winner of the *Romantic Times* award for Career Achievement in Series Romantic Suspense, she also writes mainstream suspense thrillers as Lisa Gardner.

Alicia is also proud to announce that she finally met the man of her dreams, so she'll stop holding out for that chocolate shop now. She and her soon-to-be hubby have settled down in Rhode Island, where they are raising two cats and a bunny.

Alicia loves to hear from readers! You can reach her c/o NEC, P.O. Box 1667, Framingham, MA 10701-1667.

Special thanks to Ted Johnson, Assistant Fire Management Officer Ochoco National Forest, and Lance Honda, Superintendent Redmond Hotshot Crew, for sharing their time, expertise and war stories. I am not sure any book can do the true heroics of the Hotshots justice, but I have done my best.

And to the gang from Penn—Jenn, Drew, Chris, Jon, Mark, Gabi, Parris and Michelle. Here's to all the New Year's Eves to come.

Finally, to Anthony, my love, my life, my anchor. Thank you.

Prologue

Ray Bands could count the cumulating days by the number of crumpled pretzel bags and empty diet sodas piling up on the surveillance van's metal floor. In the beginning, he'd thought absently of bringing a wastebasket for his next shift. Now he waded through the crinkling, salty cellophane without a second thought. It wasn't his van, anyway. And in his line of work, neatness didn't count.

Results did.

He stretched up his arms again, rolled his old, creaking neck, then adjusted his headphones. The screens in front of him remained static, the large reels of tapes frozen, waiting for a sound to trigger them to action. Still nothing happening. Ray propped his feet on a milk crate, opened a fresh bag of fat-free pretzels and stared at them morosely. He wanted French fries.

Ray had grown up during the days when food was just food and you were happy you got some. No fat-free this or free-range that. For God's sake, who ever would have believed that food that contained so much less—less fat, less sodium, less cholesterol, less *taste*, for crying out loud—could actually cost *more*. It defied the imagination.

But then last year, he'd started dating a granola-crunching, sassy-mouthed aerobics instructor who was a fraction of his age and so damn beautiful she took his breath away. She had him eating puffed rice cakes, lean meats and fresh vegetables. He'd given up cigarettes. He'd given up beer. He'd joined a health club where young, nubile bodies preened in front of mirrors so shamelessly he didn't know where to look.

And there were nights he woke up just so he could watch Melissa sleep, her dark hair like a satin frame around her pale, ethereal face. God, she was gorgeous. And then he would wonder what a sweet girl like her was doing with a beat-up old geezer like him. Sometimes, he thought she had to be KGB, but those days were gone, of course. No more cloak-and-dagger. No more evil empire. He'd survived it all without seeing half the glory he'd thought he would. Hell, he was four years from retirement and they'd pulled him off his current case to eavesdrop on a semiretired Wall Street investment banker.

On cue, the screens in front of him abruptly blinked to life. Sound waves undulated across the black backdrop, spiking to indicate louder noises. Brandon Ferringer was finally awake in his Manhattan apartment.

From the little the powers that be had deemed to tell Ray, Ferringer was one of those Richie Rich thrill-seeker types. In the four years since his young wife's death, he'd been running around the globe hell-bent on either adventure or suicide, depending how you looked at it. He'd just returned from Nepal, which must have been something because the man had been asleep for five straight days. Now, at last, Ray could hear him moving about.

Ray adjusted the headphones and focused on the four primary screens. The mike in the bathroom reported the sound of a shower running, then the brisk whisk, whisk of someone toweling off. Footsteps pattered down the hall, and the kitchen mike transmitted the sound of a coffee grinder roaring to life.

Brandon's cell phone was turned on. Finally getting some action, the van's reel tapes kicked to life and recorded the call. Ferringer didn't have phone service reconnected to his apartment yet. A big break for Ray. Bugging a landline phone sometimes caused interference or small clicks that gave the wiretapping away. Cellular phones, on the other hand, didn't require a bug. If you knew the frequency, you could eavesdrop or trace a call to your heart's content. Ferringer had obviously been monitored before—the frequency, serial number and PIN of his cell phone had been included in his dossier.

The ringing was staticky. The high-rises didn't always get the best reception—too many steel girders got in the way. At the other end, a man finally picked up.

"C.J.'s Mortuary. You stab 'em, we slab 'em."

"C.J.," Brandon said.

"My God!" the other man replied.

Frowning, Ray dug through the pile of empty pretzel bags until he found Ferringer's file. Who the hell was C.J., and why would Ferringer call a mortician? After a moment, Ray solved the mystery. According to the file, Ferringer had two half-siblings, Maggie Ferringer and C. J. MacNamara. They all shared the same father, Maximillian Ferringer, whose plane went down in Indonesia in 1972. His body was never found.

The MacNamara son had entered the Marines, Force Recon. Now he lived in Sedona, Arizona, where he owned a bar and worked part-time as a "bail enforcement officer."

Ray snorted. Bounty hunters were nothing but a bunch of cop wannabes who couldn't make the cut. Loser bastards, every last one of them. Then again, judging by the grainy black and white, MacNamara probably didn't do too badly with the ladies.

"Holy smokes, look what the cat dragged in," C.J. said at last. "It's been what, four, five months? How are you, Brandon, and where the hell have you been?"

"Everest."

"As in the mountain? Hell, Brandon. People die on Everest!"

"I didn't."

"Obviously God does look after fools then."

"Which you also know firsthand," Brandon replied wryly. "How are you, C.J.? And how is Tamara?"

Tamara Allistair was listed in the file as a public relations executive who currently lived with MacNamara. See file, Senator Brennan. Ray had no idea what that meant.

"Oh, we're fine. Tamara just set up shop here in Sedona, and it's going well. We've set the wedding date for September. I don't suppose you'll be in the Northern Hemisphere sometime around then."

"Actually, I'm planning on spending the next six months in Oregon. I was selected to be a hotshot."

"What?" Ray seconded C.J.'s surprise.

"Our father gave Maggie a locket," Brandon said quietly. "Did she ever tell you that? Inside, there's a picture of a beautiful woman. She's not one of our mothers."

"Surprise, surprise. Now what does that have to do with Oregon?"

"I—well, Julia—also discovered that Max had two business partners, Al Simmons and Bud Irving. Lydia says they were all best friends from Tillamook High School. They formed the partnership right after graduation, and according to the Chamber of Commerce records, it's never been dissolved. Don't suppose you know about that?''

"Maximillian and partners? Give me a break, Brandon, the man didn't even send postcards to his wives or children. Can you picture him working with two other people?''

"Al Simmons disappeared in 1970," Brandon said softly, "but I've traced Bud Irving to Beaverville, Oregon.''

"Uh, Brandon. When you say this Al guy disappeared, what do you mean by disappeared?''

"I mean I can't find any trace of Al Simmons after 1970. No taxes, no driver's license renewals, no credit cards, no bank accounts. No death certificate. As of 1970, Al Simmons ceased to exist.''

"That's not a good thing. Ceasing to exist is never a good thing.''

"No, it probably isn't.''

"Brandon..." C.J.'s sigh was audible over the line, but the brothers' argument must have been old, because Brandon cut him off at the pass.

"You think it's too dangerous," Brandon supplied.

"Absolutely.''

"You think Max has been dead for twenty-five years, why mess with it now?''

"Let sleeping dogs lie," C.J. agreed.

"C.J., don't you think it's odd that in a partnership of three people, two have disappeared without a trace? One in 1970 and one in 1972. I've been to the wreckage of Max's plane in Indonesia. There's no good reason his body wasn't found. Something is going on here, C.J. And the answer lies with Bud Irving in Beaverville, Oregon.''

On the other end of the line, C.J. was silent.

"I have to know," Brandon said quietly.

"Brandon, this isn't a walk in the park. I've gotten threatening phone calls about Max. You—"

"I may have lost my wife," Brandon stated.

"The police said she was shot by a mugger."

"She was researching Max for my family tree and then she was shot? Bloody hell, it was a mugger!" His voice was abruptly savage.

"You don't know—"

"And neither do you, C.J. Neither do you!" Brandon exclaimed.

Whoa. Ray sat back, impressed. MacNamara was a Marine, and Marines were known for their temper, but he never would have picked an intellectual Wall Street banker as the passionate type. Apparently, Brandon had inherited more of Maximillian the Chameleon's genes than either of the brothers realized.

The apple never did fall far from the tree.

And Maximillian the Chameleon had been some apple.

His sons were taking deep breaths and working on cooling their tempers.

"Let me come out there," C.J. said.

"No, you have Tamara. I won't jeopardize that."

"That's not your decision—"

"I will call you if there's a problem. Mail my wedding invite to Lydia's, would you? And C.J., congratulations, man. I wish you the best."

"Brandon…" C.J. sounded disgruntled. Then he sighed. "Just be careful, all right? I want you at my wedding, dammit. And I want my wedding day to be as happy as yours. You know?"

"That was a special day, wasn't it?" Ferringer said softly. "Yours will be special, too, C.J. Congratulations."

He hung up before his brother could reply.

The cell phone wasn't turned on again. No sound came

from the apartment for so long Ray almost panicked, but then he replayed the conversation in his mind and got a visual image of Brandon Ferringer standing at the window of his Manhattan penthouse, gazing at a world-class view of Central Park and seeing only his wife, Julia, on their wedding day.

Ray's eyes got a little moist. Christ, he was becoming a maudlin old fool. But then he started thinking of Melissa again, and wouldn't it be something to see her in wedding whites? And what would he do if something ever happened to her?

He shook his head, knowing white picket fences would never exist for a man like him. And Melissa really could do better.

He took off the headphones, found a land-line phone and dialed from memory. In his line of work, phone numbers, names and instructions were never written down. If you couldn't remember it, you deserved your fate.

"Subject's on the move," he said without preamble.

"Details."

Ray recapped the conversation. At the other end, the man fell silent. Ray wasn't sure exactly who he was. He had proper clearance and knew the passwords, which was all that mattered.

"Follow him," the man said. "Stay on him. If he gets too close, kill him."

"All right." On the road again. Melissa wouldn't like that, but what could he do? *I'm a salesman, honey, I have to travel. But don't worry. I'm four years from retirement. Just four years from retirement.*

"Make it look accidental. Incredibly so. We don't want MacNamara involved."

The former Marine, Force Recon. That made sense. "All right."

"Don't call again unless things have changed. The less contact, the better."

"Sure." Ray hung up, not required to bother with such pleasantries as goodbye. He put on the headphones. No sound. Ferringer must still be at the window. Did he miss his Julia that much? Or was he thinking about his father and how badly he wanted to know the truth?

Some things aren't meant to be known, Ferringer, not even in this day and age.

Ray began plotting his strategy. With his feet up and his mind running through a list of the best "accidents," he opened a new bag of pretzels and bit into a rock-hard mass. Traffic accidents were always suspicious, tampering with machinery better. House fires were pretty good, or electrocution. Maybe a nice shove off a cliff.

He bit the pretzel wrong and almost cracked a tooth. God, he missed potato chips.

Chapter 1

Even with the real estate agent's directions, it took Brandon three tries to find the Lady Luck Ranch. The first time, he assumed the dirt trail splicing off from the main road was a forgotten forestry path. After driving another five miles, he turned and went back. Beaverville, Oregon, wasn't that big. Downtown was a collection of six gray-weathered storefronts that could've been mistaken for a ghost town if not for the single golden pine addition gleaming on the corner.

Twenty-six people served, the dust-covered sign joked at the corner grocery deli. The new store turned out to be a cattle feed shop, its front porch and back loading docks buried beneath huge burlap bags of grain. Next to it, a hunting store boasted a dozen gleaming rifles in the windows and enough boxes of bullets to make the NRA proud. Next to it was a beat old saloon claiming to be Whiskey Jack's. *Two hundred and sixty* people served, its sign boasted.

Brandon got the impression Beaverville might be just slightly different from Manhattan.

He passed the high school. At first glance, he thought the simple three-story cabin was someone's home, but then he spotted the football field next door and discerned the fallen, two-hundred-year-old tree trunk with Beaverville High School branded into its bark. The town hadn't wasted much money on the slightly tottering school. On the other hand, the taxpayers took football seriously. The lines were freshly painted brilliant white, the wooden bleachers were carefully stained, and a decent size snack bar advertised beer, hot dogs, and Tums, all for seventy-five cents apiece.

"Wonderful," Brandon murmured. "Let the good times roll." He'd spent the whole night on a red-eye flight and the whole morning driving. After four years of rigorous hiking in the vast outdoors, he'd developed a healthy loathing of confinement. He wanted to stretch his long, lean legs. He wanted to draw real air into his scratchy throat and feel fresh wind against his face. He wanted out of his car.

He headed down Highway 26. He still didn't see any signs of a ranch.

In another couple of weeks, these dry, barren fields would be covered in lush prairie grass and pink foxglove, all rimmed by the snowcapped mountains rising majestically in the horizon. Now, however, the landscape was arid and desolate, a stark compilation of tinder-dry sagebrush and persnickety prairie grass poking out of red, dusty soil. One bolt of lightning, and the whole thing could burst into flame, walls of fire reaching two hundred feet high, sounding like a jet engine and racing eighty miles per hour. Deer would scatter and fall. Hundred-year-old oaks would burn so badly their stumps would smolder well into November.

Brandon remembered it all vividly—the heat, the smell, the roaring sound, the bloodred sun, the unquenchable thirst. The enormous awe of seeing what nature could do. Boss Hoggins, the superintendent from the White Mountains, had told Brandon that once a man saw a true wildland fire, he never was the same. Four years ago, Brandon had been in the flames. And Boss Hoggins was right—he'd never looked at Mother Nature the same way since.

Brandon hit the center of town again, scowled and turned around. *"The Lady Luck Ranch is just off the highway,"* the real estate agent had said. *"The only ranch around for miles. Just look for the sign. Can't miss it."*

"Can't miss it," he mocked. "Can't miss it."

Brandon began to contemplate wringing the real estate agent's neck.

The dirt road loomed to his right again. Abruptly Brandon slammed on the brakes and brought the car to a grinding halt, his gaze glued to one of the more impressive examples of sagebrush. Funny, but that looked like a piece of wood tangled in those prickly limbs. Say, a sign.

Brandon climbed out of his car, thinned his lips impatiently and stalked toward the offending plant. Oh, yes, that was a sign, all right. The Lady Luck Ranch sign.

"Your mother was a cactus," he informed the bush coldly, picked up the sign and stuck it on the barbed wire fence. He turned his red rent-a-wreck down the path. The car jostled over the overgrown dirt road hard enough to rattle his bones.

If he ever found this damn ranch, he was never getting into a car again.

The road wove around and around, gradually beginning to climb. The brush gave way to a thick grove of pine trees that blocked the stark sun. Abruptly, the ranch appeared.

A beat-up pickup truck sat in the circular dirt drive, colored red by more rust than paint. The wooden cabin was small, the patio dusted with yellow soil. Covered by a thick carpet of pine needles and moss, the roof sagged in one corner while the chimney crumbled dangerously. The front door had weathered differently than the rest of the house—a newer addition that already leaned on its hinges. The place obviously needed some work, and the neighboring stables didn't look much better.

But blue gingham curtains waved cheerily at the square windows. Planters rimming the patio offered red, pink and yellow tulips. Two brightly colored horse blankets were draped over the railings to dry. A rocking chair in one corner had a thick yellow and blue comforter draped over the back and looked well-used. What the place lacked in money, it made up in atmosphere. That was good enough for Brandon.

He climbed out of his car. He didn't see any sign of people, but an orange striped cat appeared, wrapping its purring form around his legs in a long procession of figure eights. After a minute, Brandon squatted to scratch the tom-cat behind his ears.

"Do you know where I can find Victoria Meese?" he asked the cat, since it was all he had to work with.

The cat purred smugly, blinking wise gold eyes. C.J. used to have an orange cat named Speedy. For years, there was nothing the Marine could wear that wasn't covered in blond fur.

"How about renting me a room?" Brandon tried again. "I'll buy you only the best cat food and fill your litter box with shredded money. Why not? I haven't had much luck getting rid of the stuff any other way."

The tomcat, no idiot, leaned against Brandon's leg and purred wholehearted approval.

"Big stubborn…" A husky voice spat a string of curses into the silence, and Brandon rose instantly, searching for the source. "Come on, into the corner. Move it. You little... I shoulda let them turn you into glue!"

Brandon followed the stream of disparaging words into the stables. The row of empty stalls gave way to the feed center. There, a blond woman in dusty Levi's and a torn plaid shirt was wrestling with a thousand-pound gelding and losing. She obviously wanted the big gray horse to back up into the covered arena attached to the stables. He obviously had no intention of doing any such thing.

"Would you like some help?" Brandon called.

She barely spared him a glance. "Nah. Doc doesn't like strangers. You step forward and he'll probably trample us both."

Brandon looked at four hard hooves the size of salad plates. He didn't take another step. In the meantime, the woman took a firm hold of the reins and tugged down the gray's head.

"Hey, you," she chastised. "Pay attention to me. Now move your big butt backward." Her voice was deep and firm, the kind guaranteed to get immediate obedience from small children and dumb animals.

For emphasis, she leaned against the horse's shoulder, pushing him along. Her long, blunt-cut blond hair swept forward, liberally decorated with straw. On the reins, her dark, dusky hands were fisted, her forearms dark and strong, her fingernails dirty and short. Compact build. Nicely curved legs. A very capable woman. And an attractive one.

With a last oomph, she shoved the gray beast into the dusty arena and triumphantly slammed the gate shut. The horse pawed the ground a few times, then shook his mane as if to say, "Well, I never!"

"Next time, I will turn you into glue." Shaking her head,

she brushed off her hands, picked up her gloves and turned toward Brandon.

"So what can I help you with?" She pinned him with a direct, blue gaze that brought his intelligence to an immediate halt. He'd never seen eyes that color before, not blue, not gray, but somewhere in between. Bright, vivid, intelligent eyes. Riveting, clear, honest eyes.

"Hello?" she quizzed. Brandon shut his gaping mouth.

"Ah, are you Victoria Meese?"

She chewed on a piece of hay jutting out of the corner of her mouth, appearing slightly wary. "Who wants to know?"

"I'm here about the rental. An agency in Redmond told me about it."

"Oh, that." She relaxed instantly, picked up two hay hooks and matter-of-factly stabbed them into a bale. The movement drew his eyes to her denim-clad legs again. "Got a one-room cabin out back," she said as she hefted the bale. "Not much to it, but it's clean and furnished. It was meant as quarters for a foreman or stable manager, but the Lady Luck Ranch isn't that lucky these days."

She dumped the bale on the ground and with two short jerks snapped the baling wire, then began peeling off leafs of alfalfa. "The cabin's a hundred dollars a month. It doesn't have its own bathroom or kitchen, but there's a bathroom in the stables and I fix breakfast every morning. If you're looking for luxury, this isn't it. But it's a sturdy little place, the bed's comfortable, and spring around here is worth seeing. Are you interested?"

"I don't require luxury," he told her honestly. She was walking down the center aisle, depositing bundles of alfalfa to the four waiting horses as she went. At the last stall, the horse blew softly into her hair, scattering hay. She smiled at the oversize beast and patted his shoulder.

''The lease agreement is simple,'' she called to Brandon. ''Just pay me one month up front and give me four weeks' notice before you move. I'll need you to fill out some forms—name, permanent address, employment, Mr...''

''Ferringer. Brandon Ferringer.''

''What brings you to these parts, Mr. Ferringer?''

''I am a hotshot,'' he said quietly.

''What?'' She straightened abruptly against the stall, startling her horse and apparently herself. ''*You're* the last hotshot?''

Beaverville didn't have much, but from spring to fall it was the premiere spot for training and deploying hotshots around the country. When the big wildland fires broke out, the Smokejumpers parachuted into the hard-to-reach areas and launched the first wave of attack. The hotshots followed like ground-force Marines, hiking through rugged terrain with twenty-five pounds of equipment on their backs, clearing the brush, digging the fire trenches and working, working, working while the roaring flames stained their faces black.

''I'm going to be a hotshot,'' Brandon agreed, confused by her reaction. She still looked flustered.

''*You're* the hero from New York?''

''I'm...I'm from New York.'' Hero? How had that got out?

Victoria was waving a hand as if to clear the air. ''Sorry, I'm making a mess of this. I know all about the hotshots, you see. My brother Charlie also made the crew. Beaverville's team is only eighteen people, and with sixteen returnees, only two slots opened up. Charlie got one, and according to the rumor mill, some hero from New York got the second.''

''Oh,'' Brandon said with feeling. He'd forgotten about the rumor mill. The forestry service was notoriously cliquish, with everyone knowing everyone and talking about everyone. Except for Brandon. He was officially the outsider in a world unaccustomed to outsiders.

Victoria was giving him a frank up and down. "If you don't mind me saying, you're not what we expected. For starters, you should be ten years younger."

"I'm thirty-six."

"That old? Charlie's twenty-two."

Brandon made a face. "They're probably all kids, aren't they?"

"Hardly a soul over twenty-eight," she assured him. "But then, none of them can say they rescued two kids in the middle of a blowout."

"It was luck."

"Really? I'd say taking on a wildland fire in the Presidential range was less about fortune and more about a death wish."

Brandon didn't comment. That fire had happened only six months after Julia's funeral, so she might very well have a point.

"Well," Victoria said when it become apparent he wasn't going to elaborate, "that must have been some experience, Brandon Ferringer, because Superintendent Coleton Smith hates to take outsiders onto his crew, but he accepted you. Two hundred applications for that slot, men he knows and has personally worked with on the district crews, and he chose you."

Brandon smiled wanly. "I'm in good shape, even for an old guy."

A wry gleam suddenly appeared in Victoria Meese's clear gaze. "Oh, I won't argue that." She gave him a sudden, flashing grin. "Boy, you are going to have a fun summer. Come on, hotshot. I'll show you the cabin."

True to Victoria's description, the cabin wasn't much.

Built as a miniature of the main house, it had the same aging roof. Inside, however, he found a decent-size room that was well-maintained and smelled of lemon wax. The furniture was old, probably garage sale bargains, but Victoria had done her best with it. A hand-sewn blue gingham slipcover brightened up the couch, while an old blue and green quilt decorated the double bed. The cabin didn't offer a kitchen, but an old yellow counter against the back wall provided a sink and an outlet for a hot pot. Mostly, the small quarters offered a stunning view of the back pasture framed by the mountains. Dappled with sunlight, two new-born foals kicked and frolicked close to their mothers' protective forms.

"What do you think?" She rested against the doorjamb, her arms crossed over her chest, her gaze patient as he inspected the room.

"It's perfect, Victoria."

"Please, call me Vic. Only my mother calls me Victoria. And my brothers when they're trying to get my goat."

"A lot of brothers?" he guessed.

"Six. Three older, three younger. I didn't exactly grow up playing with dolls."

"But you had the best arm on the Little League team?"

She grinned unabashedly. "Exactly. Listen, I'm happy you're interested in the place, but there are a few things you should know." She straightened in the doorway and suddenly got down to business. Brandon waited obediently.

"My father is the sheriff around here," she said levelly. "You might as well know that, because he's going to conduct the background check from hell on you. In Beaverville, we don't have any secrets."

"I don't have anything to hide."

"Okay. Two, I have an eight-year-old son."

"Pardon?" She didn't look a day older then twenty-six.

"I'm twenty-seven," she said crisply, as if reading his thoughts. "That makes it no less stupid, but a little more legal—"

"It's none of my business—"

"Damn right. But for the record," she took a deep breath and spoke more quietly. "I have a great son. A fabulous kid, and I really want to keep him that way. So, while this place is yours, I do ask that you set a good example. No drunken, disorderly, loud parties, no, um, well, women."

He said, "I'm a thirty-six-year-old widower. I'm not exactly into wild parties, and don't worry about women."

"Oh." Her expression softened instantly as people's always did when he said he was a widower. At least Victoria's gaze didn't look pitying. Her blue eyes had merely gentled in a philosophic, understanding sort of way.

"That's hard," she said.

"It was a tough time."

"Well." Her tone became brisk. "That brings me to the last consideration. My ex-husband didn't die—he went to jail for two years for dealing dope. I got a restraining order against him, but he was paroled last week, and sooner or later, he'll come around."

"You think he'll try to kidnap your son?"

"Ronald?" She shook her head vehemently. "Oh, no, he has no interest in parenting. It's money he wants. My father is keeping as much an eye on him as possible, but if you see a dark-haired man around here, feel free to grab a shotgun. My brothers are all blond, and they're the only men who should ever set foot on this property. I'm sorry, but don't keep anything of value in your cabin. I can't run a ranch and sit guard on the house, and if Ronald does come by…" She shrugged, and that pretty much said it all. "There you go, Ferringer. All dirty laundry is on the line."

"And it's quite an impressive assortment," he said respectfully.

"Not bad for a twenty-seven-year-old, huh? So tell me, Ferringer, are you interested in the place?"

"The cabin is perfect."

"Really?" She sounded genuinely shocked, then caught herself. "Huh. I'm not sure if that makes you crazy, or just nice enough to have around." She glanced at him again, more contemplative this time, and suddenly, something in the air simply caught.

Brandon's gut got a rolling, tight feel he hadn't experienced in a long, long time. His breathing grew shallow. He became hyperaware of the smear of dust of her high cheekbone and the way her red lips parted in shock.

He was startled. She was startled. And damn, for a moment he did want to cross the room, encircle her waist...

Brandon cleared his throat. Victoria quickly looked away. "Um. We're all set, then?" he asked.

"Huh. Hmm. Well," she said, and took a deep breath. "I'm gonna fetch the paperwork," she announced abruptly. "My father will check you out ASAP."

"Fine." He still sounded hoarse. "Um...may I borrow the bathroom in the stables to clean up? I've been traveling since eight o'clock last night."

"Oh. Sure. Need anything?"

"I'm fine, thank you."

"Okay." She pushed away from the doorjamb hastily, and they were both happy for the distance. "My son will be home from baseball practice around six," she called as she headed for the steps. "You'll know when he arrives by the sound of the earth shaking."

"Got it."

She made it halfway down the steps, then halted. He was

staring. He had the tingling feeling along his spine again. He found himself leaning forward.

She turned abruptly. "Would you like to join Randy and me for dinner? If the security check works out, of course. It's...it's always good for everyone to know their neighbors."

"Neighbors. Of course. That would be nice. It is good to know your neighbors."

"Yeah. Neighbors. See you around seven." She took off and disappeared inside the house. He finally expelled the breath he'd been holding. Belatedly, he shook his head as if that would rattle his thoughts into order.

It wasn't like him to react in such a way to a woman. It just wasn't. And yet here he was, struggling for a second breath.

From the day he was born, Brandon had been different. Other children laughed, other children played, other children invented wild, nonsensical games. Not Brandon. He'd been quiet, somber and unbearably aware of the tension in his family. His most vivid memory of his father was Max striding out the front door saying, "Time to deal, time to deal."

Max hadn't dealt well. He'd squandered the family estate, cheated on Brandon's mother and left behind a legacy of bitterness. And from the time he could walk, Brandon had known it was his job to fix things. He was the oldest son. He needed to make things right.

He went to Wharton on a scholarship and graduated with honors. Then he worked hundred-and-twenty-hour weeks on Wall Street for money, money, money. He bought back the family estate when he was twenty-five. He built the perfect *GQ* life. He did everything he thought he was supposed to do. And his mother informed him he was just like his father—a cold, materialistic, workaholic.

There was nothing in Brandon's life to prove her wrong.

The thought banked the last of the embers in his mind, and his shoulders tightened with a familiar tension. He should go jogging. In the last four years, he'd discovered that if he ran far enough, fast enough, hard enough, sometimes he could escape his demons.

Instead, he stood silently on the wooden porch in springfilled Oregon and thought of Julia and how she'd looked in that ridiculously short pink waitress uniform the first time he'd met her. She'd been so flustered, she'd poured steaming coffee onto his silk tie. Then she'd started to laugh as she'd tried valiantly to repair the damage. Then, somehow, he'd started laughing, too. Stuffy Brandon Ferringer giggling over coffee spilled on his two-hundred-dollar tie.

He'd never realized how much Julia had brought into his sterile existence until she'd died. He'd never realized how much she made him laugh until he was alone in the silence.

He'd never realized how much he'd loved her and how little he'd given her until he stood at her grave and realized his mother was right. He was like his father. He'd married a woman, he'd loved a woman and he'd given her nothing of himself.

More than C.J., more than Maggie, Brandon was Maximillian the Chameleon's child.

Later, after a long, hot shower and badly needed nap, Brandon unpacked his single duffel bag while a spring sunset washed the world with shades of gold. In the distance, Victoria called to her horses. Her son arrived home with a high-spirited roar of greeting and the sharp snap of the screen door slapping shut.

Brandon removed the sweatshirts and jeans from his duffel bag, piling them onto the quilt until he came to the waterproof pouch tucked securely in the bottom. He opened it slowly and carefully placed its precious contents on the bed—the heart-shaped locket Maggie had received from their father and a slim, bound blue book titled *Tillamook High School, 1955.* The locket contained the portrait of a beautiful woman no one could identify. The high-school yearbook offered pictures of Max with his two best friends and business partners, Al Simmons and Bud Irving.

After four years of investigating, these were the only clues Brandon had to his father's enigmatic life and death, as well as a mysterious phone call C.J. had received six months ago from a voice he didn't recognize. The caller had wanted to exchange information of Max's life in return for C.J. backing off a case. C.J. being C.J., he had said no.

We've been watching you for a long time, the voice had said. *You're almost as good as your father. You're just a little too straight.*

Had Maximillian been involved in something illegal? Had Max's plane crash in Indonesia been accidental? *Was Maximillian even dead?* Twenty-five years later, his body had never been found.

Footsteps came running up the wooden porch in rapid staccato, sounding like a thundering bull. Brandon moved quickly, sliding the yearbook and locket beneath his mattress just as Randy Meese's small, wiry form filled the doorway.

Randy had his mother's blond hair covering his head like an unruly mop. It might have been carefully combed once, but now strands stuck out in every direction as befit an energetic, sports-crazy, horse-crazy eight-year-old boy. His face was liberally covered with freckles and he was missing one front tooth. The gapped smile fit him.

He rolled back on his battered sneakers, stuck his grubby hands through the loops of his faded, dust-covered jeans and gave the new guy a thorough once-over.

"Huh," Randy declared at last, his voice high-pitched. "I'm supposed to invite you to dinner." He scowled fiercely so Brandon would know Randy was still contemplating extending the invitation.

"I see," Brandon said and waited patiently.

Randy wriggled against the doorway, using the doorjamb to get at an itch on his back. His red flannel shirt was brand-new, uncomfortable and two sizes too big so he could grow into it. From what he understood, his father was a decent-size man so he had a solid future of growing ahead of him. Good thing, too. It was hard to be intimidating as the man of house when you were only four feet tall. Randy was strong, though, and tough. His baseball coach called him fierce.

"Mom says you're gonna be a hotshot," Randy stated. He narrowed his eyes like Clint Eastwood did when interrogating bad guys.

"That's right."

"You're too old," Randy said flatly. Jimeeny, the guy was *at least* thirty, definitely one step from the grave.

"That seems to be the consensus," Brandon agreed.

"What's consensus?"

"Um, it means other people have said the same."

"Then why are you doing it? My uncle Charlie says only the leanest, meanest bast—uh, guys are fit to be hotshots. You're just old."

Brandon did his best not to wince. "Yes, I think we've covered that. But for the record, I've done a thing or two."

"Like what?"

Brandon contemplated the boy. He recognized the intense look, the determination to be tough. Randy was the eight-year-old man in the family. Brandon respected that.

Brandon squatted. He spoke man-to-man. "I've gone scuba diving in open seas."

"That's just water."

"I've hiked the volcanoes of Indonesia. The ground shakes and pops beneath your feet. You have to watch your step. One wrong move, the hot lava bursts beneath you and sprays sulfur all over your legs."

Randy appeared slightly more interested. "Oozing rocks, huh?"

"I've done peak bagging," Brandon said sagely. "Do you know what peak bagging is?"

"Peak bagging? What's a peak? Does it have fangs? Does it growl? Can it tear you from limb to limb?"

"Not quite. A peak is the top of a mountain. The very tippy-top most people never see. You know how early explorers—"

"Lewis and Clark."

"Yes, Lewis and Clark. They went into hard, brutal terrain most people would never attempt to cross. Peak bagging is like that. You hike up tough mountains and rough trails most people wouldn't be able to handle. You have to be in a great shape, have strong legs, good lungs. You have to be willing to keep climbing even when your whole body wants to stop.

"Then, when you reach the top of the peak, you've bagged it. Some people bag the different peaks of the Appalachian Trail. Some people try to bag the fourteen-thousand-foot peaks around the globe. Then there are peaks over twenty thousand feet high, so tall and so cold, you have to bring your own oxygen."

"Have *you* done twenty-thousand-foot peaks?"

"Yes," Brandon said quietly. "Everest."

"Mount Everest!" Randy's eyes went saucer-wide. "Did you make it to the *top*?"

"Not quite. The weather took a turn for the worse. But we were close."

"What was it like? Did it hurt? Was it hard?"

"The hardest thing I've ever done," Brandon said honestly. "And it was the most beautiful place in the world. Everest is twenty-nine thousand and twenty-eight feet tall, give or take ten feet because of snow. Up that high, the whole world is thick and white and the sun glints blue off the ice caps. It's like walking on top of the world, through the clouds."

"I bet it was dangerous," Randy said shrewdly.

"It was dangerous."

"Did people die?"

Brandon hesitated. "It was dangerous." Two men in their team had died. Sometimes Brandon still dreamed of the men's frozen blue faces and wide-open eyes. Sometimes, he dreamed that they were him.

"Keeewl," Randy drawled breathlessly. "Wait till I tell Mom!"

He leapt off the porch, went racing pell-mell across the yard, then came to a skittering halt that churned up plumes of red dust. "You're supposed to come, too," he called. "It's dinner!"

"Oh," Brandon said, having not understood that part. He straightened slowly, feeling suddenly hesitant about approaching the main house and sitting down with Randy and Victoria. It would be such a cozy scene. Homey, comfortable. Those were things Brandon hadn't felt in a long, long time.

"Hurry up!" Randy yelled from across the yard. His impatient look clearly stated that if they didn't eat absolutely, positively *now,* the food would magically disappear and they would both starve. Brandon got moving.

Randy scurried up to the front porch then waited, propping open the door with his hip and working the laces of his sneakers. "No shoes in the house."

"All right." Brandon removed his worn hiking boots and placed them side by side by the door. Randy tossed his tennis shoes in two different directions. One landed beneath the rocking chair.

"Gotta wash up before dinner. Do the back of your neck, Mom checks."

"I see."

Randy led him to the utility room just inside the door. A big old metal sink, rimmed with eight kinds of disinfectants and cleansers, loomed. Randy took up a position on the right side. Brandon went left. They stood shoulder to shoulder, preparing for battle.

"The trick is to lather up good," Randy informed him. "Specially 'cause then you smell like soap, and if you smell like soap, she won't look so hard."

"Good point."

Randy scrubbed his face so hard his freckles should've come off. Then he passed the lumpy bar of soap, and Brandon lathered up. Under Randy's watchful gaze, he washed the back of his neck, too, finally earning the boy's nod of approval.

Victoria found them a moment later, Randy hunched over the sink, his face soapy and water sticking his oversize red shirt to his thin shoulders and bony little-boy's frame. Beside him, Brandon filled out the room with the unmistakable form of a man. Wet spikes of hair rimmed his crinkled blue eyes. Beads of water trailed down the smooth line of his square-cut jaw and dampened his blue chambray shirt. His lean fingers gripped the soap, squishing white suds across the back of his bronzed skin and drawing her gaze to the rippling strength of his forearms.

"Oh, my," she whispered, stomach tightening. She'd told herself the moment in the cabin had been a product of her imagination. Obviously she'd lied, because here was Brandon Ferringer, damp and soapy, and heaven help her, she was growing warm all over.

Her son was looking at her curiously. She whisked herself to attention. "I mean, oh, my, it looks like you're both ready for dinner."

Randy promptly thrust out his hands and face. "I'm washed up! Time to eat."

"I smell like soap," Brandon said modestly.

"You put on a new shirt," Randy accused Victoria shrewdly. "Why'd y'change your shirt?"

Uh-oh, she was busted. She'd hoped her son wouldn't notice, but fat chance of that. Like any good eight-year-old, Randy only ignored things that could be used against him in a court of law. She squirmed beneath her own child's gaze, twisting the hem of her shirt. The shirt wasn't much, just an old plaid shirt like the rest of her wardrobe. Of course, it was lavender and she'd been told it highlighted her eyes, but that had nothing to do with it.

Her son was still staring at her, astute enough to make Torquemada proud. "Uh, my other shirt had hay on it," she tried.

"Your shirts always have hay on them."

"Gee, you're all washed up. Why don't you go sit at the table now?"

"Okay!" The promise of food sent Randy bolting from

the room. Child-rearing was definitely ten percent skill, ninety percent blatant bribery.

Victoria turned toward Brandon, hoping she looked natural, figuring she probably didn't. Ferringer, on the other hand, looked great. When he'd arrived this afternoon, he'd looked too grim, worn around the edges. Now, however, his shoulders were down, his face was relaxed. She'd recognize her son's handiwork anywhere.

"Isn't he something?" she said.

"I like him," Brandon said promptly and looked a little dazed. Yep, Randy had that affect on people.

She began to relax, but Brandon took a step forward, she inhaled instinctively, and her pulse skittered out of control. Lord help her, he did smell like soap. Good strong spicy manly soap. She swore it didn't smell like that on her brothers.

"Thank you for the dinner invite, Victoria. Generally I just eat alone."

"No problem," she said in a voice that was two octaves too high, then dug her fingernails into her palm. Dammit, she was too old and too sensible for this. Sure Brandon Ferringer was a good-looking man in that rugged outdoorsy sort of way, but she had a ranch to run and a son to raise. She was beyond the stage of being easily impressed by the male half of the species. Now, if he knew how to train horses, rebuild a ranch or grow money on trees...

"Mom!" Randy wailed from the kitchen. She smiled. Oh, yeah, hers was the glamorous life.

"That's our paging system," she informed Brandon.

"Highly effective."

"Oh, you haven't heard anything yet. Let's eat."

"Wonderful." He fell in step beside her. "I'm really looking forward to this, Victoria," he said somberly. "I washed the back of my neck, you know."

Chapter 2

It was nice to have a man at the table again. And by that she meant a man, as in a *man*—someone who was not a blood relation, someone who didn't tousle her hair, slurp food or drive her crazy with adolescent antics. Someone who sat up straight, said please and thank you and ate with such quiet dignity even Randy was shocked into practicing table manners.

Brandon Ferringer sat in a hard wooden chair at her beat-up round oak table, oblivious to the stir he was creating, while she studied him shamelessly from beneath the cover of her bangs. She'd made a deal with herself. As a practical woman, as a red-blooded twenty-seven-year-old who still had a pulse, dammit, she wasn't allowed to dream, but she was certainly allowed to stare. And what fine staring it was.

Brandon Ferringer certainly looked like he'd climbed mountains and scaled new worlds. His craggy face was windburned, his brown hair sun-streaked. His dark blue eyes were permanently crinkled from squinting toward dis-

tant horizons while his palms bore pads of thick yellow
calluses from gripping ropes and pounding tent pegs. In his
worn jeans, his simple blue chambray shirt and his thick
black hiking socks, he still emanated the capable, graceful
ease of a strong, virile man who'd gone the distance and
somehow found himself there.

And tonight, having passed her father's background
check, Brandon Ferringer would be sleeping in a cabin fifty
feet from her bedroom window. Buck naked, would be her
guess. He looked like a man who would never tolerate pa-
jamas.

She vehemently stabbed a pea with her fork, splitting it
in half. *Don't think about it, don't think about it, don't think
about it. You got a son to raise and a ranch to run and
two new foals to train and bills to pay and feed to buy
and—*

"Mom," Randy exclaimed. "Are you gonna pass me the
potatoes or what?"

Victoria passed the mashed potatoes. Of course she was
paying attention. The kitchen lapsed into the comfortable
silence of three hungry people devouring a hot meal. She
studied Brandon again. So far, he seemed to honestly like
the fried chicken.

Cooking wasn't exactly her thing. After being up at the
crack of dawn running errands, managing the horses and
trying to keep up with Randy, the evening meal was generally simple, hot and representative of four food groups.
She didn't have time or inclination for more.

Once, when she'd been sixteen or so, she'd been young
enough or naïve enough to envision herself as a Western
version of Mrs. Cleaver. She would tend horses, raise children, bake big hearty meals while her husband ran the
ranch. In Beaverville, Oregon, where there wasn't much
else to do on Friday nights, she and the other girls in her

high school class had spun their fantasies. She supposed statistics, small-town boredom and youthful ignorance were impossible to escape, however. By the time Victoria was seventeen, the first of her friends was pregnant. Her senior year, they all seemed to come down with it, as if it was a contagious disease. At nineteen, just two months after graduation, Victoria caught the plague herself.

She and Ronald had made a go of it, like most of their friends. They'd found each other irresistibly attractive—love at first hormones—and getting married and having kids was pretty much all they'd expected out of life, anyway. Then Randy had arrived, squalling, demanding, breathtakingly beautiful—and Ronald had bolted for the first exit he could find. Diapers weren't his thing. Crying babies weren't his thing. The prospect of failing such a small, delicate new life *definitely* wasn't his thing.

Hanging out with his buddies, drinking, joking, getting into bar brawls at Whiskey Jack's was so much more his style. Victoria tried to tell herself boys would be boys. God knows her brothers had sowed some wild oats. Her father was the one who'd finally told her about Ronald's drug problem. Victoria just hadn't wanted to see the signs.

Luckily, her parents hadn't raised her to mope, and her brothers hadn't conditioned her to hide. She'd given Ronald one last chance to clean up his act, and when he emptied out their meager savings account for dope, she'd kicked his sorry ass out of the house and gone at it alone. And her family had stood by her one hundred percent because that's what families did.

Her parents cosigned her mortgage on the ranch and helped with the down payment. Her brothers assisted with the larger projects and made sure Randy never suffered from a lack of male attention. The house could be more, of course—cleaner, nicer, fancier. But the roof didn't leak and the hot water ran if you hit the pipes just right. The money could be more, as well. She couldn't afford the fancy baseball shoes and gloves the other boys on Randy's team wore. Instead of a new encyclopedia set or deluxe computer, Randy had a 1972 world globe she'd picked up at a garage sale. One of these days, she was going to have to remember to tell her son that that big thing marked Union of Soviet Socialist Republics no longer existed.

But there were good things, too. There was Randy. The best. She wouldn't trade her son for the world, and if she had to do it all over again, she'd make the exact same mistakes just so she could hold him in her arms and hear him cry in his exasperated voice, "Mom!" She and Randy made a fine team.

And she wondered if, sitting in a beat-up old kitchen, eating a simple ranch-style dinner, Brandon Ferringer thought the same. According to her father's background check, Brandon used to be some Donald Trump-style New York investment banker. He rented a penthouse apartment in downtown Manhattan, owned more gold cards than Victoria had horses and had earned enough degrees and honors to wallpaper a house.

He could afford to stay at a place a lot fancier than her one-bedroom cabin, and he could do a hell of a lot more than work six months a year for ten bucks an hour in the middle of a wall of flames.

The man must be addicted to adrenaline in the worst way. And Victoria was afraid she already knew his type—except for the money, he wasn't so different from her rowdy, stir-crazy brothers, after all. And just like them, just like all the men it seemed she knew, he wasn't the kind of man who stuck around.

"How's the chicken?" Victoria asked Brandon at last.

"Excellent." He was cutting into his third piece. She'd

never seen anyone eat fried chicken with a knife and fork before, but he made it look quite elegant. Beside her, Randy gave it a go and sent his drumstick skittering onto his lap. Unperturbed, he plopped the piece of chicken onto his plate and tried again.

"May I please have more peas, Victoria?"

"Who's Victoria?" Randy asked, still wrestling with his drumstick.

"I'm Victoria."

"You're Vic. Or Mom. But he can't call you Mom. Only *I* can call you Mom."

"Mr. Ferringer can call me Victoria, then." She didn't mind it, the way he said it. The accent, of course.

"You don't like Victoria—"

"Randy, it's fine."

"Victoria's a girl's name." Randy scowled.

"I need to find the duct tape," she murmured.

"The peas?" Brandon requested politely once more.

She passed the peas and offered a rueful smile. "Dinners around here are a little informal. Generally it's just Randy and me...I...me. Well, we're a pretty casual household."

"Oh, I don't mind. It reminds me of my grandmother."

"Is your grandma in England?" Randy asked with fresh interest. "I looked up England. It's on a whole new incontinent."

"Continent."

"Yeah, that."

"My grandma doesn't live in England," Brandon said, "but that's where I grew up so I'm happy you could find it on the globe. More Yanks need to be able to locate the mother country, you know."

Randy beamed. Brandon picked up his fork. Victoria rolled her eyes. Yanks, indeed.

"Actually," Brandon continued, "my grandmother,

Lydia, runs a dairy in Tillamook, on the coast, right here in Oregon. Have you ever eaten Tillamook cheese?''

"Oh, yeah." Randy made a face. Oregon cities weren't as exciting as English ones. At the wise age of six, he'd already declared that he was going to leave Beaverville 'cause it was too boring. Victoria had hoped it would take him another six years to figure that out.

"Tillamook is a beautiful place," she said levelly. "I've been there twice, and it's so...so *green*."

Brandon nodded. "Most definitely. My grandmother came from Texas during the Depression. They traveled for weeks, and she likes to say that the minute she saw the rolling green hills and the mist-shrouded mountains, she knew she'd found home. My father grew up on the farm. After his plane went down, she made sure myself and my two half-siblings, C.J. and Maggie, spent our summers there, as well, so we could learn about Tillamook and each other. Those were wonderful summers."

"Your grandmother sounds like a very smart woman." Something had come over Brandon's face. He looked...homesick, as if he still missed the days of his youth, sometimes even ached for them.

"I'm done," Randy announced.

She tore her eyes from Brandon to Randy. "Eat your peas."

"I ate two of them."

"I know, now try two *bites* of them."

Randy rolled his eyes and gave Brandon a long-suffering look, seeking an ally. But Brandon piled peas onto his fork, scooped them into his mouth and made a great show of enjoying each and every one of them.

"Gross," Randy muttered, but grudgingly followed suit. Victoria gave Brandon a grateful smile.

"My sister still lives in Oregon," Brandon said after a

moment. "Her husband programs CD-ROM games for your computer. His name is Cain Cannon. Maybe you've heard of him. His biggest seller is Break Out."

"I don't have that," Randy announced. "I don't have a computer." He gave Victoria an injured look.

Even more than a new baseball mitt, Randy wanted a computer. Last week, he'd gone so far as to explain how they could keep the ranch finances and horse-breeding records on it. One of his best friends, Arnie, had a computer and he did everything on it—school reports, surfing the Web. *Games.* Victoria was no dummy.

"No, we don't," she said firmly. "Computers are a major investment. However—" she caught her son's eye so she would have his full attention "—I was thinking that this summer you could help me train one of the foals. With the right training, she'll be worth a lot of money come fall. We could sell her. Maybe after we deducted the cost of feed, breeding and training, there would be enough money left over to buy…oh, I don't know. Say, a computer."

"Oh," Randy said, his eyes already widening with the possibility. "Neat! Great! Cool!" He whirled toward Brandon like a mini tornado and expelled in a rush, "Our foals are royalty. They're beautiful. They got *bloodlines*! We saved for *two years* to breed our mares with Sir Henry. Now we got two re—recent—revent…"

"Regents."

"Regents out back. Have you seen them? I'll show you after dinner if you'd like. They're named Mary and Libby and they already come when they're called. They have papers they're so fancy—I don't even come with papers. And Mom's gonna train them and they'll be worth a fortune. My mom is the best trainer in Beaverville. There's no one like her." He whipped around to Victoria and beamed so big she felt twenty feet tall. The thing that never failed to

amaze her about her son was that in his eyes, all her dreams
had come true. She was a hero.

"I'll work them with you," he said in a rush. "Every
day. It'll be great. Before or after baseball, though, of
course, right? I can't miss practice."

"We'll work them in the morning, then."

"I'm going to get a computer and play games!" Randy
chortled. "It'll improve my hand-eye coordination so some
day I can be a jet fighter." He cocked his fingers, lined up
his sights and took out the mashed potatoes with a hail of
imaginary bullets. "I'm gonna be the best jet fighter pilot
in the world!"

"That will be great," Brandon said seriously.

"The computer isn't for games," Victoria intoned.

"I'm gonna be a jet fighter!" Randy roared again.

"Fine, fine, Ace. Now eat your peas!"

After dinner, she served apple pie and black coffee.
Brandon insisted on doing the dishes, so she sat at the table
and watched. Not a bad deal. Eventually, Randy dragged
out his homework and piled it on the table. He was learning
to multiply mixed numerals, and both of them were having
a hell of a time with it. Victoria had passed grade school,
but these days, she had no idea how. Surely the most con-
vincing argument against having sex was that someday you
would have to help your children with their homework.

She labored through the first problem set with half her
attention on her son's efforts and half her attention on Brandon Ferringer's body. When she and Randy got the first
four equations wrong, she supposed she shouldn't have
been surprised.

"You don't have to find a common denominator," Brandon said abruptly from the sink.

"What?"

"For multiplication of fractions, you multiply the numerator and denominator straight across. Finding a common denominator is for addition.''

"But don't you have to invert the second fraction?"

"That's division.''

"Oh,'' she said.

Randy looked like he was ready to drop out of school. Frankly, she didn't blame him.

"I could help you, if you like,'' Brandon said.

Randy perked up. Brandon set the last battered plate in the drying rack, wiped his hands on an old olive-green towel and came on over. He flipped the chair backward, then straddled it so he could stick his legs out and rub his sore quads.

"May I?'' he asked, and took the textbook from Randy who was only too happy to relinquish it. "Math is rather my thing. Wall Street investments these days are all about exotic derivatives and exponential equations.''

"I don't even understand what you just said,'' Victoria said honestly.

He flashed her a slow smile. "Most people don't.''

"Just a teeniest bit arrogant, hmm?''

"That's a kinder word than most people use.''

He picked up Randy's yellow, number 2 pencil, and scrawled numbers across the lined paper as fast as any computer, then just as abruptly slapped the pencil back down.

"Keeewl,'' Randy breathed.

"All right. Let me walk you through it.''

He did, and by the end of the lesson, even Victoria was qualified for grade school once more.

"I used to help my half-siblings a lot,'' Brandon said by way of explanation, finally climbing out of his chair. The hour had grown late. Both Victoria and Randy should be in bed by now. Instead, Randy was looking at Brandon with the largest case of hero worship Victoria had ever seen and

she was wondering at just what point the evening had run
away from her.

"I...uh...thank you," she said at last.

"No problem."

"Will you help me again tomorrow night?" Randy
wanted to know.

"I don't know." Brandon Ferringer looked bewildered,
as if he hadn't bothered to think that far ahead. The look
restored Victoria's bearings. That's right, she knew this
man and this situation after all. She spent too much time
with strong, virile men who only traveled with one duffel
bag.

She rose up, ruffling her son's hair. "Come on, Randy,
time for bed. Mr. Ferringer has to get ready for hotshot
training so we can't take up too much of his time."

Her son looked on the verge of protest. He scoped her
out, searching for signs of weakness, but when she merely
thinned her lips, he relented with one of his "Aw, Mom,"
shrugs.

"Brush your teeth. I'll be in in a minute."

Randy nodded, made it half out of the room, then surprised them all by returning to give Brandon a quick, fur-
tive hug. Now red all the way up to the tips of his ears, he
bolted.

Brandon appeared stunned.

"He's at that age," Victoria said at last. "You'll probably want to set some limits with him or you'll end up with
a second shadow."

"That age?"

"He's eight years old, realizing that all the other kids
are bringing fathers to the ball games and not just uncles.
He's getting into sports and wanting to know what M-E-N
are all about. It's hard for him. I give him all I can, you
know, but frankly, I don't understand the Y chromosome

that well myself. Why *do* men slap each other's butts after a touchdown? It's a mystery to me."

She smiled ruefully. Brandon, however, God bless him, wasn't fooled.

"It must be difficult," Ferringer said gently, "but if a layman's opinion means anything to you, it seems to me that you're doing great."

"Thank you, I try."

He smiled, she found herself smiling back. Their gazes locked, held. Victoria couldn't even tell what was between them anymore. Sparks, emotion, chemistry, friendship. It beat the hell out of her. She just knew her stomach was plummeting and her pulse accelerating and for a crazy instant, she was angling back her head, the way a woman did when she was hoping a man would kiss her.

And Brandon took half a step forward. His eyes narrowed. His lips parted. He leaned down just a fraction, and they hovered somewhere in between.

Abruptly, they both drew back.

"I should be going to bed," Brandon said briskly.

"Me too. My bed, I mean. The one down the hall. That bed, of course. Yes." She shut up.

Brandon was nodding sagely, as if she'd actually said something intelligent. "And me, to the cabin. I have to get up bright and early, start training. Six months as a hotshot."

"Six months," she repeated emphatically.

"Six months," he agreed.

And between them both, that said it all. He made it to the door. In another awkward moment, he stuck out his hand.

"Thank you for dinner, Victoria," he said formally.

"Oh, any time."

She shook his hand soberly. They both nodded as well-meaning adults. He walked away to his cabin and she re-

mained standing in her house, her hand fisted at her side
so she wouldn't do anything stupid such as call him back.

"He's just passing through, Vic. He's just passing
through."

Victoria and Randy rose at the crack of dawn, downing
a quick breakfast of hot instant cereal and orange juice.
Generally Randy tended the chickens and horses on weekend mornings, but he'd been invited on a nature hike with
Arnie, so he and Victoria had swapped shifts. She packed
his lunch while he filled his water bottles, then he was off
like a shot, leaving Victoria alone in a house that was suddenly much too quiet.

She checked the bucket of corn next to the back door.
Corn was running low. The horses needed more oats. She'd
have to make a trip to the feed store. She grimaced. The
one thing about animals—they just kept eating and eating
and Victoria's bills just kept climbing and climbing. Sometimes, she felt that as hard as she worked, she was on a
giant treadmill, sweating bullets and never getting ahead.

She looped her fine blond hair back into a ponytail,
scrubbed her face, and grabbed the bucket to feed the hens.
The coop had been moved last week, a traumatic event for
chickens, and they'd just started laying eggs again yesterday. Today, she found three more eggs, not bad. She figured it would take another week for everyone's nerves to
settle down. In the meantime, she had enough eggs to make
French toast tomorrow for her and Randy's traditional Sunday brunch. Afterwards, they'd head to church, and then to
her parents' house for a table-groaning feast.

She headed for the stables. The sun was just beginning
to come up now, the pastures washed with dew and the
clean, crisp air reddening her cheeks. It was quiet out,
peaceful and sparkling. In the distance, she heard birds

chattering. The wind carried the fragrance of old pine and new grass.

Mornings were her favorite time. Everything was fresh, everything was new, and she was absolutely content with her life. She had a great family and a wonderful son. She owned a ranch and trained horses. She lived in Beaverville, Oregon, where the sky was a vast blue landscape interrupted only by soaring pine trees and verdant mountains. It was quiet, it was small, and it was the most beautiful place on earth.

She sauntered into the stables with a smile on her face and a whistle on her lips, and got her hours' worth of chores done in forty minutes. With her bonus twenty minutes, she might as well go into town and blow her feed bill once and for all. She wouldn't be a rancher if she didn't have debt.

Walking back to the house, however, her eyes strayed to Brandon's cabin. No signs of life emerged. It was only 7:00 a.m. She didn't think city people moved much before nine on Saturdays.

She was lingering. She didn't want to linger. Of course, she didn't want to dream about Brandon Ferringer either, and that hadn't stopped a torrent of erotic images from swamping her sleep last night. She sighed, chewed on her bottom lip, and in the quiet of the morning, wondered what to do with herself.

She was attracted to the man. Then again, she hadn't had sex in so long she'd probably lost all circulation in vital parts of her anatomy. Beaverville wasn't exactly crawling with virile young men, either. Frankly, Brandon Ferringer was handsome, intelligent, had buns of steel and was sleeping fifty feet from her bedroom window.

All right, the man had sex appeal. What did it change? She wasn't some footloose, fancy-free young girl. She was a responsible, hard-working single mother looking for a bit more than a midlife crisis.

Sometimes she did still fantasize about falling in love, getting married and being part of a whole family once more.

She went into the house, grabbed her field coat and headed for the truck. As Victoria's mom liked to say, stop mooning and get to work.

She spotted Ferringer, however, just as she drove to the top of her driveway's incline. He was at the bottom of the drive, running uphill at a fast clip that had his breath billowing. He'd dressed for the brisk weather—a pair of thick navy blue runner's pants, a navy blue turtleneck, and a red, fleece vest to maintain core body temperature. Now, however, the vest was completely unzipped, his shirtsleeves were pushed up to his elbows and his chest sported a dark stain of sweat.

He showed no signs of slowing, his long, limber legs sprinting up the bumpy path like an antelope. Some people ran for pleasure. Some people ran for fitness. Judging by the look on Brandon's face, he ran for pain. His jaw was tight, his lips thinned. It was obvious he wouldn't stop until he'd proven whatever it was he had to prove this early on a Saturday morning.

Victoria slowed the truck and unrolled the window. In tight clothing, Brandon's lean, rangy build provided an eyeful, long, limber muscles wrapping his limbs like thick sailor's rope. He was going to make one hell of a hotshot.

He finally crested the hill and slowed to a stop beside her idling truck, his breath coming out in gasps.

"Morning," she said brightly.

He leaned over, pressed his elbows into his thighs and gulped air. "Morning," he gasped.

"That's quite a pace."

"Need to do…six minute…mile. For hotshots."

"I see," she said with the right level of seriousness—
Charlie had informed her that everything about the hotshots
was serious. "And what are you at now?"

"Can run…the mile and a half…in nine. Requirement
is…eleven."

"Then you're all set."

He grimaced. "Want to run it in eight." He dragged
another deep breath and finally straightened. Thin lines of
sweat streaked his craggy face and spiked his hair around
his eyes. His face was flushed from the exertion. He looked
good.

"I'm the old guy," he said bluntly, finally catching his
wind. "And the outsider. The requirement may be to run
a mile and half in eleven minutes, but if you're anything
above nine, your team laughs at you. I'll need to be even
faster than that. I have more to prove."

Victoria nodded. She didn't doubt that he was absolutely
right.

"Where are you off to?" he asked at last.

"Going into town. Time to buy some feed. Yourself?"

"No plans. Where's Randy?"

"Off on a nature hike." She paused. "If you need anything in town, you're welcome to join me."

"Oh I don't want to slow you up," he said immediately.

"All right, have it your way." She put her truck in gear,
and immediately he changed his tune. For some reason, she
thought he might.

"Actually," he was saying now, "I would like to get to
know the town."

"I'll give you the full nickel tour."

"I need to shower first…"

"It's no bother," she assured him. Of course it was a
bother. Waiting for a man was always a bother. Sitting in

the front seat of her tiny truck with Brandon would be a definite bother. And yet she was smiling and he was smiling, and most likely they were both idiots.

"Just give me ten minutes?"

"Ten minutes it is."

"Victoria…thank you." He sprinted off to his cabin, his long legs effortlessly finding the rhythm.

She stared at his butt. He had a tight, firm, nicely shaped butt. Oh for God's sake. She slapped her hand against the steering wheel and sank low on the bench seat. It didn't help. She still saw him in her mind's eye, and she knew the minute he climbed into her pickup truck, she would flush.

And maybe, if she were lucky, he would, too.

Chapter 3

Victoria drove like a madwoman. She barreled her truck down the bumpy dirt driveway with no regards to its ancient age or groaning protests. While Brandon clutched the dusty dashboard for dear life, she casually swung them on the main highway and thrust forward at near light speed. She seemed to be enjoying the experience very much, her bare lips curved, her freshly scrubbed face untroubled.

"The seat belt does work," she mentioned casually.

"Too late," he murmured, and sought it out with trembling hands. She was grinning openly. At least he was amusing her.

This morning she wore what appeared to be yesterday's jeans with a fresh flannel shirt in shades of brown. Over the top, she'd thrown an old white wool sweater with thick worsted braiding and a hole in the left shoulder. Her face wasn't marred by an ounce of makeup. Her fine, silky hair was pulled back in a simple ponytail, illuminating her light gray-blue eyes.

He'd seen women in silk and he'd seen women in cashmere, but he'd never seen a woman as down-to-earth, bonedeep beautiful as Victoria Meese.

He'd returned to his cabin last night with the best of intentions. He was here in Beaverville because of his father and needed to get cracking. He'd pulled out the Tillamook yearbook and stared at the pictures of Bud Irving and Al Simmons as if he could sear them into his brain. He needed to find Bud Irving. He needed to solve the riddle of Maximillian the Chameleon.

He'd thought of Victoria and the way she smiled at her son. He'd pictured the way her hips swayed slightly as she swiftly covered ground with her dirt-eating stride. He'd replayed the way her brow crinkled as she tried to work out mixed numerals with Randy.

He'd lain on his bed, feeling wired and disoriented and anxious. He'd tried to rein in his thoughts, but they came back to Victoria again and again, and each time, his nerve endings trilled and his head got light and he wanted to see her again.

He hadn't felt like this since the day in the coffee shop when he'd met Julia. That night he'd returned from work equally frazzled. He'd paced his apartment, entertained wild plans and tossed them out one by one as he sought the perfect way to approach this delightful woman. Finally, he'd buried her in flowers, launching a six-month whirlwind courtship of roses, dinners and jewelry. He'd had money and he'd poured it on her lavishly.

Poor Julia, who'd loved cheap perfume and tacky trinkets.

But it had worked, and she'd married him with a laugh and a smile, and he'd felt like the luckiest man on earth.

And now he remembered the years after. The night he'd come home at two in the morning after a crazy month of working unbelievable hours on a bond-financing project. Julia had been waiting up for him, listening to the radio in the dark. The song "You Don't Bring Me Flowers Anymore" had played, and she'd started to cry.

He'd brought her two dozen roses the next day. He'd tried to come home earlier, say 10:00 p.m. instead of 2:00 a.m. And he'd watched his marriage begin to fall apart, though he could honestly say he had never loved his wife more.

He wasn't any good at relationships. He was lousy at love. He was better off climbing mountains and fighting fires.

"Here we are," Victoria sang out cheerily. "Downtown Beaverville. Don't blink or you'll miss it."

She slowed the truck to a light sprint, and Brandon yanked his mind to the bright spring morning and the row of beat-up trucks pulled up to wooden sidewalks like modern-day horses. Beaverville bustled first thing on a Saturday morning. Big, tough men lumbered down the streets, hitching up old jeans and feeling their back pockets for cans of chew. Even Whiskey Jack's had people passing through its doors. Brandon hoped it meant the bar served breakfast, but judging by one man's swagger, he couldn't be sure.

Did Bud Irving hang out at a place like Whiskey Jack's? Or maybe the feed store or the general store or the pharmacy? Beaverville wasn't that big...

Victoria jerked the brakes, dug in the back tires and swung her old truck into a neat one-eighty next to the feed store. Red plumes of dust billowed up, then abruptly she killed the engine and the world finally settled down.

"You can let go of the door now," Victoria said innocently and hopped out.

Brandon climbed down just as a short, middle-aged man with jet black hair and jowls appeared. Victoria introduced

him as Joel Logger. Judging by the way his belly strained
his red-checkered shirt, Joel enjoyed a good beer. His worn
denims sagged precariously low, barely captured by a thick
leather belt with a huge silver belt buckle and the will of
God. Joel was saved from slovenliness, however, by a
beaming smile, intelligent black eyes and a firm, hearty
handshake.

"So you're the New York hero?" He rocked on his
heels, working a toothpick tucked in the corner of his
mouth and inspecting Brandon. "I hear you saved two
kids."

"That was a long time ago."

"Ferringer doesn't like to talk about it," Victoria said,
her gaze fixed on the feed store's big yellow price tags.
"British reserve and all."

"Brit, huh? Well, welcome to Beaverville. We got no
city pollution and no city crime. 'Course, we got no city
entertainment, either, but the baseball team's turning out
pretty good. After that, I recommend a drive into Bend.
Better bars there. Just don't tell Jack."

"I'll keep that in mind," Brandon assured him. Jack
must be the Jack of Whiskey Jack's fame.

"Ferringer's here to work, not barhop." Victoria tapped
her foot impatiently. "Joel, please tell me you're not serious about these prices."

Joel grinned and led the way inside where he and Victoria began haggling in earnest.

Brandon left them to check out the store. It was huge,
overflowing with feed, farm gear and even a small selection
of John Deeres. It was a popular place, with a dozen people
milling the aisles, checking out cattle medications and new
sprinkler heads. Brandon examined each person as dis-
creetly as possible, only to discover that all farmers looked
alike to him. Every man in the group wore faded jeans,

cowboys boots and plaid, and Brandon had only a forty-year-old image to work with. It wasn't enough.

He returned to the back door just as Victoria and Joel finished dueling and shook hands. While Victoria signed the credit slip, Brandon hefted the bags of feed into the back of the pickup truck.

"I could've done that, you know," she announced as she came down the stairs and realized what he'd done.

"Yes."

"I didn't haul you around for your muscle."

"I'm sure it was for my British charm."

She scowled and climbed behind the wheel. Some strands of silky blond hair had slipped free of her ponytail, curling around her cheeks. She blew them back with one fierce huff.

"Thirsty?" she asked abruptly.

He eyed her carefully. If he didn't know any better, he'd say she was suddenly nervous. "Maybe."

"Ever have a chocolate soda, Wall Street Man?"

"Can't say that I have."

"All right, what the hell." She abruptly popped open her door and hopped out. "Come on, Ferringer. Tom's got a real ice-cream parlor in the back of the general store. Makes the best chocolate sodas around. My treat."

"You don't have to—"

"My invite, my treat." She took off down the street, and Brandon had no choice but to follow.

The general store was just a few doors from the feed store. A tiny chime sounded their arrival, but no one stood behind the cash register. Plowing through narrow aisles that bore everything from Band-Aids to barn boots, Victoria led him straight to the back where the store suddenly sprang open into a white, brightly lit space. Sure enough, it looked like an old-fashioned ice-cream parlor, with a long Formica countertop, red vinyl stools and bare bulbs rimming the top.

"Tom!" Victoria boomed, and the back door was promptly pushed open. A trim, gray-haired man bustled through, wiping his hands on his apron.

"Vic, good to see you."

"How's my favorite soda man?" Victoria clasped his hands over the counter, and the two exchanged dazzling smiles. Brandon was beginning to think they'd forgotten all about him until Tom's gaze slid past her to him.

"So *you're* the New Yorker." Tom thrust out his hand and shook vigorously. For someone who was in his late sixties, his grip was firm and strong. Judging by his erect stance and penetrating stare, Brandon pegged him as a retired military man. A good one.

"Brandon Ferringer, right?" Tom winked. "I got my sources. I'm considered Beaverville's version of the front-page news. And for God's sake, Vic. It's not fair for you to have kept him to yourself. I'm the gossip mill around here. If I don't know things first, people stop passing by."

Victoria laughed. "It's true," she told Brandon, "Tom's lived here for as long as I can remember, and nothing happens that he doesn't know about. So if you're cheating on anyone or hiding from the law, don't tell Tom."

"I took over Beaverville's paper when I moved here fifteen years ago," Tom informed Brandon proudly. "Of course, with a circulation of only twenty-five, it couldn't last forever. Now I thrive on gossip, and you're the headlines around here. I heard you're some kind of hero."

"That's what people tell me," Brandon said wryly. He eyed Tom curiously. The man spoke friendly enough, but his gaze was sharp, almost assessing. There was an alertness to his stand that didn't fit with a general store owner making idle chitchat.

"If you don't mind me saying, you're not what I expected," Tom said.

"Too British?" Brandon quizzed politely.

"Too many gray hairs."

"I prefer the term blond highlights."

"Then I'm a California surfer dude."

"Way cool," Brandon said with such a straight face Victoria cracked up and Tom began to chuckle.

"Oh, yeah, you'll do just fine around here. Have a seat." Tom gestured to the red vinyl stools, his expression was perfectly charming. Perhaps Brandon's imagination was getting the better of him, after all. He took a seat next to Victoria and began to relax.

"I assume you both want chocolate sodas?" Tom said, heading toward the ice cream.

"Victoria tells me your chocolate sodas are the best."

"Victoria? Oh, Vic. Sure, sure. And she's one of my better customers."

Victoria blushed. "Don't tell Randy," she muttered.

Brandon waited until Tom was scooping out the chocolate ice cream, then said as casually as possible, "Say, have you ever heard of anyone named Bud Irving?"

Tom froze with his hand inside the ice-cream carton. Victoria stiffened.

"Bud Irving?" she asked incredulously.

"Why are you interested in Bud?" Tom asked carefully.

The relaxed mood was definitely gone. Apparently, the subject of Bud Irving was a shocking one. Brandon proceeded slowly. "Bud was an old friend of my father's. I'd heard he might be in the area."

"Oh, Bud's in the area, all right," Tom said, resuming plopping ice cream in the old-fashioned mugs. "And so are his surveillance cameras, his Dobermans, his sharpshooter rifles. Bud's, uh, Bud's a little bit socially challenged."

"Bud's crazy as a loon," Victoria added bluntly. "Holed himself up on the top of his mountain, ranting about everyone who's out to get him. He's got more feet of barbed wire than common sense, and when he comes to town, he talks to people who don't exist."

"Bud probably needs to see a doctor," Tom said more diplomatically.

"Bud saw a doctor. Then he said the doctor was out to get him, too." Victoria turned to Brandon. "Last year, we voted Bud the person most likely to climb a clock tower and shoot young children. My father keeps an eye on him. When Bud does decide to come into town, my father makes him leave the rifle at home. You don't want to get involved with Bud Irving."

"Oh," Brandon said. He wanted to sound casual, but it came out strained, and once again, he felt Tom's scrutiny. He looked at the counter. So the last tie he had with his father was a crazy old man suffering from paranoid delusions. He wondered if he should be surprised.

Tom abruptly slid the two chocolate sodas down the counter. "Vic's probably right," he said quietly. "I would stay clear of Bud Irving."

"All right," Brandon said. "All right."

The front bell chimed, so Tom excused himself. Victoria leaned over and took a deep, appreciative sip of her frothy soda, but her gaze was on Brandon's face.

"How old were you when your father died?" she asked.

"Twelve."

"And you remember the name of his friends?"

"When you don't have much to remember, you keep what you have."

"I guess," she said, but he knew she didn't believe him. Finally, she turned her attention to her soda and sipped gustily.

"Did your husband bring you here often?"

"Nah, Ronald didn't waste his thirst on chocolate sodas. He was strictly a Bud man."

They lapsed into silence, drinking their sodas and staring at the bulb lights. Victoria seemed happy with her soda. Brandon didn't taste his at all. He was thinking of barbed wires and Dobermans and high-powered rifles. He was thinking of crazy Bud Irving and all the secrets his father still wouldn't share.

Arriving at the ranch, they discovered a young man with unfashionably long blond hair and a goatee longing on the front porch, the orange tomcat purring smugly on his lap. As the truck pulled up, he unceremoniously dumped the cat on the ground and stood, stretching out a lean, limber body.

Brandon was afraid he already knew who the man was. Sure enough.

"Charlie!" Victoria boomed, sliding out of the truck as it was still rolling to a halt. "When are you gonna remove that dead rat from your face?"

"I'm just too stylish for this family," Charlie drawled, crossing his arms over a thin blue T-shirt with the word Mercedes stretched over his well-toned torso. He gazed at Brandon with frank, appraising interest. "So you're the hotshot." He made it sound like a challenge. His expression was bland.

"Oh, stop staring," Victoria snapped. "Next thing I know, you two will be dueling on the delta. Listen, there's two hundred pounds of grain in the back of the truck. Put some of that testosterone to work on it."

"Aye, aye, sis," Charlie responded drolly, then shook his head. He meandered toward the vehicle, his gaze still locked on Brandon. With a swift movement, he found a bag and hefted it effortlessly over his left shoulder. Still looking at Brandon, he wrapped a sinewy arm around a second fifty-pound bag, grunted and slung it over his right shoulder. He staggered, then stood triumphantly, his blue eyes gleaming.

Brandon got the signal loud and clear, and most likely the next six months would kill him. With a mental sigh, he sidled up to the truck and took up the gauntlet. He grabbed the first bag and tossed it over his shoulder. Not bad—he could do this. Shifting his weight, he got his right arm beneath the last bag, grunted, staggered and through divine intervention wrestled it onto his shoulder.

He tottered, caught his balance and stood. Sweat streaked his face. He met Charlie's stare eye to eye.

"Brandon Ferringer. Pleased to meet you."

Charlie's face split from ear to ear into a beaming grin. "Now you just gotta carry them to the barn," he said innocently, hitched the bags for better balance and set off.

Brandon winced. Victoria was watching him. Charlie was waiting for him. A man really had only one choice. He pivoted sluggishly toward the barn, his already tired legs groaning beneath the hundred-pound burden, and got going. If he could hike Everest, he could do this. Of course, his thirty-six-year-old body still hadn't quite recuperated from all that.

He wheeled into the barn slightly off balance, spotted his target, took a step forward, almost fell and caught himself against the stable wall to keep going. Son of a... The feed center loomed ahead, Charlie already leaning back with his arms akimbo, smirking. Brandon made a beeline for the home stretch, and with a last grimace, dumped his load.

Behind him, Victoria began to clap. "Congratulations, you're both he-men. Is now the time to tell you that the corn goes next to the house?"

Brandon was pretty sure he was going to die. But Charlie

just slapped him on the back and scooped a bag off the ground one-handed.

"Don't worry, old man, I got this trip. I need you to have enough energy left to run."

Charlie wasn't kidding. Brandon changed into sweats, and while Victoria muttered about thick-skulled Neanderthal men, the two hit the trails.

Charlie set a fast pace, but Brandon had expected that. His legs protested—they were tired and more accustomed to distance than speed. Generally, Brandon started hikes at the back of the group but ended the day at the front as the younger, stronger men succumbed to their unrealistic pace. Slow and steady, legs of steel, that's what got you up a mountain.

Hotshots needed endurance, to be sure, but when a fire blew up at ninety miles an hour, hotshots also needed speed.

Charlie leapt a small stream. Brandon got a stitch in his side. He ducked his head and ignored it, even as his breathing labored. *Focus, Brandon, focus.*

He blanked out the whipping pine trees and spicy, dusty air. He blanked out Charlie's effortless sprint and the rugged, tricky ground. He thought of Maximillian, and the casual way he'd walked out the door one day and never come back. He thought of his mother standing in the foyer and saying his father's plane had gone down. The devil had finally caught up with Max.

And he thought of Julia, and how she must have bundled up to go out for a walk that cold winter's day. She'd been working on a special birthday present for him, putting together a family tree. She'd been researching Max and the partnership he'd formed with Bud Irving and Al Simmons almost forty years before. Was she thinking of that as she walked through Central Park? Or was she thinking of the bright blue sky? Or was she wishing that Brandon would give in to her pleas and stop working so hard?

And did the mugger say, "Stop investigating Max," right before he pulled the trigger?

"Okay, okay," Charlie gasped.

Brandon's mind jerked to the present. The younger man had slowed to a cooling pace. The trees no longer whipped by so fast, and the hard, dusty ground had grown smoother beneath their feet.

"Take it easy," Charlie exclaimed. "You've proved yourself, Ferringer. Now slow down before you hurt something. Don't want to burn out before Monday."

Brandon slowed. It burned to exhale. His left side ached. He leaned, rubbing it with his hands. His legs had turned to rubber and his thoughts were still all over the place.

Charlie finally slowed to a walk, and they moved along the trail together in silence, listening to various birds sound their calls while chipmunks darted around their feet.

"So why are you doing it?" Charlie asked at last.

"Doing what?"

"Becoming a hotshot!" The younger man glanced at him impatiently. "Come on, my father did the background check on you. Word's out all over town that you're some independently wealthy Ivy League investment banker. Why the hell does a rich executive want to become a low-level federal employee?"

Brandon shrugged. "The same reason everyone else does, I suppose."

"No, that's not true. We are in for the money. Let me tell you, there's not much else *I* can do that pays me ten to twelve bucks an hour."

"When you sit too long, do your legs hurt?"

"Oh, yeah. And my knees crack like brittle twigs."

"When you're indoors for more than a day, do you feel like you can't quite breathe?"

"Yeah."

"And when you go more than a day or two without hiking or jogging, can you no longer sleep at night, your legs burning to move?"

"Oh, yeah."

"Then we're doing it for the same reason," Brandon said quietly. "Because I'm like that, too."

Charlie appeared to ponder his words. They reached the end of the trail, turned wordlessly and headed for the ranch. It was a beautiful day, the sky so blue, the soaring pine trees so green. Brandon didn't know how to live without this world anymore, and in that way, he did fit in with the men and the women of the forestry service perfectly.

"You know," Charlie said, "Victoria's been through a lot. She got a real raw deal with Ronald. I mean, a real raw deal."

"She told me."

"She didn't deserve it. She's a good person, you know. An amazing mother. Have you seen her with Randy?"

"I like them both very much."

"That's good to know. We're very fond of her, you see. She has six brothers, did she tell you that? I'm one of the smaller ones—but fast. Our dad's the sheriff," he continued casually. "He wears a gun."

Brandon picked up the subtext loud and clear. He said just as conversationally, "I have a younger sister, too. Her name is Maggie. My brother, C.J., and myself are very protective of her. A few years ago, she was kidnapped from downtown Portland by an escaped murderer, Cain Cannon. I flew here from New York to offer a five-hundred-thousand-dollar reward and to negotiate her release. C.J., a former Marine, brought his collection of guns."

Charlie's eyebrows hitched. "And did you get her back?"

"We like to think that we helped. The truth, however, is that Maggie saved herself. A rather spirited girl, our Maggie turned out to be. C.J. and I never would've imagined.... Well, suffice to say, I think Maggie and Victoria would like each other a great deal."

"Huh. So where's Maggie now?"

"She lives near here. In fact, she's married to Cain Cannon, the escaped convict."

"You're kidding me."

"No. And she was right about him, too. He's one of the best men I know." Brandon sighed, then offered a small smile. "Women simply defy the imagination."

"You know," Charlie said finally, "you're all right, Ferringer. You're honestly all right."

"Well, I try."

They kept walking while the sweat dried on their faces and the sun rose higher in the sky.

Brandon didn't go to the house that night. From his cabin he could see the light blazing in the kitchen and could imagine Victoria and Randy sitting at the table, exchanging stories of the day and wrangling playfully over who should eat more vegetables. He heated up soup on the hot plate and ate it straight out of the pot with the spoon on his Swiss Army knife, deliberately keeping his distance. Randy was at "that age," Victoria told him, that impressionable age where he might mistake a drifter for a future dad. Brandon owed Victoria at least the decency of trying to prevent that.

Later, he saw the lights go on in the arena and went out to find Victoria working one of her horses. He stood in the shadows, not wanting to interfere. She rode like an extension of the beast, going around and around, teaching the horse to stop with a click, turn left, turn right, back up, move forward. He'd never seen anything like it.

The air grew musky and hot with the scent of sweating horseflesh and human exertion. He remained watching, wishing there was something he could say to reach this woman as she flew by.

He slept poorly that night, with too many dreams he woke up unable to recall.

In the morning, he made himself get to work. In twenty-four hours, the hotshot training would start. For the first two weeks, they'd have daily doubles, workouts in the morning and afternoon. In between they'd have classes as well as routine forestry service work. Hotshots were guaranteed forty hours of work a week—clearing brush, digging fire lines, repairing fences or trails, whatever needed to be done. Once fire season hit, they would all work a hell of a lot more.

He needed to get equipment. He should stock up on food. He should make sure he had enough clean socks and underwear. He should get focused.

When he came out of his cabin Sunday morning, Victoria's truck was gone. He hiked into town rather than risk his rent-a-wreck. The walking stretched his legs. He bought a better backpack from the general store, fresh hiking socks with the extra thick toes and heels, loaded up on canned soup and powdered milk and hiked to the ranch.

He ate another fine meal of minestrone soup, sitting on the edge of his bed and reading the firefighter's handbook on wildland fire fighting.

Later, he sat on the front porch and stared at the sky.

When Victoria's rusty truck barreled into the yard, he was pathetically happy. Randy darted out first, wearing his good jeans, which were still dark blue, and a fancy Western dress shirt with mother-of-pearl snaps. He raced to Brandon's cabin, saying, "How are you what are you doing can you help me with my homework now?" in one big rush. "Mom said I wasn't supposed to bother you too much," Randy stated. "You gotta get ready for tomorrow. Charlie says the first two weeks are hard, and then you guys'll be traveling all the time. I wanna be a hotshot some day."

Brandon gazed over Randy's head to Victoria, who lingered by the truck, her features obscured by twilight. Her blond hair was down, forming a pale, silky curtain around her shoulders. Like Randy, she wore her good jeans, combined with a nice red silk blouse. He should've known she wouldn't wear dresses even to church.

He should've known that he'd find her even more attractive this way. He dropped his gaze to Randy.

"I can help you finish the problem set tonight," he said soberly. "After that, I don't know. Charlie is right. The next few weeks are going to be very busy."

Randy seemed to accept that readily enough. In his mind, hotshots probably spent their free time flying to the rescue and leaping tall buildings in a single bound.

"Cool. Come on." Randy dashed for the house.

Brandon walked, taking the time to casually stroll by Victoria. This close, he could see the shadows the falling night had dusted over her face. Her light eyes glowed more gray than blue.

"You look very pretty tonight," he said somberly and walked away.

Behind him, she expelled her breath sharply, and for the first time all day, he smiled.

Chapter 4

Superintendent Coleton Smith was a tough son of a bitch. Late fifties, whipcord lean, he had a fanatical gleam in his dark eyes and the fire stamped into his face. His left cheek bore a flat, shiny brand, as if he'd been struck by a hot iron. Tendrils of scar tissue dug furrows through his cropped gray hair. His left ear was gone completely, the flaps of skin rebuilt just enough to channel the sound waves into his eardrum. Down his neck, across his collarbone, down his left arm, the fire had oozed like rivulets of lava, searing away the man's skin and leaving its own particular kind of smooth, plasticky scars in its place.

On Coleton's left hand, only three fingers remained. They were clumped together as if they were still hiding from the encroaching flames.

"Mann Gulch, 1949," Coleton Smith barked at oh six hundred Monday morning, pacing before their seated forms, "twelve Smokejumpers dead. Storm King Mountain, 1994, fourteen firefighters—nine Prineville hotshots—dead. This won't happen again, and in the next two weeks, I'll tell you why. I'll pound it into your brains, I'll squeeze it between your eardrums until the next time a slow moving creeper blows out, you people will know exactly what to do.'' Superintendent Smith slapped a red hunting cap on his head, obscuring half his scars. "Now get off your asses, and let's see what you got.''

He ran them hard, ten men and eight women hitting the dusty, rocky trails and trying not to sprain an ankle. They were an eclectic mix of size and shape, age and sex. Some people had spent the winter outdoors or at least in a gym, and they were already lean, mean machines, sprinting to the front and setting the pace. Others had spent the last six months behind a desk and had a thin layer of winter insulation dulling their edges. In the coming weeks, that fat would be wicked from their bodies as if it was water.

Brandon hovered somewhere in the middle of the pack, knowing he didn't have the speed to play with the young bucks like Charlie, but having too much to prove to drop all the way to the back. Endurance was the ticket. He would never be as fast as the young people, but he was most likely the most aerobically fit person present. Hiking developed good lungs, and hiking up seventy-degree slopes at twenty-five thousand feet qualified you to blow up a balloon with a single, powerful puff.

All he had to do was ignore his tired leg muscles.

He focused on the trail, not the man stumbling to his right or the woman clutching her ribs behind him. He ran and tried to pretend he didn't feel Coleton Smith's black gaze pinned to his back, waiting for him to fail.

"Being a hotshot isn't about glory. It's five percent fighting fires and ninety-five percent hard work. Even if you beat a wildland fire in a matter of hours, mop up can take days—long, hard days trudging through a hundred acres of soot and ruin, seeking and extinguishing every last ember in every last tree trunk and twig. Welcome to the glamorous life.''

After the six-mile run, Coleton passed out the Pulaskis, shovels and chain saws. He split the crew in half, sending nine off to build a trail while the remaining nine began thinning patches of the forest, pulling out brush, felling dead trees—called widow makers by the experienced crew—and hoeing grass, dead pine needles and old leaves off the ground. After an hour, Brandon's arms ached from wielding the chain saw and his face was streaked with sweat. Beside him, Charlie labored in silence, looking strained. A few of the others, however, joked and laughed, obviously at ease with the work.

At noon, Coleton showed up, inspected their efforts and informed them they were done. He'd heard the Redmond crew did aerobics to build endurance, and so would they. Fit firefighters better tolerate heat, he informed them. They acclimate faster, work with a lower heart rate and body temperature and don't become sloppy or careless with fatigue. And, if things got ugly, they had the reserves left for sprinting down the escape route.

''Before we post up,'' Coleton threatened the crew with a scowl, ''you will be the fittest hotshot team in this state, or I'll send Richard Simmons to your house personally.''

That scared them all into action. At twelve hundred, Charlie and Brandon were in the gym raising their hard-toed boots to the beating rhythm of Jane Fonda's smiling commands. Lift one, lift two, lift three, lift four, inhale, lift five, lift six, seven, eight...

By the time they showered and ate lunch, even the pros were dragging. Coleton gave them just enough time to down black coffee and high energy bars, then led them to the forestry service's tiny broom closet classroom to begin the required sixty-four hours of education in Crew Boss, Urban Interface Fires, and Intermediate Fire Behavior. Coleton started with fire behavior, his personal favorite, and they tried to stay awake. It wasn't easy.

"A fire is nothing but a chemical reaction called rapid oxidation. For it to happen, three elements—heat, fuel and air—must be present in the right amounts. You want a fire to go away, then you yank an element. Hey, Meese, what are you yawning about?"

Charlie snapped to attention. "Uh…"

Charlie looked at Brandon, Brandon looked at Coleton. Coleton hunkered his scarred head between his shoulders, creating an extra roll of smooth, shiny skin that wasn't pleasant to look at. Coleton had lived in Beaverville for twenty years, and young children still refused to walk by his house.

"Okay, folks, listen up. Here are our two rookies, who obviously don't think they need to listen. So tell us, freshmen, the team is called into a fire. What do you do?"

"Follow the lead of the crew boss," Charlie said weakly.

Coleton narrowed his sights on Brandon. "What about you, Ferringer? I hear you went to some Ivy League school in downtown Philly. Learn anything good about wildland fires in downtown Philly?"

"No."

"No, huh? Big-shot Wall Street guy, fancy degrees, and all you can say is no?"

Brandon remained quiet.

Coleton approached, his black gaze narrowed, his three clumped fingers slapping against his thigh. "You're a bookworm, aren't you, Ferringer?"

"I read."

"You read about fire? You look at the textbooks? There are some good ones out there."

"I have glanced at a few."

"So tell us, rich Brit, what are the factors that influence fire behavior?"

Brandon kept his gaze pinned on the far wall. He said calmly, "Fuel characteristics, weather conditions and topography."

"You got a fire, a slow-moving creeper in a canyon. Midday. Sun is bright red, warm front hovers over the canyon, terrain is a forty-degree incline covered by light fuel. Narrow river runs down the center of the canyon. There is no wind. What do you do?"

"Call the national forecaster and ask about approaching cold fronts."

"You call. One is moving in. What do you do?"

"Get out."

"Get out? What do you mean get out, Ferringer? It's a slow-moving creeper. Why, I bet you and Meese could take it yourselves. Besides, there's a town at the end of the canyon. Gonna let all their homes burn? Fine federal employee you are."

"There's a town?" Brandon said. "Then evacuate it."

"Evacuate it?"

"Immediately."

Coleton stopped right in front of him. Those mangled fingers thrummed his thigh again and again. No one in the room spoke. No one moved. Abruptly, Coleton bent down. "Well, rich Brit, at least you read the right book."

The superintendent straightened and strode to the front of the room. "So tell us, Meese, why does your good buddy Ferringer want out of the canyon so fast?"

"Blowout," Charlie said quietly, giving Brandon a look of reluctant admiration. "The cold front will hit the warm front, kick up winds of fifty miles an hour, at least, the oxygen will hit the small grass fire and blow it up." The scenario was one all hotshots and Smokejumpers knew intimately. If they hadn't learned it from analyzing Mann Gulch, they'd learned it firsthand from Storm King Mountain.

"What do you do then?"

"Drop tools and run for the nearest safe zone."

"In that topography, where's the safe zone?"

Charlie paused, thinking hard.

"The other side of the water?" Coleton pressed.

"No, the wind will jump the fire over the water. The other side of the canyon will go, as well."

"What about in the water?"

"Too hot. You'll be smack in the middle of several hundred degrees. No good."

"Outrun it, over the top?"

"If you could get over the ridge, you'd be okay, but at that slope, the fire will move uphill at over a hundred miles an hour—not even Michael Johnson could win that race. You'd be overtaken before you were even halfway up."

"So what do you do, Meese, say your prayers?"

"Find the black. You'll always be okay if you keep a foot in the black."

"Finally," Coleton growled and flung his hands into the air. "This is what fifty years of fire fighting has taught us hotshots. You can predict fire, you can manipulate fire, but some days, you won't get it right. And then…you find the black, a burned-over area. It has no more fuel to feed a fire, so there you'll be safe. If you can't find one, start one. Light a cross fire, and as soon as a patch is burned, drop down, pull your fire shield over yourself tightly and weather the storm. When all else fails, find the black. Are we clear?"

Everyone was clear. Traditionally, wildland fire fighting wasn't that dangerous. Deaths were more likely to happen from helicopter or plane crashes on the way to sites than on the ground. But then there were the incidents such as Mann Gulch or Storm King Mountain, when the fire got out of control too fast. When whole crews lost their lives and whole communities got to mourn.

Those lessons were not forgotten.

"Okay, so let's talk fuel," Coleton snapped. "And let me show you all the lovely charts you get to memorize…before Meese falls asleep."

Thursday night, Brandon didn't crawl back to the Lady Luck Ranch until almost nine o'clock. He stood in the back of the stables, staring at the shower with longing. Yesterday, they'd started weight training. Brandon had never lifted before. Now his pectorals hurt, his deltoids hurt, his quads hurt, his biceps, his triceps, his glutes and his calves. If he had it, it ached.

And his mind swam with such stimulating charts as "Dead Fuel Moisture—Time Lag Relationship to Fuel Size," "Fuel Flammability by Time of Day and Aspect" and "Relationship Between Air Temperature, Fuel Moisture Relative Humidity and Time of Day." He was trying to remember how fast different fuel types burned, the differences between northern and southern exposure and the impact on fire behavior as the day moved from morning to noon to night.

People who thought hotshots were empty-headed thrill seekers had never glanced at the textbooks. The information was detailed, technical and precise, and the price for forgetting was high.

Brandon kept thinking it shouldn't be a problem for his analytic mind. If he could compute bond prices for purchasing after issue and selling before maturity, he ought to be able to handle fuel considerations and topography charts. No such luck.

Four days into training, he wanted to crawl under his bed, curl into a ball and sleep for a week. He hadn't felt so fatigued or overwhelmed since Everest, and at least then he could blame it on a mountain.

"Wow, you look like hell." With effort, Brandon twisted his exhausted body from the shower and discovered Victoria standing in the aisle. She was leaning against one of the stalls, wearing blue jeans, a ratty gray sweatshirt and a grin. He hadn't seen her or Randy since Sunday night. He'd told himself he didn't mind. He'd lied.

"At least you're still standing," Victoria continued conversationally when Brandon remained too shell-shocked to speak. "Mom says Charlie comes home every night, wolfs down three servings of everything and keels over face-first onto his empty plate."

Brandon said, "I'm standing?"

Victoria laughed and moved closer. He caught a whiff of apple shampoo, and something tightened in his chest. Her hair was in a ponytail, swept from her face. He wanted to pull out the rubber band and feel the silky strands wave over his sore, bruised palms.

"So tell me, hotshot, how is it?" She stopped right in front of him. He swore he could feel the breath from her words whisper across his windburned cheeks.

"I killed my whole team," he blurted.

She merely cocked a brow, her eyes gleaming with gentle humor. "Not bad for a day's work."

"I keep forgetting they're there," he continued like an idiot.

"Want to start at the beginning?"

"Coleton Smith—the superintendent—"

"I know Coleton."

"He's split us into crews of four to five and given us various drills. To pass, everyone on your crew must succeed. We're learning teamwork, you see. Today, we had to clear brush, dig a fire trail, then he shouted, 'Blowout,' and we had to run to the safety zone. I cleared. I dug. I ran. I made it to the safety zone. Everyone else fried."

Victoria winced. "Ouch."

"My teammates stopped talking to me, then Coleton yelled at them that they had no choice—a team was a team was a team. Then they certainly started talking, but I won't repeat what they said." He ran a hand tiredly through his hair. Bits of pine needles rained down, and he grimaced. "What a mess. Coleton thinks I've spent too much time in New York and I might as well give up now. This evening, he had me clear a quarter-acre patch of forest alone so I would learn to appreciate my team members. Rather like beating erasers after class, but more painful. Bloody hell." He sighed.

Coleton must have stayed late, too, because as the sun set and the world grew dark with dusk, Brandon became aware of someone's gaze pinned upon his back. It had been a lonely, eerie feeling in the middle of the rapidly darkening forest. He'd set up more lanterns than necessary and had still been so frazzled he hadn't inspected the chain saw before turning it on. The chain had been half off, and the starter motor ripped it from the gears with violent force, flinging it left and by the grace of God embedding it in a tree trunk instead of Brandon's leg. His hands had shaken for a long time after that. He'd waited for Coleton to materialize and lecture him, but Brandon had remained alone in the lantern's glow, his shoulders hunched warily and his gaze uncertain.

Victoria was speaking. "Well, do you think you'll remember your team members next time?"

Brandon hesitated. He'd been wrestling with that question since the incident without coming to an acceptable conclusion. He confessed quietly, "I don't know."

Her expression grew curious. "Why do you say that?"

"I...I grew up as a single child, Victoria, from the stoic, British upper class. I'm better at math than most mathematicians. In school, I was the chap who enjoyed algebra. People like me...well, I wasn't generally invited to play in other people's circles."

"You play with Randy nice enough."

"He's Randy."

"You volunteered to help him with his homework. You did the dishes. You helped Randy with his homework again on Sunday night. I don't know, Ferringer, but so far you seem appallingly well-adjusted and just all around nice to me." She shrugged. "But that's just my opinion."

"Oh." He looked away. He was blushing, definitely blushing. The more he tried not to, the darker he grew. He wasn't accustomed to being characterized as the nice guy. C.J. was nice. Maggie was sweet. Brandon was...smart. This nice business, however, felt good.

"How's Randy's math?" he asked.

Victoria grimaced and shrugged. "I wish I had your mathematical mind. Well, with a bit of luck, we may both pass grade school yet."

"And the foals? Have you started training?"

"Not yet. We're still in the getting them accustomed to people phase. I may start them both on a lunge line soon, see how that goes. That's about it for Randy and me. Frankly, your last four days have been more exciting than ours."

"Routine's not a bad thing."

"Funny comment, coming from you."

His lips twisted wryly. "I suppose it is."

She leaned forward abruptly. It caught him off guard and he didn't know what to do. He was unbearably aware of her scent—apple shampoo and alfalfa, spring air and horses. Her face was clear tonight, no smudges of dust to mar her pale, perfect complexion. And her eyes bore into his, frank, honest, clear. That was the thing about Victoria. Her gaze was always direct, never coy, never manipulative, never sly.

She stared him straight in the eye, and Brandon felt it like a one-two punch. He sucked in his belly, stopped breathing and thought she looked so beautiful and so pure and he was standing there covered with sixteen hours of mud and sweat.

"I'm filthy," he exclaimed without thinking.

She laughed. "I like you tired and worn-out, Ferringer. It makes you blunt."

"I need to shower. I can't figure out how to raise my arm to turn the damn thing on."

Her smile grew. "So maybe you need a little help?"

"Maybe." He was breathless, staring into her cornflower blue eyes.

She moved slowly, each motion deliberate, her gaze never looking away. She lifted her arm—he saw her breasts, high, nicely rounded, shift and press closer. She reached above his shoulder—he felt the soft, worn cotton of her sweatshirt brush against his cheek. She leaned over—he watched her lips approach, part slightly and moisten.

She turned on the shower behind him, and fringes of spray dusted his hair. He stood there unmoving. This close, there was no denying it. The spark between them was real, deep, earnest. He was thinking back to that moment in her kitchen four nights ago, when he'd almost kissed her simply because it seemed so right.

And now her lips were parted, and once more he felt the pull.

He wanted to hear his name on her lips: Ferringer. No one called him Ferringer, but he liked the way she said it, as if it were a challenge.

"Why do we keep doing this?" she whispered.

"I have no idea."

"Ferringer..." she whispered.

He came undone.

He yanked her against his body, hard. One moment for her to protest, then his lips were upon hers. Fierce. Raw. Yearning.

Victoria dug her fingers into his scalp and held on for dear life. She was a big girl and she knew better, but at this minute she didn't care. She'd been thinking about Brandon Ferringer for four long nights, staring at his cabin window, watching the light go out and imagining him stripping down to smooth, rippling bare skin and lean hard muscle. She'd been picturing him crawling between worn cotton sheets buck naked. She'd been contemplating the feel of those sheets sliding over his long, sinewy form and Lord, she was tired of being sensible.

He thrust his leg between hers, suckled on her lower lip, and she thought of singing *hallelujah!* and ripping the flannel from his back.

His cheeks rasped against hers, roughened by twenty-four hours of beard and the great outdoors. His tongue snaked over her lips, delving boldly in the corner, then sneaking its way back up, until she groaned, parted her lips and angled her neck for more. He plunged in and consumed her.

From far away, she heard someone moan. Then a soft sigh, a needy gasp. She was rubbing her pelvis shamelessly against his hard thigh, feeling his hands smooth over her lithe build. He palmed her bottom, and she bracketed his collarbone hard enough to welt his skin.

It wasn't enough. She should've realized that with this man, it would never be enough. His hands were rough, callused, bold. They would feel divine against her naked skin, squeezing her nipples, slipping between her thighs. Oh, Lord...

Suddenly her eyes were wide-open. She was watching him kiss her, seeing the need, the genuine desire, and she was thinking of hot torrid nights in the back of Ronald's truck, the way their hormones burned like wildfire and the way reality splashed her as a bucket of ice water nine months later. Cause and effect. Thinking with her heart instead of her head.

Oh, Vic, what are you doing?

She planed her hands on Brandon's shoulders, stiffened her spine and pushed him away.

"Easy partner."

Brandon stood stock-still, his breathing labored in the silence, his fingers still curled around her waist. She couldn't bring herself to move. His eyes had darkened to almost midnight blue. They glittered, storm-tossed and hungry in his lean, angular face.

He released his grip so abruptly, she almost fell. He backed away from her, raking his hands through the waves of his sun-streaked hair. Then suddenly, the dark, passionate, needy Brandon Ferringer was gone. Two blinks of an eye, and the Brit retrieved his reserve and shuttered up.

"You're right," he said stiffly.

"I am?" Her fingers lingered on her lips, which were bruised and swollen. Holy smokes. It didn't feel so great to be right. It felt lonely. Already, Brandon was stalking away, putting more space between them.

She drew another deep breath. Her brain cleared further,

the world coming into sharper focus. Her horses blew
gently in the barn. The air smelled like alfalfa and horseflesh. A cat purred from on top of the horse blankets.

"I guess I should be going in now," she said. Her hands
were shaking, so she stuck them in her back pockets.

Brandon just nodded, his features tight.

"Oh for heaven's sake," she burst out abruptly. "We
can't walk on pins and needles around each other. We need
to talk about this."

"Oh, no we don't." Brandon shook his head vigorously.
"I'm an Englishman. I don't need to talk about *anything*.
You have a son to raise. I have…I have… You have a son
to raise. I'll leave you alone."

"But dammit, I don't want you to leave me alone. Ferringer," she took a step forward, then halted when he froze.
"Ferringer, I'm too honest for my own good and we both
know it, so let me just get this out. You're staying in a
cabin fifty feet from my bedroom, you're the best-looking
man Beaverville has seen, and I haven't had sex since
Moses walked the earth. I'm a little bit attracted to
you."

"My cabin is fifty feet from your bedroom?" Good old
Wall Street Man sounded like he was strangling on his own
tongue. Apparently, he'd never contemplated that
before.

"Oh, yeah," she assured him matter-of-factly. "And I'm
guessing you sleep buck naked. But if you do wear clothes,
don't tell me. A healthy fantasy life is all I got left."

Brandon's face grew ever darker. "You're trying to kill
me! Don't you realize that all I can think about now is
what you wear to bed!"

"I figured we might as well be in the same boat."

"I don't want to be in any boat. I want to fight fires, do

my investigation and find another damn mountain to climb!''

''Do your investigation?''

''Nothing!'' he said immediately. ''Dammit! I have a certain level of reserve. You can't just go around saying such...such things!''

''Kind of messes with your mind, doesn't it?''

''Victoria, so help me God—''

''Oh, Ferringer, I don't know what to do any more than you do. I certainly didn't plan on being this attracted to my new tenant. I honestly haven't felt this way since I met Ronald, and as pathetic as this sounds now, there was a time I thought the sun rose and set on that man.'' Her tone calmed. She took a deep breath, and the spark abruptly left her face. ''I'm just...I'm just not ready for this. I can't afford to make that mistake again.''

''Then turn around and walk away, Victoria. Because I'm tired and I've had a long day and I...I *want* you.''

Oh, my. Her lips formed the words soundlessly. She hesitated for a second, still living dangerously, then her resolve broke and she beat a hasty retreat. She was determined to be smart this time. Dammit, she was twenty-seven, practical and a single mother. She was a darn pillar of the community!

''Victoria.'' She was almost out of the barn, but that one word stopped her. She closed her eyes, knowing she was weak.

Ferringer stood in the middle of the aisle, looking grim, looking fierce, looking *frustrated*.

''I loved my wife,'' he said abruptly, his face unreadable. ''I *loved* her. There hasn't been anyone since. Four years, Victoria. Don't push me too hard.''

She swallowed thickly. ''I'm sorry.''

''And your bedroom is just across the way....'' His eyes

closed. She watched his fists clench, and the thrill that shot through her was nothing short of primal.

"Yeah, Ferringer. I know. Lord, I know."

She gave up on composure and fled.

In the stables, moment followed moment. Finally, Brandon pulled himself into the shower and let the cold spray sting his face.

As he toweled off and slipped into a pair of sweats in the privacy of his cabin, he told himself it was for the best. He and Victoria were ill-suited in so many ways it defied the imagination. She and Randy needed a good husband and father.

Brandon wasn't qualified for either position.

He was a loner. He was a hiker. He would be a good hotshot—he would figure out this team thing—and he would talk to Bud Irving. And in September, mission accomplished, he would find some new mountain to climb until some night he could go to sleep without dreaming of Julia, or Max, or his mother's voice telling him he was just like his father.

Saturday, he would pay a visit to Bud Irving. That's what he'd come to Beaverville for and that's what he would do.

But he never got the chance.

"Hell, rich Brit, are you all right?"

Brandon opened his eyes slowly. The bright, cloudless sky hit him hard enough to hurt. He winced, squinting, and groggily made out two of his teammates, the woman, Barbara, and the small, wiry man everyone called Woody.

"How many fingers am I holding up?" Woody held up his hand, but it swam before the blue, blue sky, and Brandon thought he was going to be sick.

"Oh, he's not doing well." Barbara was taking his pulse,

her gaze on Woody. Barbara evidently didn't like Brandon much. She hadn't forgiven him for running ahead on the escape route and leaving them all behind. Now, however, she looked concerned. Then it occurred to Brandon that he was flat on his back on the ground in the middle of the day and he had no idea how he'd gotten there. Surely a hotshot shouldn't be lying around. If Coleton saw him...

He struggled to sit up, and both his teammates grabbed him. The world spun again. He went pale as a sheet.

"Easy, easy, easy," Woody was saying. Far away, Brandon could hear yelling. Natasha was running toward them.

"What the hell happened?"

Henry was after her. "God, I've never seen anyone fall like that. Is he all right?"

Barbara was holding him up. He tried to say he was fine, never better, but his lips wouldn't move. Vaguely, he remembered working up the slope. It was Friday. They were practicing building fire lines. He'd been digging down to mineral soil. A tree was above him. And then the air had been split by a giant cracking sound and someone had screamed. Barbara had screamed.

He'd looked up. He'd seen green. He'd jumped and the world went...

"We gotta get him back to command central." Woody took charge. "Ferringer, tell me if this hurts."

Brandon said no to everything until Woody got to the back of his head. The lump just above the indent of his spine had already swollen to the size of an egg and hurt like bloody hell. They clustered closer, debating the options, and as if in a fog, he watched their lips chatter, chatter, chatter.

It was unseemly, these people hovering over him. He should be keeping a stiff upper lip, set an example for little

C.J. and Maggie. Otherwise they might realize he missed their father, too, and then they would cry. He was the oldest. He must set the example. Max had left him first. Maybe it was all his fault, after all. He was the oldest. Must be responsible.

Don't cry. There's a good chap, don't cry. Never show fear.

All these people were still clustered over him.

"Go ahead," he said thickly. "I just…need another moment. I'll…be…in a minute."

"Nope," Barbara said firmly. "One person fries, we all fry. Come on, guys."

Suddenly arms were around his waist, helping him up. He was leaning on Woody's shoulder. The guy wasn't that big and had been working all day. He shouldn't have to bear such weight. But they were all there, passing him around like a rag doll as they limped to command central.

One person fries, we all fry.

He heard his father laughing in the back of his head. *It's only about you, it's only about you!* Max was screaming.

He tried to say no, and Barbara looked at him with concern.

"My father," he croaked.

"Shh," she said.

Then she wasn't Barbara anymore. She was Victoria, whom he'd kissed and wanted to kiss again. She was leaning over him in his cabin, putting a cold washcloth on his head and telling him it would be all right, everything would be all right.

He wanted to draw her into his arms and knew he shouldn't. He wanted to hold her close and bury his head against the sweet, apple fragrance of her hair. He wanted to cry but he had no idea why. *Swallow it down, swallow it down. Be a man.*

Must set the example. Must be responsible.

"Trust me," Victoria whispered. "Just trust me."

I can't. I can't.

"I'm sorry," he croaked. "So sorry." But then he was talking to Julia, who stood so far away while the world turned black.

Chapter 5

"I think he's dead."

"He's not dead, Randy. He just bumped his head...violently." A diffuse brain injury, Doc Matthews had diagnosed. In other words, Brandon Ferringer had a concussion.

"His face looks ugly."

"Well, those tree limbs aren't kind."

"He isn't breathing much."

"He's just resting, Randy. Listen, honey, according the doctor, we need to wake him up every hour and ask him his name and the day of the week. You know, I think you might be just the man for that job."

"Oh keeewl!" Randy clapped his hands, making Brandon, lying on the bed, wince. "He's alive!" Randy screeched.

Brandon opened his eyes and pinned Victoria with a long-suffering stare. She merely smiled, but when he wagged his finger, she dutifully approached his bed. The first time, she couldn't hear him, so she bent lower. Then she made out his words.

"I...will...get you for that."

"Death threats, huh? Yeah, you'll be all right, Ferringer."

Propped against the counter, Charlie began to chuckle. "Told you his head was too hard to be felled by one measly bump." Charlie approached, the three of them crowding around the bed and making Brandon feel like he should be delivering his last will and testament.

"So how are you, buddy?" Charlie asked seriously. "Got a headache, dizziness, nausea?"

"Shouldn't have drank so much Scotch," Brandon mumbled. "Head. Ow."

"Actually it was a tree. A big tree."

Brandon looked at Charlie blankly. He felt like he'd been asleep a long time, and his head was filled with shadowy, tortured images he couldn't place. He'd been running after Julia. He had a clear memory of calling his wife's name. He looked at Victoria, and she immediately glanced away.

Slowly, he raised a hand and touched his face. His cheeks burned. His jaw was covered with myriad scratches. His fingertips zigzagged from scab to scab until they reached the fiery, pounding lump at the back of his head. He already knew better than to touch. He let his hand fall and tried to focus on seeing only one of everything. No use. He groaned.

"Yeah," Charlie joked weakly. "But wait till you see the other guy."

"A tree," Brandon whispered hoarsely. "I was attacked by a tree?"

"Keeewl." Randy looked impressed.

"Looks like someone started cutting down a dead oak," Charlie explained. "But for some reason, they didn't finish.

The oak was barely sitting on its trunk, then you came around, pounding at the ground, and over she went. Coleton's livid, man. Ripping through the crew like a fox in the henhouse. So far, everyone insists they didn't go near the tree, but he doesn't take no for an answer real well. Coleton's been decent about this. Called the doctor for you himself, and one way or another, he'll figure out who downed that tree.''

"Am I...am I off the crew?''

"No, man. Your team brought you back, everyone working together and making Coleton happy. For a New Yorker, you got their loyalty fast enough.''

Brandon grimaced. He wasn't convinced it had anything to do with him.

"The doctor says that with a little R and R, you'll be as good as new. Luckily, you chose Friday to wrestle with the oak, so you got all weekend. On Monday, Coleton and the doc will check you out. If you're all right, you're back in. If not...there is a list of alternates.''

"I'll be all right,'' Brandon said. The throbbing picked up in his temples, however, forcing him to clutch his head.

"Oh, for God's sake,'' Victoria said, sighing, "you're growing a doorknob out the back of your skull. Don't be so stubborn.''

"I'll be all right.'' Bloody hell, he hurt.

"Men. Stubborn, driven, foolish.'' Randy looked at Victoria with obvious interest, and she bit off her tirade. "Sweetheart—'' she ruffled her son's blond hair "—next time you wake up Ferringer, clap really loud.''

"No! No need—''

"Oh, of course there is. We don't want to be lax about our duties, do we, Randy?''

"The doctor says we gotta check on you,'' Randy

chirped. "Make you follow my finger and tell me the day of the week. What day is it?"

"Armageddon."

"Wow, he's not very good at this. That's not even a word. What do I do if he gets it wrong?"

"Clap louder."

Randy began dutifully to comply, but Charlie took pity and intervened. "Later, buddy."

"I need to practice."

"You'll have plenty of time for practice," Victoria said sweetly. "All weekend."

Having won the battle, Victoria took her son's hand and stomped out of the room, leaving Brandon to contemplate his crimes. He'd ticked her off, all right. He just had no idea how or why. What had he said while he was unconscious? And why did he feel so guilty?

"Wow," Charlie said as if reading his thoughts, "she really likes you."

"*Likes* me? I'm afraid you're gravely mistaken."

"Oh, no. I haven't seen her this enamored since she stuck bubble gum in Ronnie's hair in third grade."

"She had a crush on Ronald all the way back to the third grade?"

"Oh, yeah. For Vic, Ronald was always the one. Mooned over him from the day she saw him. Ronald pretty much ignored her, but then in high school... I still remember the first time he asked her out. Her sophomore year. She came home looking as if she'd won the lottery. I pulled her hair, and she didn't beat the hell out of me." Charlie's voice drifted off. Abruptly he shook his head. "Well, when life decides to throw you a curveball, it sure seems to know how to pick the best one."

She was angry. She couldn't decide if it was at herself or Ferringer, so she was taking it out on her kitchen floor.

Eleven o'clock on a Friday night, Randy safely tucked into bed, Victoria attacked stains that had probably existed since the Depression and scrubbed as if her life depended upon it.

Damn machismo men.

She blew her hair out of her eyes, squirted on more bleach and rubbed vigorously. Didn't they have any idea what it was like for a woman to have a man *carried* to the house, his face covered in blood and his body unconscious? And then to sit there, so helpless, waiting for the doctor to finish examining, to tell her he really would live, after all, and still there was nothing she could do but wait?

So she puts her horses on hold, she puts her ranch on hold, she puts her life on hold to sit in a damn cabin and wait for said broken man to open his eyes.

And what does Brandon Ferringer focus on? What question consumes Brandon Ferringer as the lump on his skull grows and his vision becomes blurred? *Will he still be a hotshot. Is he still a hotshot!*

She grabbed steel wool and lit into the stain until her knuckles burned.

Men had too much testosterone. That was the problem. If there was any justice in the world, God would throw out the whole lot of them and let women start over in the labs. Women would produce something driven by more than hormones.

Brandon Ferringer made enough money to support himself. He had enough degrees to be anything he wanted. But no, he had to pick one of the riskiest jobs. He had to be a thrill seeker camping out in her cabin.

She gave up on the stain, now pared down to a pale shadow and looked for fresh targets.

She didn't get Ferringer, she just didn't. She didn't know what drove him so hard when at the same time he could show such patience with Randy and such compassion with her. When she'd told him to think of Randy, he'd understood. When she'd broken off a kiss so hot her lips had seared, he'd listened.

And when Charlie had brought him home and laid him out on the bed, he'd whispered Julia's name.

She stopped scrubbing the floor. She sat there in the sea of soapy water and felt sorry for herself.

She couldn't resent his dead wife. He had a right to miss her and a right to mourn. Victoria was feeling hurt anyway. She couldn't think of any man right now who, when hurt or unconscious, whispered her name.

She sighed, squared her shoulders and picked up a sponge. *Dammit, Vic, get to work.*

She moved to the left-hand corner, where an amazing composite of grime had accumulated in the shadow of her refrigerator, and resumed scouring. It wasn't any use. She hadn't been able to stop thinking about Brandon Ferringer since the day he arrived, and tonight wasn't any different. Last night, she'd dreamed of him stripping off her nightgown, nibbling on her throat and whispering *Victoria, Victoria, Victoria* until she'd wanted to *consume* him.

Instead, she'd woken up sweaty and frustrated in the middle of tangled sheets. What was it about her that made her attracted to the wrong kind of men? Sure, Ferringer wasn't a drug addict or thief, but he wasn't so different, either—still just a guy passing through.

What had Brandon meant last night about his "investigation"? Did he really think she was so stupid she didn't notice a slip like that? First he was asking questions about Bud Irving, which was strange enough given Bud's sociable personality. Then he was saying it was because Bud was his father's best friend. Did you really remember the names of your father's friends—particularly when your father died fifteen, twenty years ago? If it meant that much to Brandon, why hadn't he come to Beaverville before?

Oh, yeah, Ferringer was up to something, all right. Wonderful, wonderful, wonderful. Adrenaline-addicted, danger-thirsting guy with secrets. Yeah, she could really pick 'em.

She should just—

She froze, her hand halting midmotion, the water soaking into her jeans. There it was again. A sound. Rustling, outside, where there shouldn't be.

She took a deep breath. She glanced out the window, where the world was dark but she was clearly silhouetted by the kitchen light. Slowly, she crawled toward her ancient refrigerator. Using it for cover, she stood and peeked.

It took a moment for her eyes to adjust. She heard the noise again, someone working their way out of the woods alongside Brandon's cabin. And then she saw him, a black shadow materializing by Brandon's cabin.

A dark, unknown man beginning to approach her house.

Victoria went for her rifle.

Brandon was sleeping badly again. Tossing and turning on the old bed and hurting himself each time he moved. Sometimes he dreamed he was on fire, a burning twig pressing against the back of his skull. Sometimes he saw his father striding out the door. *Time to deal, son. Time to deal.* A lot of times he saw Victoria working with her horses, and stood on the sidelines, unable to approach.

He kept waking up in a sweat, groggy and disoriented and knowing he needed to get his butt out of bed, and then he'd go tumbling down into troubled dreams once more.

The fifth time, he roused so violently, he jerked awake, clutching his head. He swung his feet over the side and sat up before he could fall into the abyss. His fingers rubbed his temples and tried to force the migraine into the back of his skull. His stomach rolled queasily.

And outside his cabin window, a tree limb snapped.

His breathing stopped. He grew perfectly still, focused on the window. There. A footstep. Someone was outside, in the back, by the fringe of the woods.

Someone was out there.

His thoughts blew apart on him. He remembered the chain ripping off the saw. He heard the crack of the giant tree falling. He felt the branches snatching at his face. Two big accidents in just two days. What were the chances of two major accidents in just two days?

Someone was out there.

He couldn't get his body to move. He was a New York investment banker. He was a hiker, a wildland firefighter. What was he supposed to do?

Something other than sit on the bed and analyze. Later, you think, rich Brit. Now, you act.

He stood. The world spun crazily, and for a minute he thought he'd be sick. Then his flailing hand landed on the wall and he leaned against it heavily. The wall was straight, the wall was sturdy. He used it to support himself while he inched toward the window.

The intruder was stepping toward the cabin, trying not to make any noise and doing a poor job of it. If subtlety was any judge, this guy wasn't a pro. Brandon took a deep breath. The nausea was receding, the dizziness, too. His head still ached, but standing, moving, thinking about anything other than the lump cracking his skull seemed to help.

He made it to the window and peered out, finally discerning a shadowy figure halfway between the cabin and the house. The man was creeping along with exaggerated footsteps, as if he'd seen too many movies.

What the hell? Brandon gave up on doubts and grabbed

his jeans. Concussed or not, he had to do something. He yanked on his hiking boots and prepared to intervene.

"Oh, for God's sake, it's you, Ronald!"

Brandon emerged from his cabin just in time to see Victoria appear on the front porch, flash on the lights and position the shotgun against her shoulder. Caught in the flood of light, the man froze, looking on the verge of peeing his pants.

"Vic," he croaked. "God, you're not going to shoot me, are you?"

Victoria was already lowering the gun. She looked disgusted. "Of course not! Though it's through no help of your own. What the hell are you doing, skulking around a woman's yard?"

Ronald hunched his shoulders and gave her a beseeching look. At one point, that expression had probably worked for him. Now it didn't sit well on his lined face, his cheeks puffy and his eyes bloodshot. At one time, he had probably been handsome. Now he looked thick and bloated, a man who'd fought the battle and lost.

"Go home, Ronald," Victoria said. "I don't have anything to give you, and you already stole what there was to take."

"Ah, gee, Vic, can't you give a guy a break? I'm off that stuff now. Swear to God, cross my heart and all that." He tried the puppy-dog look again, but it just didn't wash.

"Go home before you wake up Randy. It's the least consideration you can give."

Ronald shifted uncomfortably. He couldn't meet his ex-wife's gaze. "I'm trying," he mumbled.

"That's good, Ronald."

"I miss you."

Victoria didn't say anything.

"It's not my fault," he suddenly blurted in a belligerent tone. "My daddy was an alcoholic, too. It's in the genes. You can't fight your genes."

"You always have a choice, Ronald."

Ronald seemed to deflate. "I miss the old days, Vic. Don't you remember the old days? We'd cruise around in my pickup truck and look at the stars. Drinking Old Milwaukee and waiting for the sun to come up."

"We were eighteen and stupid."

"Nah, we were wild, we were real, we were something. Don't you remember? I was the big man on the football team, and you were my doll. We were the couple. Everyone wanted to be us."

"Ronald, you don't belong here. You need to go home."

"Ah, hell, Vic. You always were a hard-hearted bitch."

Victoria's expression didn't change. "I'm going to count to ten. If you don't leave by then, I'll call the sheriff."

"Your daddy, you mean. Always running to your daddy—"

"One—"

"Just gimme a couple bucks. For old time's sake."

"Two—"

"I won't bother you again. I swear."

"Three—"

"Come on, you gotta have something stashed away. You always had something stashed away. No one could prepare for a rainy day like Vic. Superwoman, supermom. Ain't no man good enough for you—"

"Four." Her chin came up, but in the glow of the porch lights, Brandon could see the tears in her eyes. He'd had enough.

He took two steps forward and caught Ronald by the shoulder so hard the other man jumped and squealed.

"Get off her land," he said without preamble. "She may

have something against shooting her ex-husband. But I don't.''

Ronald bolted. He ran from the yard as if his tail was on fire and there wasn't enough water in the world to put out the flames. And just as quickly as it began, Brandon and Victoria stood alone in the shadows, her rifle propped against her legs, his arms reaching for a tree to steady himself.

Awkwardness set in. Brandon gave up on the flimsy sapling and leaned against the rusted-out truck, trying to think of something to say. He'd witnessed something too personal, intruded upon Victoria's inner sanctum and upset the natural order of things. She stood stiffly, looking straight ahead with her chin up and her lips thinned.

''Are you...are you all right?'' he asked finally.

''Oh, sure. Never better.'' But her expression made a liar out of her words. She set the rifle against the side of the house and slumped on the porch steps, wrapping her arms around her knees. The light washed over her face, exposing her high cheekbones, and the tears that still threatened her lovely blue-gray eyes.

He wanted to hold her. He wasn't sure she would let him. He approached the porch instead and wordlessly sat beside her. She offered a tight smile.

''Not exactly the finest example of the male species.''

''I think he'd been drinking.''

''Probably. Ronald does his finest thinking under the influence.''

''Victoria,'' he began, but couldn't think of what exactly he wanted to say.

''Well, he's not so wrong,'' she stated after a moment. ''I am hard-hearted.''

''You are not hard-hearted, Victoria.''

''Oh yes, I am. I married that man, Ferringer. No, I worshiped that man, spent most of my younger days with the world's largest crush on him. Loved him, adored him. Became his wife and bore his child. And now... Now I look at him and feel nothing.'' She turned toward him. ''Do you know how strange it is to look at someone you once loved enough to promise until death do us part and feel nothing?''

''It happens, Victoria. People fall in love. People fall out of love. It doesn't mean you're hard-hearted.''

Her expression said she wasn't convinced. He gave up on good intentions and wrapped his arm around her shoulder. She stiffened, of course. He could feel the battle within her clearly, pride going head-to-head with need. Abruptly, she turned to him, her head relaxing into his shoulder, her arm curving around his waist. She felt warm and pliant, soft and strong. He'd kissed her, but he'd never really held her. It felt better than he'd imagined.

His throat grew tight. It had been so long since he'd held anyone. Years since he'd seen his sister, Maggie, and broken his self-imposed exile with a hug. Years since he'd allowed himself to reach out and remember how poignant an embrace could be.

You're still an I, Brandon, I need us to be a we.

I'm sorry, Julia. I didn't know. I just didn't know, and now I'm trying so hard to learn, and it's too late.

''You still love your wife,'' Victoria whispered as if reading his mind.

''Yes.''

''You called her name, you know. When you were unconscious or asleep or whatever, you called for her.''

''I was dreaming that I saw her. I was trying to catch up with her. There were things I wanted to say.''

''It's hard when someone dies.''

''Yes.''

''Unfinished business, I suppose.''

"A lot."

Victoria gazed at him curiously. "How long were you married?"

"Three years. I was working as a bonds trader on Wall Street. Julia was a waitress in the coffee shop on the corner, where we would spend most of our lunches...if we took lunch."

"You married a waitress?"

"She was working her way through school, earning her doctorate in nineteenth-century European history. Julia was a research fiend. Someday, she would've made a great professor."

"Did she get sick?"

"She went for a walk in Central Park. The police think it was a mugger."

He had too many doubts to say more. About a mugger really shooting a waitress. About Julia researching Maximillian and then suddenly turning up dead. He didn't believe in coincidence.

"So your wife was shot," Victoria was saying, "New York became an ugly place, and you hightailed it out of there. Traded in prime rib for trail mix?"

"Something like that."

"Something? Come on, Ferringer, it's almost midnight, the stars are clear and you just met my wonderful ex. Humor me and tell me more. Please."

He said clearly, "The money's not mine, Victoria. Not really. The big money, the money your father sees, comes from Julia's life-insurance policy. She died, and I received a million dollars. You have no idea how hard it is to get rid of that kind of money."

"You're trying to get rid of it?"

"I worked too hard," he said abruptly. "All through the marriage. Julia kept asking me to come home, to spend more time with her, but I...I liked working. I wanted the money, the power. My father had bankrupted my mum's estate, but I bought it back when I was twenty-five and I became rather hooked. I was going to be everything he wasn't—rich, successful, self-made. Instead, I became everything he was—cold, remote and self-centered. And I married a great woman and I failed her.'' His lips twisted. ''Just like Dad.''

''You're an intense man, Ferringer.''

He nodded somberly. ''I am, and I have this nasty habit of learning everything too late.''

Victoria studied his face. He'd retreated from her, his thoughts someplace dark and tortured. In his mind, was he a little boy again, watching his father ruin his mother's estate and feeling helpless? Or was he thinking about his dead wife and the time he felt he should've spent with her? She had wondered what drove him so hard, and now she knew. Brandon Ferringer was wearing his father's hair shirt. He'd been trying to absolve his father's sins since he was a little boy, and now he was an intense, brooding man who was much too hard on himself.

She moved closer and tightened her arm around his waist.

''You were twelve when your father died?'' she asked quietly.

''Yes. He was an importer-exporter who traveled a great deal. His plane went down over Indonesia. They never found his body.''

''You know, Ferringer,'' she said softly, ''I think I know why you're having problems with teamwork.''

''Do you?'' He was staring at the night sky.

She tilted her head on his shoulder, her hair pillowing her cheek. ''I read a lot about children growing up with only one parent—you know, for Randy's sake. He asks a lot more questions about his father these days, and I don't really know the best way to say Daddy has a dope problem. Well, one of the things all the studies talk about is that children who lose a parent for whatever reason often develop trust issues. Basically, it's impossible for a child not to feel as if his parent failed him. In Randy's case, he'll probably wonder why Ronald didn't love him enough to give up dope, straighten out his act. Frankly, I wonder that all the time. Even if a parent dies, a child can't help feeling abandoned. Parents are supposed to be there for you unconditionally, and once they're not, you can't fight the feeling that they failed you. It seems safer to depend on only yourself.''

Brandon looked troubled.

She continued gently, ''You said yourself that you're a bit of a loner. Your work was solitary, and when you left it, you took up hiking—one of the few sports where you don't need anyone. Not a teammate or a competitor or a coach. It's just you and the mountain. Brandon, the hotshots are your first team, aren't they? And suddenly, after thirty-six years of depending on only yourself, you're supposed to rely upon and trust a group of total strangers. That's scary. No wonder you're having problems.''

He glanced away sharply, his fingers abruptly steepled and tense. ''So what do I do, Victoria? Fail them the way I failed Julia? Make yet another mistake?''

''No. Give it time. Understand how you got these fears and try to work your way through them. You're a capable guy, Ferringer. I've seen you with Randy, with Charlie. You're a great guy.''

He was silent for so long, she thought she'd alienated him. Then he said suddenly, fiercely, ''Victoria, next time Ronald tells you that you are hard-hearted, shoot him.''

''Oh.''

''Don't let him treat you like that. Don't let him talk to you like that. You are the most generous, compassionate woman I know.'' He turned toward her, and the fire in his intense blue eyes took her breath away.

She couldn't swallow. Good Lord, her thoughts and emotions were in total disarray. She wanted to hold him. She wanted to wrap her arms around his lean waist and nestle her head against his shoulder. She was trying to tell herself it was hormonal, while the rest of her was wondering if she and Ronald had ever had conversations like this, and if they had, would they have made a difference?

''I should go,'' Brandon said hoarsely.

''No!'' she cried without thinking, then caught herself and fisted her hands.

Their gazes held in the half-light of the porch, both of them stark, both of them raw.

''I want to kiss you again, Victoria. You don't want that.''

''Maybe I've changed my mind,'' she babbled. She wanted to grab his shirt so he could never walk away.

''It's the moment. You're caught up in the moment, I'm caught up in the moment. And in the morning? You deserve more than I can give you. I don't want you to look at me later and have only regret.''

She couldn't deny it. She wanted to, but she couldn't. Brandon's arm slipped from her shoulder. She bit her lip so she wouldn't protest. Her gaze was locked on his face.

He paused. His fingers, featherlight, brushed wisps of her fine, blond hair. He traced a path down her cheek and stopped to wick a bead of moisture from her lashes. Then his thumb came to rest on her lips. She was trembling.

''You are so beautiful,'' he whispered.

Don't go, don't go, her mind begged. *Practicality be damned, I want you to stay. Make me feel pretty....*

Brandon pulled away. He moved to the center of the yard where his face could no longer be read, and she pressed her fists against her stomach.

"Good night, Victoria."

It took her much longer to reply. "Good night."

Chapter 6

Brandon woke up slowly, when the sun was already high in the sky. His morning started where his evening had left off—with his body rock hard and aching. He was already reaching for Victoria, who had haunted his dreams. But then he opened his eyes, and his bed was empty and he was alone with the sun streaming over his legs and the emptiness raw in his gut.

Ex-husbands, hard hearts and trust issues. Their conversation whirled around his aching head in teasing snippets, and finally he squeezed his eyes shut.

New day. Same old business. Get over it, Brandon. Get over her.

He pulled his ancient body out of bed. He still had a headache, but as a type-A anal retentive, he'd certainly suffered worse. Otherwise, all arms and legs seemed to be operating within spec.

The pile of dirty clothes on the floor earned his grimace. He needed to find a Laundromat. He needed to find Bud

Irving. He needed another week's worth of sleep. He settled for pulling on a pair of jeans that really needed a wash. Stepping onto his front porch, he promptly encountered Randy.

The young boy was sitting on the edge, swinging his feet and looking like he'd been there awhile.

"Mom said I wasn't supposed to wake you up anymore," Randy explained. "She said you were feeling better, and I had to let you sleep."

"That was kind of her."

Randy cocked his head and eyed Brandon's bruised and battered face with open skepticism. His gaze narrowed. "What day is it?"

"Saturday."

"What's your name?"

"Randy Meese. I'm eight years old and love baseball."

Randy grinned wide enough to stretch his freckles and reveal his missing tooth. His ears stood out like jug handles beneath his tousled hair. "The doc said you might have am...you might not remember things. He didn't say you'd think you were me. If you're me, will you do my chores?"

"I don't know. What are your chores?"

"On weekends, I feed the chickens and the horses. I also get to muck stalls. I hate mucking stalls."

"Can't say that I blame you. I have to do laundry. Want to do my laundry?"

"I don't know how," Randy said soberly. "I'm only eight. Where are y'goin?"

"Ah, to the stables. Thought I would wash up."

"My mom's not out there."

Brandon paused, his mouth parted like a fly trap. Belatedly, he snapped his jaw shut. It wasn't that obvious. Brandon was never that obvious. Randy was most likely saying the truth, observing the truth, reciting the truth. Brandon scowled.

"I just wanted to wash up," he said curtly.

Randy wasn't fooled. "My mom is pretty."

"Uh…"

"She's good with horses, too. My grandpa swears she's the best horse trainer around."

"Mmm, okay."

"She's a little weird about eating vegetables, but my grandma is the same way. I think maybe that's a *woman's thing.*" Randy nodded sagely.

"Ah." Brandon was officially flummoxed. "I see." No, he didn't. He was in over his head and looking around desperately for the escape hatch, or at the very least an eight-year-old's on-off switch.

"I think you should go out with my mom," Randy announced matter-of-factly. "She always says Beaverville doesn't have any good men that aren't a relation, but you're new and you're not an uncle. You oughtta do."

Brandon decided to take a seat. He swung his legs over the porch next to Randy and let them dangle.

"Well," he said at last, his tone serious, "I'm very flattered. I happen to like your mother a great deal. I like to think she likes me. But it's not a boyfriend-girlfriend kind of thing." More like a mad, passionate, hot-blooded, steam-pouring-from-the-ears kind of thing. "Er, we're friends. For example, you're friends with what's his name, Arnie. And I'm friends with Charlie."

Randy digested this. "Charlie and Arnie aren't as pretty as my mom."

"Well, yes, that's true."

"They're not so good with horses, either."

"Ah, but do they make you eat your vegetables?"

"Oh," Randy said, eyes widening. "Aha."

Brandon began to breathe easier. Four years of formal forensics training in Oxford's private boarding school, followed by two years of debate at Wharton, and he was almost ready to take on a farm boy. How much did his Wharton degree cost again?

Randy said abruptly, "I saw my dad last night."

"What?"

"I woke up hearing some noise, and when I looked out my window, there he was."

"Oh." Brandon didn't know what to say.

"My dad's a drunk," Randy said quietly. "His daddy was a drunk, too, and that's why I don't have a second grandpa—he drank too much whiskey and hit a tree. You shouldn't drink and drive."

"You shouldn't drink and drive," Brandon repeated.

"I don't want to be a drunk. I'm never going to drink. It's evil, and I don't ever wanna make my mom cry the way my daddy did." Randy's lower lip was suddenly trembling. Brandon understood. Growing up wasn't easy. Watching your father disappoint your mother made it even worse. And feeling as if you had to fix everything and heal your mother's pain was almost unbearable.

Certainly nothing Brandon had done had ever been good enough. Caroline was still bitter and angry and resentful. Brandon no longer phoned home because he'd run out of things to say.

"Have you, uh, have you told your mother this?" Brandon suggested softly. "I find her rather easy to talk to, myself."

"I don't wanna worry her." Randy rubbed at the corner of his eyes furiously. "She's got a lot on her mind, you know."

"She's your mum, Randy. That's what she's there for."

"Do you tell sad things to your mom?"

Brandon faltered. Talking to his mother was the conversational equivalent of putting his head on the chopping block. But Caroline wasn't anything like Victoria. Caroline's hatred of men extended to her son, whereas Victoria...

Victoria would give up her afternoon to tend some fool's head wound even when she had a whole ranch to run. Victoria would give her life for her son and the brothers and family she held dear. Victoria was fierce, loyal and generous, and the man who finally earned her trust and respect would be the luckiest man alive. And that man had better take damn good care of her or Brandon would—would...

"I talk to my grandma," he told Randy. "When I'm upset, when I have too many things on my mind. She listens." He added in a low mutter, "And I should call her soon."

"Does that help?" Randy wanted to know.

"It helps."

Randy's feet swung faster. He seemed to contemplate the advice. "Maybe...maybe I could."

"Victoria would like that."

"You think?"

"I think."

Randy nodded. He stuck his fingers through his belt loops. "I could tell her, I guess. You know, so she'd feel like I was *sharing*. Grandpa tells me *sharing* is another one of those *woman things*."

"And how." Brandon sighed.

They sat together a minute longer, listening to the silence like men. Randy pulled up a slender stalk of prairie grass, shucked the outer skin and stuck the stem into the corner of his mouth. Brandon thought of the cold, stone foyer in Hampton Court where his mother had told him that Max's

plane had gone down with a smile twisting her thin, blood-
less lips.

After a bit, Brandon went into his cabin, slid on a pair
of sweats, and regardless of doctor's orders, began to run.

At one o'clock, Brandon stood in front of Beaverville's
tiny Wash-n-Fold, attached to Tom's General Store. He'd
procrastinated about doing his laundry as long as possible—partly because laundry wasn't his thing and partly because some traitorous part of him mooned over Victoria
like a sixteen-year-old schoolboy, convinced that if he just
lingered around his cabin long enough, he could catch a
glimpse of her.

Apparently Victoria had marshaled her defenses after last
night, however, because his pathetic vigil had yielded no
sightings. Not even a glimpse of sun-highlighted blond hair
or worn plaid shirt. Not a sneaking grin or firm, curving
line of well-shaped legs.

He'd just wanted to say hi, he thought defensively. Give
a neighborly hello. Certainly after last night's conversation
they were something more than mere acquaintances.
They'd shared moonlight and personal intimacies. He understood about her husband. She understood about his dad.

He'd started gazing at her lips again.

God, he was hopeless.

Belatedly, he tore his attention to the line of coin-
operated washers and contemplated strategy. In Manhattan,
he dropped off his meager clothes downstairs, the doorman
sent them out to the corner cleaners, and they returned magically washed, pressed and folded. In Nepal, he'd hunkered
down on rocks and scrubbed his fleece and wool beside the
grinning Sherpas who thought the foreigner's love of soap
was funny.

In the last four years, he'd taken care of his chores on

his own and through many means—except for a Laundromat.

He rustled through his pockets until he came up with a handful of quarters and spent the first three on a little box of white detergent that promised "outdoor freshness." Having spent a great deal of time outdoors, Brandon wasn't sure if his clothes should smell like trees or mud but was willing to give it a try.

If memory served, he was supposed to divide his clothes between whites, lights and darks. The three piles looked small and insignificant on top of the yellow industrial washers. He kept his whites out and threw the lights in with the darks. Good enough.

He was just tossing them into the machines when Tom stuck his head through the doorway.

"Don't do that!"

Brandon froze, his red Patagonia vest in his hand. He looked wildly from side to side. "Do what?"

"Wasn't that a light blue T-shirt you just put in?"

Brandon nodded.

"Uh-huh." Tom leaned against the doorjamb and made himself comfortable. "Add bright red to that, and you'll have streaks through all your light-colored clothing."

"You know how to do laundry?"

"'Course. Been doing it all my life. Never married." He eyed Brandon with that too-penetrating stare. "Want some help?"

After a brief hesitation, Brandon agreed. Tom dumped his clothes out and sorted them into dark darks and all others. Then he tossed the piles into two separate machines, picked cold wash for the darks, warm wash for the lights, and plugged in quarters.

"I have quarters," Brandon said immediately.

"Don't bother. It's on the house."

Brandon was uncomfortable. There was something about Tom Reynolds. He seemed friendly and he seemed casual, and Brandon kept thinking both of those appearances were a lie.

"Take it from me," Tom said conversationally, "laundry's not hard once you get the hang of it. Funny that a bachelor like you has never washed clothes before."

"I generally send them out."

"Oh, that's right. The rich man." Tom smiled to take the sting from the words, but Brandon stiffened anyway. "How's the training coming?" Tom nodded toward his face. "Looks like the other guy is winning."

"I had a small run-in with a tree."

"Yep, I already heard. Probably knew the news before you regained consciousness."

Brandon didn't argue. He didn't know how long he'd been unconscious.

"Coleton's pretty unhappy," Tom said. "It's not wise to make a man like Coleton unhappy. He's a tough one."

"I gathered that."

"You know how he got his scars?"

"No."

"Neither does anyone else. Rumor is a fire in Montana that got out of control. Some say he went back for his buddy, but his buddy didn't make it and Coleton lost half his face. Coleton won't talk about it. Showed up here twenty years ago, walking through the streets without even a hat on and staring everyone in the eye. That's Coleton's style. Take it or leave it. We've all gotten used to him over the years. Of course, every now and then some poor kid bursts into tears or runs away screaming. Coleton never apologizes."

"Why should he?"

"Oh, some would say he should have plastic surgery or at least make an effort to cover up his ears."

"It's his face, his scars."

"True, true. But some people think he's maybe a bit too fond of them. They can do amazing things with plastic surgery these days. Makes you wonder why he's never looked into it."

Brandon shrugged, trying to figure out where this conversation was heading and not succeeding.

"Personally," Tom drawled, rocking on his heels, "I think Coleton is perfectly aware that the scars make him appear scary, and he likes the fear. When he says jump, people around here jump. He talks about fire, and people shut up and listen. Those scars have made Coleton a big man around town."

"I suppose."

"The one thing everyone learns from Coleton is to be careful. For example, it's a dangerous thing to be digging a fire line by a half-dead tree without checking it out first. Kind of like starting a chain saw without inspecting the machinery."

Brandon stilled. He stared right at Tom. Only two feet separated them, and suddenly that space was tense, uncomfortable…dangerous.

"I see," Brandon said at last.

"I'm not sure that you do."

"A man should be warier? Look out for accidents?"

"Some men seem more accident-prone than others," Tom said.

"Why would one man be so accident-prone?"

"I don't know. I hear rumors that he's asking questions, that some people are uncomfortable. Lots of folks believe the past should be the past."

"Like Bud Irving?"

"Especially Bud Irving."

"I should leave now," Brandon said abruptly. "Give my clothes time to wash."

Tom nodded. He narrowed his dark eyes, the corners deeply creased in his tanned, weathered face. The man had one of the best poker faces Brandon had ever encountered.

Slowly, he moved back. Brandon had made it to the doorway when Tom spoke again.

"Be careful, Ferringer. It's not me, you know. I'm just hearing murmurs about things I don't like to hear. And I'm not one to believe in accidents."

"How long were you in the military?" Brandon asked bluntly.

Tom looked him in the eye. "Not the military, Ferringer. But it was long enough."

Brandon was breathing hard by the time he got outside. The spring sun slapped him in the face and stunned him. He'd thought it would be dark. Storming and sinister. Instead, it was a cheerful Saturday afternoon in downtown Beaverville, and people were bustling on the plank sidewalks, eyeing the collection of pickup trucks and lingering over tractors. A young boy and girl went dashing by, the towheaded girl shouting at her brother to stop.

Brandon wiped the sweat from his brow and took a deep breath. He didn't understand Tom Reynolds. Friend or foe? Storekeeper or crackpot? Beaverville wasn't as simple as it seemed.

And Brandon didn't have any answers. He knew Tom thought chain saws and trees weren't accidents. But who? How? Why?

In the bright spring afternoon, Brandon headed for the town library. For some reason, he was having to think hard to walk. His limbs felt weighted down, the world slightly out of step. He staggered at a corner, earned curious glances, shook his head and plunged down the street.

Beaverville's public library was in a new three-story building set behind the high school and announced by an impressive wood-carved sign. Across the street, the high school baseball team was practicing and Brandon could hear the distant cheers of pep squad girls, loud and distorted across the too-bright sky.

Only five cars were parked outside the library. Apparently, book vaults weren't a popular spot on a sunny afternoon.

Brandon climbed the steps and gripped the warm brass doorknob. His hand was shaking. He stared at it until it stopped.

There's nothing to fear but fear itself.

He felt unsettled. He opened the door and thrust himself into the cool, dim interior. For one moment, he couldn't see. His eyes blinked owlishly. But then they adjusted, Brandon looked up, and the whole world tilted off its axis.

He fell with a soft thud and never felt a thing.

"Sir, sir, are you all right?"

Brandon opened his eyes. A woman was peering at him, her thin face wrinkled like fine parchment paper, her gaze a watery blue. Glasses dangled from a chain around her neck, and she smelled like White Shoulders perfume and cedar mothballs. Librarian. The perfect librarian.

Brandon's gaze went past her, to the painting on the wall in the foyer. The oil portrait. The beautiful blond woman looked over her shoulder with a sad, ethereal smile and a delicate grace that would go forever unchanged. Brandon knew. He'd found the miniaturized picture of that painting in Max's locket.

He squeezed his eyes shut, but the image was etched into his eyelids.

"Are you all right?" the librarian quizzed again in her high, wavering voice. Her gold name tag identified her as Miss Elsie.

"Sorry," Brandon muttered. "My head. Dizzy."

He managed to sit up, and the world spun. He was on fire. Moisture poured from his skin. The librarian looked at him with concern. "I'll call Doc Matthews."

"Already saw him. Yesterday." Brandon winced. "I have a concussion. I probably pushed myself too hard."

Miss Elsie thinned her lips. "Are you Brandon Ferringer, young man? I heard all about that accident yesterday in training. Just dreadful! You should be home in bed right now, not darkening the doors—not to mention the floors—of my library."

Brandon opened his mouth to argue or apologize, he couldn't figure out which, but his stomach rolled queasily and he snapped his mouth shut, afraid he'd be ill.

Miss Elsie stood authoritatively and brushed off her hands. "Well, that's it. I'm calling Doc Matthews and I'm calling Sheriff Meese. They'll take care of you."

"Please." It was all Brandon could manage to say, but it stalled her. He gestured weakly toward the picture. "Who...who is that?"

"Ashley Jacobs, of course. The Jacobses built this library. Fine people, never deserved what happened—"

Brandon staggered to his feet. The pain was receding, the sweating, too. He seemed to be in the middle of a dream, watching himself move from somewhere high up, where he was no longer connected to his body. He was staring at the picture. Examining the brass plaque. Ashley Jacobs, 1939—.

So she was still alive. Thank goodness she was still alive.

He would find her. He would ask her about Max. It was terribly important that he ask her about Max.

He staggered toward the door.

"Mr. Ferringer—"

"I'm fine, I'm fine," he was muttering. He burst into the bright afternoon, and red lights exploded in front of his eyes, but he was running and no longer noticed.

He was at the Laundromat. His motions were hazy. He put his clothes in the dryer. He turned on the dryer. He watched the clothes begin to spin and thought he would vomit. Then he heard footsteps and figured Tom Reynolds was coming to get him. No, not Tom, crazy Bud Irving with his high-powered scope rifle and pack of Dobermans. Or maybe it would be beautiful Ashley Jacobs with her sad, sad smile.

I know why Maximillian never came back, she whispered. *I know why Maximillian didn't love you enough to stay. I know why. I know why.*

He left the Laundromat. He got into his rental car, started the engine, then realized he couldn't see—there were too many spots in front of his eyes. He crawled out, wavered and couldn't remember what he was doing.

Bud Irving. The name came through the red haze. Find Bud Irving.

He set off with uncoordinated footsteps, having no idea where he was going. From far away, he realized that people were staring. Then he was in front of Whiskey Jack's, and the smell of deep-fried food made his stomach roll.

He slipped down the steps, shimmied into the alley where the shadows were cool and staggered resolutely ahead.

"Oh, my Lord, call Sheriff Meese," someone said from behind him.

Brandon wondered what the sheriff had to do with it. And then he pitched forward face-first and passed out cold.

"Stupid, stupid, stubborn, stubborn, stupid, stupid."

Brandon opened his eyes. He was in Kansas, he thought blankly. "Auntie Em?"

Victoria stopped pacing at the foot of the bed. Her head shot up, her blue eyes widened, then narrowed. "It's about bloody time!"

Brandon thought that should be his line, but couldn't make his lips move. His body had melted on him. He had sunk into the mattress as if it was a porous sponge and there was no getting back. He was drenched in sweat.

Victoria stalked to the side of the bed, torn between genuine concern and the desire to throttle his reckless hide. "How *are* you?" she quizzed.

"Dead."

"No kidding. Jogging with a concussion. Stubborn, thick-headed... My father said he hadn't heard of anything so stupid since Charlie tried to climb to the top of a fifty-foot pine when he was four. You're lucky you're not in a coma."

Victoria grabbed a glass, dumped in some water and held his head while he drank. When he was done, she soaked a washcloth in a basin of cool water, then laid it over his forehead. He realized for the first time that it was dark outside, that his laundry was miraculously dry and folded on the floor, and that Victoria carried deep purple shadows beneath her eyes.

"Time?" he whispered. He wanted more water but didn't have the energy to ask. He felt as if he could drink a river, then request an ocean.

"Midnight."

His eyes widened. He looked at her almost fearfully.

Dear God, he'd lost the whole day. What had happened to him?

Victoria sighed. The anger left her all at once and she sat on the edge of his bed, her shoulders coming down. "You had a concussion, Ferringer," she said softly. "That's basically a fancy word for a bruised head. When you ran, you aggravated it. The bruise swelled, and a pocket of fluid pressed against your brain. You went from a mild concussion to a major concussion. Basically, you got a serious fever, became disoriented and threw up all over the back of my father's squad car when he was called to pick you up. You're going to hear about that, too, you know."

"I'm sorry."

"Doc Matthews has a few choice words for you, as well, Brandon. You need to stay in bed. Give yourself a chance." She stood abruptly, her face tight and her body edgy. "What kind of man goes running with a concussion? Just what are you trying to prove? Brandon Ferringer, you scared the living daylights outta me!"

Her voice had risen to a shout. He made no move to protect himself against it. "Thank you for picking up my laundry," he said.

"Tom did it," she growled, refusing to be mollified so easily.

"Oh."

"Tom told me I oughtta chain you to the bed with handcuffs. I thought he might be on to something."

"I shouldn't have run," Brandon said finally, turning away to look out the dark window. "I didn't feel that bad. Just a minor headache."

"*Just a minor headache,* says the Man of Steel. Let's see, yesterday my brother brought you home unconscious and missing half your face and we discussed trust issues. Today, my father brings you home unconscious, violently

ill and worse off than yesterday. Should we revisit last
night's conversation?''

"I didn't know, Victoria. I just…went for a run." He
looked at her as sincerely as he could. She was standing in
the middle of the room, one arm pressed against her stomach. He wished she would come back to sit on the edge of
the bed. He wanted to hold her hand. He had the sudden,
intense need to weave his fingers into hers and hold on
tight.

"Are you okay, Ferringer?" she asked quietly. "I mean,
are you *okay?*''

"I have too many questions and not enough answers,"
he whispered, and the oil portrait flashed in front of his
eyes. *Sad, sad Ashley Jacobs, how did you know my father?*

"Is this about your investigation?"

"What?"

"Miss Elsie said you came to the library. On a Saturday
afternoon?"

"I'm a geek," he whispered weakly. He wasn't ready to
talk about it yet. Max, the locket, the yearbook—they were
the only parts of his father he had left. It was terribly important that he solve the riddle. He had to know what had
happened to Julia. He had to know what had happened to
himself.

*I don't want to be like my father. Victoria, Victoria, I
don't. I want to be a better man. Must learn to be a better
husband, brother, son, father. Victoria. Victoria…*

His lips refused to form the words. The thoughts buzzed
through his mind like angry, stabbing hornets, making him
wince.

"You and your damned British reserve," Victoria
growled but she sighed and returned to the edge of the bed.
He immediately moved his fingers toward her hand.

"Ferringer, I can't keep having them bring you home on
a stretcher. It's giving me gray hairs."

"I know." His fingers were very close to her now. Just an inch more. He shifted.

"For crying out loud, try to spend more hours of the day conscious. It sets a good example for Randy."

"Yes." He made contact. Slowly, he threaded his fingers through hers. She didn't pull away, and her hand was warm and her skin soft. She felt solid, the way he knew she would. She grounded him.

He looked at her wordlessly and saw the last of the defenses crash in her gaze. "You're no good for me, Ferringer," she murmured, "absolutely no good." But then she leaned over, brushing her lips over his forehead, kissing the soft sweep of his eyelashes, whispering her lips over his cheekbone. He moved his head slightly, and she kissed him gently, giving them the reassuring contact they both needed.

At last she pulled away. "I'm so sorry," he said again, and they both knew he meant it.

"Yeah," Victoria sighed. "Yeah." She feathered his hair. She wanted to be angry with him. She'd spent the last six hours stoking a pretty good rage, but now he was conscious and he looked too pale and weary to beat up. She wanted to hold him instead, feeling a tenderness she generally reserved for her horses and her son. She brushed her fingers down the flaxen beard roughing his cheeks. He exhaled lightly over her hand. He looked exhausted.

Last night, she'd vowed to keep her distance. Instead, she'd gotten to play nursemaid once again, tending his prostrate form and wondering what things made him mutter in the dark.

Something about Maximillian the Chameleon, who kissed the girls and made them cry. But then he'd stated that he wouldn't cry, couldn't cry. Must be strong for Maggie and C.J., there's a good chap.

Whatever he had been thinking, it had upset him a great

deal, making him pitch and roll. Twice she'd shaken his
shoulder and he'd quieted. The third time, he'd resisted and
she'd finally crawled into bed and held his fevered form
against her. He'd turned to her immediately, buried his head
against her shoulder and whispered her name.

Whispered her name.

She doubted he remembered what he'd done, and she'd
promised herself she would never tell.

"Randy told me he spoke to you this morning," she said
at last.

"Did he?" Ferringer was staring at her too intensely.
The fever still? Something more? She fastened her gaze on
the floor.

"I hadn't realized he was awake last night, when Ronald
came. What a mess."

"I'm sure you handled it well."

She made a face. "I tried, at any rate."

"What did Randy say?"

"He's worried about becoming an alcoholic. I told him
that was fair. But I would help him and his uncles would
help him and his grandparents would help him and he had
an awful lot of people in his corner who thought he was a
very special boy, so he'd be all right. The sins of the father
don't have to be the sins of the son, or any of that gar-
bage."

Brandon didn't say anything, but the intensity of his gaze
ratcheted up another notch. Her breathing was no longer
steady. The silence frayed her nerves.

"Well," she announced too brightly, "I should let you
get some sleep. No moving tomorrow, Ferringer, doctor's
orders. I'll send Randy in here to sit on you if I have to."

She tried to stand, but he didn't relinquish his grip on
her hand. Finally, she looked at him.

His face was too lean, his cheeks hollow, his eyes
smudged. This close, she could see the demons dancing in

his eyes, the regret and need that flayed him bit by bit, night after night. He looked raw around the edges, and his mind was savaged and hurt. The first time she shut off the lights, the monsters would spring from their hiding places and devour him.

"Please," he said. She didn't pretend not to understand. He needed her. Really, truly *needed* her. She squeezed her eyes shut and felt herself being torn in half.

"Oh, God, Ferringer. My mother always told me the devil would get me in the end."

"Please," he said again.

"I...I can't. Randy."

"Of course," he whispered. "Randy. You're absolutely right. And that's important. Protect yourself from me. That's important."

He wasn't making sense, but his fingers released their grip. Victoria bounded up before she lost her resolve. She kept looking at him, though. It wasn't right to leave him like this—so vulnerable.

She did want to hold him. She wanted to be there for him when the lights were turned down and his dreams grew harsh. She wanted to stroke his cheek and tell him it would be all right, because when he said her name she felt pretty. And last night, he'd put his arm around her when she really needed to be held. And he'd told her she wasn't hardhearted sincerely enough for her to believe him.

He gave her things he probably didn't even realize, and when he was wounded and raw, she was going to walk away. They both knew it was the only choice she had. And God, did it hurt her.

"I'll bring you breakfast in the morning," she whispered.

He nodded slowly. "That would be nice."

"Ferringer, take care of yourself, all right?"

He didn't reply.

She turned out the light and left him alone with the demons that lurked in the dark.

Chapter 7

"**D**ay of the week?"

"Monday."

"Your name?"

"Smokey the Bear."

"Very cute, Ferringer. Shut up and listen to the doc." Coleton was in a bad mood. Then again, Brandon had yet to see him in a good one.

"Follow my finger. Uh-huh. Does this hurt? How about this? And this." Brandon winced sharply, which Doc Matthews took as a yes. The older man put down his clipboard, looped his stethoscope around his neck and sighed.

Brandon stiffened. It was 0620 Monday morning. The rest of the hotshots would be arriving in ten minutes for the morning run. He wanted to know, in or out. Fish or fowl.

"Yep," Doc Matthews said, "you were right, Coleton. This one's got a skull like a bowling ball. He'll take a lickin' and keep on tickin'."

Coleton grinned, twisting his scarred cheek grotesquely and creasing his scalp. He slapped Brandon on the shoulder. "Not bad, rich Brit. Not bad."

Brandon relaxed, but only slightly. His gaze kept going from Coleton to Doc Matthews with barely disguised wariness. He'd had all day Sunday to contemplate his "accidents" and Tom Reynolds's words of warning. Flat on his back, with only Randy as company, Brandon had replayed every detail of the chain saw and the falling tree. He'd thought of the sensation he'd had that night of being watched, the jolt of seeing Ashley Jacobs's picture hanging in the town library and the information that Bud Irving was a delusional, gun-happy, crazy man. All roads led to Beaverville.

He was on to something, he just had no idea what. Instead, he'd developed a thin glaze of paranoia that made everyone suspect—Bud Irving, Ashley Jacobs, Tom Reynolds, Coleton Smith, Doc Matthews, Sheriff Meese. As the day had gone on, his list of potential suspects had grown longer. The fact that Randy had been reading an R. L. Stine book to him probably hadn't helped.

"No running for the next few days, of course," Doc Matthews continued, making notations on the chart. "He can do light weights, mild work, but no heavy machinery just in case he has dizzy spells again."

"What about classroom training? Wouldn't want to strain anything."

"Now, Coleton, I've seen his IQ, and I've seen yours, and I can honestly say, he's in no danger from you."

Coleton grinned again. "Son of a bitch, doc."

"How can I help my team if I'm not allowed to run?" Brandon interrupted.

"You can play crew boss," Coleton said easily. "You ought to know management, rich Brit."

Brandon looked at the doctor.

"That would be best," Doc Matthews agreed. "You'll be perfectly fine, but you're going to need a few days. When does the crew post up?"

"Classroom training is complete Friday," Coleton told him. "We'll do the fit test then."

"Well, as fit as Mr. Ferringer is, a few days off from running won't keep him from qualifying. I've never seen lungs as good as his. Everest, huh? When the crew gets calls, he'll be ready."

Doc Matthews turned his attention to his charts, his old face guileless. Coleton, however, looked pleased with himself. Because Brandon was going to be all right or because for the next few days, Brandon would be slowed? Brandon's thoughts were making him dizzy.

"Ever lead a team?" Coleton quizzed. "Ever made a decision under real *fire*, with life and death hanging in the balance?"

"No."

"Good." Coleton slapped him hard on the back. "You'll like it, rich Brit. Builds character."

Brandon didn't come home until seven o'clock, his limbs leaden and his temples pounding. He stood beneath the stinging needles of the hot shower hoping it would hammer the tension from his shoulders. His mind was full, trying to remember the structure of command center, the functional and regional chain of command, the different units and divisions that would all be deployed and coordinated to combat a major fire.

He was thinking of the proper strategies for determining fire lines and laying hoses, the things that could get his crew into trouble and the things that could save their bacon.

He was thinking that he had the phone number for the Jacobs family, straight from directory assistance.

He stepped out of the shower and toweled off. He pulled on his black sweats and a white turtleneck. He walked through the dark yard all by himself, wondering if he really felt eyes upon his back, or was it just his overactive imagination? He could see the kitchen light on in the main house. Victoria and Randy were sitting down for dinner.

He hadn't seen Victoria since Saturday night. She'd never brought him breakfast as she'd promised on Sunday. She'd had Randy do it, instead. He supposed he understood.

He wondered what they were having tonight, sitting together at the comfortable old table in the warm, cheery kitchen. More fried chicken and mashed potatoes? Would Randy eat his vegetables?

Brandon heated up split pea soup and ate it with dry crackers and baby carrots. He unburied the phone number from his duffel bag and stared at it. He should call. Say he knew Maximillian Ferringer. Wait for Ashley Jacobs's reaction. Bud Irving might be the town loony, but apparently the Jacobses were pillars of the community, an old rich family whose money had built the library and kept the 4-H Club and Little League teams afloat.

He rinsed his soup pan with a pitcher of water and put away the crackers. He'd gotten crumbs everywhere. He swept them up. The phone number still sat on his pillow.

He finally got out his cell phone, the cabin having no phone service of its own. Just call. Reach out and touch someone.

He sat on the bed, phone in his right hand, number in his left. He couldn't do it. He just couldn't do it.

He didn't want to know the answers, he thought suddenly, with a wave of panic that startled him. What if C.J. was right? What if Maggie was right? What if their father was a no-good smuggler? Ashley Jacobs might confirm everything. And then there would be no place to hide. The truth would be out, raw and irrefutable.

Maximillian the Chameleon had been a self-centered, money-hungry, materialistic, no-good con man.

And you're his son. You're his son.

The one he left as soon as the money was gone.

He stood too fast. The world spun, and he grabbed the wall. Then his head cleared, blood flow evened out, and he moved quickly. He shoved the phone into his duffel bag. He buried the locket beneath the mattress and shoved the phone number beneath his dirty laundry, where maybe he would forget it completely.

It wasn't enough. He didn't want to be alone in the damn cabin anymore with the walls closing in and the night too dark. He said to hell with it all and headed for the stables.

He wanted to see Victoria. For the last few days, all he wanted was Victoria.

"So let me get this straight. You get conked on the head by a tree you didn't even notice. You violate doctor's orders and make your head injury worse, and now you're in management?"

"Basically...yes."

"Sounds like the federal government to me."

Brandon allowed a wry smile. His gaze was latched upon her figure like a starving man, and though he'd been here for ten minutes, neither of them was exactly comfortable.

She'd stilled at first sight of him, the hyperawareness washing over them both. He'd remained twenty feet away, afraid that if he came closer she'd bolt. After another tense moment, her gaze had returned to the horse she was preparing to ride, and Brandon had pounced upon the first neutral subject he could find—work. So far, so good.

"What exactly does a crew boss do?" Victoria asked, stretching to better position the saddle on Doc's back. She wore gray riding sweats that fit her like a second skin. Every time she twisted, Brandon lost his train of thought.

"Um...directs the efforts. When our team is called out, we'll be put in charge of a section of a fire line, building it, maintaining it. The crew boss helps plan the best area for the line, keeps an eye out for trouble and coordinates his team's efforts with everyone else's. If things get dicey, he'll make the call to evacuate. Then he makes sure everyone gets out."

"Uh-huh. Aren't you guy who let his team burn last week?" She adjusted the stirrups.

"Yes. And thanks for pointing that out."

She looked him in the eye, and the tension ratcheted up another notch.

She snapped the stirrup in silence, and they both flinched while the horse pranced.

She said, "I just wondered how you felt about it. Last week, you were struggling to be part of a team, today you're leading it. That's a big jump for a man who considers himself a lone wolf."

"It's a big jump."

She waited, and when he didn't elaborate, she shook her head. "Fine, forget I brought it up, it's none of my business." She resumed tightening the saddle, her hand yanking the leather strap through the buckle with unnecessary force.

"A leader should be selfless," Brandon said, abruptly taking a step forward. "I don't think I'm selfless."

"What do you think you are?" She took a step back.

"Self-centered," he told her. "Remote. Someone more comfortable with thinking of himself than others." He was close to the horse now. She circled to the other side, but his gaze was locked on her bent head. The horse danced nervously.

"Ferringer, you are not selfish. I don't know who saddled you with that rap, but they shouldn't have. So there." She yanked on the saddle buckle, grunting as she cinched it tight. "These days, you got some allies."

She made the mistake of looking him in the eye, and the saddle almost burst into flame.

Their breathing accelerated. The stable was suddenly hot and musty and damp.

"It was the tree," he murmured in the hushed stillness. "Surviving a falling tree seems to garner a man some respect."

"Ha!" she said, but her voice was breathless.

"Don't knock it until you try it."

"What about the woman who nurses you back to health and sends her son to strap you into bed, huh?"

"She served beyond the call of duty. She deserves a reward."

"A reward? Us starving ranch owners and single moms have unbelievably refined tastes, you know. I can't be bought off with just any old trinket."

"What about a kiss?"

The question hung in the air. Her gaze fell to his lips helplessly, and even as her body shifted, wary and edgy, the tip of her tongue moistened her lips. "Damn," she muttered. "Damn, damn, I'm not going to do this! I am not eighteen!"

She whirled abruptly, stalked two steps, then whirled again. "I'm gonna ride my horse, Brandon Ferringer. That's what I came out here to do, and that's what I'm gonna do. So get out of my way. I need to saddle up."

She stormed to his side, as he was standing on the left. She moved like a tornado, grabbing the saddle and fumbling to get her foot in the stirrup. At the last minute, she pinned him with a look.

"Help me up," she growled. It was not a request.

Wordlessly, Brandon knit his hands into a step and offered it. She planted her foot and swung up, her hip against his cheek, her leg pressed against his chest. He could smell laundry detergent and apple shampoo. He could smell a light, wafting fragrance of musk.

And though he knew he shouldn't, he curved his fingers around her calf, feeling the warm, firm flesh. Slowly, his fingers crept up.

"I'm going to ride," she said in a strained voice.

"Uh-huh." He explored the shape of her knee, charting it as he would a detailed map. He found a spot behind her kneecap, pressed it and heard her gasp. He wanted to plant his lips there. He wanted to traverse every inch of her well-curved legs with his lips, his tongue, his teeth.

"Step…step back."

"Uh-huh." His fingers arrived at her thigh, feeling her quiver. Her legs were strong, well-toned and beautifully shaped. He dug his fingers in slightly, and she sighed helplessly.

"You're tense, Victoria." He caressed her leg.

"Just a little."

"Hard time sleeping?" He curved his fingers toward the inside of her thigh.

"Just a little."

"Me, too."

"That's because you beat yourself over the head with a tree." Her back was arching. Her eyes had fluttered shut. His fingers crept up.

"You don't want me at all?" he whispered.

"Not at all," she gasped.

"Then I don't want you just as much."

"What are you doing?" Her voice grew definitely strangled as his fingers finally reached the apex of her thighs and he cupped her with his palm and pressed lightly.

"I've missed you," he said softly, surprising himself. "I didn't mean to miss you. I didn't mean…"

He shifted closer, his voice suddenly too raw, and her hand snapped around his wrist.

"Enough!"

Her breathing was ragged. So was his. The horse pranced away nervously, and the contact was finally broken.

"Damn you, Ferringer," Victoria said. Her eyes were squeezed shut. He could see the longing etched clearly in every aching line of her face. Then her eyes flew open, and she shook her head vehemently. "You're making this too hard on both of us. I can't…I won't!"

Abruptly, Victoria clicked her tongue and Doc shot forward into a trot, churning up plumes of dirt as he bounded by. Victoria leaned over the big beast's neck, muttered a few words of encouragement, and they went flying, her golden hair mingling with gray mane, her expression saying she had no intention of stopping. She rode as if she was pursued by the devil himself, and once again, Brandon understood.

She was right. Absolutely right. And dammit, he wanted her anyway. He *burned.*

Not until Brandon left the stables did Victoria slow her mount. Moisture stained her cheeks. She felt as if she'd been through a wringer, as if her bones had been crushed.

"What doesn't break us makes us stronger," she muttered thickly. "Oh, bloody hell."

She was fighting a losing battle and she knew it. Friday night, she stood in front of her closet contemplating her lone dress and trying to be strong. They were going out for a celebration dinner. Brandon, Charlie, her whole family. Fourteen people, only one of whom she wasn't related to. She didn't need to wear her dress.

Her brothers would tease her if she wore the dress.

She fingered the red cotton material anyway, remembered Ferringer's hand kneading her thigh and snatched back her arm as if she'd been singed.

Jeans. Definitely jeans. Loose jeans. And some old ratty T-shirt so he'd know once and for all that she wasn't staying up late mooning over him. Not Vic. She was much too strong for that kind of prattle.

Dammit, she was staring at the dress again and scowling so hard her face should be permanently wrinkled. Men were evil.

She sat on the edge of her bed. Her shoulders were tight, her whole body knotted with tension. She hadn't seen Brandon Ferringer since Monday night, but that didn't seem to affect things. She was unbearably conscious of every move he made. What time he came home—late—what time he turned off the light in his cabin—later—how long she swore she could feel his gaze across the fifty yards—a long time.

She knew from Charlie that he'd gotten a clean bill of health on Wednesday and was doing better. He was paying more attention to his crew members and Tuesday had stayed late to help Barbara become more comfortable operating the chain saw. Barbara was married, Charlie added casually. Her husband was there the whole time.

Then Randy had asked permission to seek help on his homework, not returning until almost nine and announcing straight off that they should have Brandon over for dinner more—the man only got to eat soup by himself. Randy thought canned soup was worse than even Brussels sprouts.

Victoria had sent her son to bed after informing him that Brandon was a big boy—he could take care of himself.

He'd pulled in the driveway Thursday night just as she and Randy were sitting down to a hot, hearty meal of beef Stroganoff. She'd stuck to her guns. Randy had given her reproachful glances all evening. No one could deliver guilt like an eight-year-old.

Now it was Friday, and she couldn't avoid Brandon anymore. Today, the hotshot crew would complete the required classroom training and then have the fit test. Assuming that everyone passed, the team would be posted up. They would officially be on call.

Charlie had assured her that they would all pass the fit test. You just had to run a mile and a half in under eleven minutes, then pass the step test—step up and down for thirty seconds without elevating your heart rate beyond the target zone. No big whoop for lean, mean hotshots. Charlie's real goal was running the mile and a half in six minutes. Brandon thought he could do it in seven. No doubt they were egging each other on as much as possible.

Men.

Her gaze was back on the red dress. It was simple, belted at the waist with a flared skirt that whirled around her legs, perfect for dancing. And there would be dancing. Her parents didn't take their children anyplace that didn't offer a good Western band. Did Ferringer like to dance? She could imagine his hand spread on the small of her back, guiding her through the elaborate steps.

"They're here, they're here!" Randy yelled from the foyer. He was already decked out in his red-checkered cowboy shirt and freshly polished Sunday boots. "Mom, Mom!"

"Coming!" she called, and without giving herself an-

other chance to think, grabbed her lavender blouse and a
fresh pair of jeans.

"It was incredible, you should've seen it!" Charlie was
exclaiming in a rush as Victoria stepped into the yard. Twilight was falling, the assembled group of her parents and
assorted siblings cast in shadows. Even then Brandon stood
out, freshly showered, his dark blue Oxford-cloth shirt
rolled up to his elbows.

"At the quarter-mile mark, Barbara twists her ankle on
the track and goes down. She gets right back up, but she's
limping. She can't run. Still, eleven minutes for a mile and
a half isn't bad, and Barbara's in good shape. It won't be
graceful, but she figures she'll half-walk, half-trot it. But
her ankle's worse than she thought. It starts to swell—she
can't walk. In fact, she's more or less hopping along, trying
not to stare at Coleton, but hell, we know what's going on.
She's not going to make it. Now she's trying not to cry.

"Then all of a sudden, who goes sprinting onto the track
but Ferringer. He comes up right behind Barbara, swings
her into his arms and runs with her to the finish line, where
he politely sets her down and she hops over all by herself.
Ten minutes fifty-five seconds. 'Teamwork,' Ferringer
chirps. 'My crew is done.'

"And Coleton, Coleton's so floored he gives it to them.
'What the hell,' he says, 'at least someone has been listening to me.' It was unbelievable. Barbara will most likely
give Ferringer her firstborn child. You know—" Charlie's
gaze slid toward Victoria "—unless he gets any better offers."

Her parents laughed, and there was a general murmur of
appreciation while Victoria scowled at her youngest
brother. Charlie and Brandon showed off the new pagers
clipped to the waistbands of their jeans. Now that they were

posted up, they were required to be within one hour of deployment and five minutes of call back. They were hotshots.

Her father slapped Brandon on the back. "Not bad for the man who yiffed all over my patrol car. Still can't get the smell out."

"Sorry about that."

"Ah, well, glad to see that you're feeling better. Sounds like Beaverville's lucky to have you. Now let's go eat. My treat."

"I get to ride with Brandon!" Randy whooped, and the divvying of cars began.

Victoria stayed over to the side, trying to pretend she didn't notice who went where. But when Brandon calmly climbed into her truck, she wasn't surprised.

"I like playing with fire," he said conversationally.

"Bah, humbug," she replied.

"Mind if I interrupt?"

Sarah and Victoria both looked up. Sarah was Victoria's sister-in-law and currently eight months pregnant with her and John's second child. With her round face, chocolate brown eyes and rich mahogany hair, the half Native American was a startlingly beautiful woman. She was also sick of being pregnant and was telling Victoria all about it in no uncertain terms.

"I miss sex," she'd just got done announcing. "I know I'm as big as a house and I'm supposed to be feeling all nurturing and maternal, but dammit, I miss sex."

So far the conversation wasn't helping Victoria's state of mind.

"I was wondering if you would like to dance, Victoria," Brandon murmured when both women remained staring at him wordlessly. "I thought I would give this Western two-step a try, but I imagine I'll need some help."

"We're talking," Victoria said rather rudely. The plate in front of her was piled high with stripped rib bones. She loved barbecued ribs and could eat them by the dozens. Of course, that kind of shamelessness was easier when it was only her brothers who noticed.

"Oh, no, go ahead," Sarah said quickly. She flashed Brandon a winning smile. "I'm done moaning about my lack of a sex life now." Her brown eyes twinkled. Brandon's cheeks flushed red. No one in Victoria's family was very bashful. So far, Brandon was holding up surprisingly well.

"Mmm, uh, well, yes, then. Victoria, shall we dance?"

"No one says *shall* anymore," she muttered, but she accepted his outstretched hand. Big mistake. His palm was callused and hard, his fingers warm. She was suffused with the image of that hand tracing her breast, and the pang of desire was so potent, she missed a step and almost fell on her butt.

Brandon caught her around the waist, steadying her. "I wasn't expecting to be able to do that until we got on the dance floor," he muttered in her ear. "But this works."

She yanked away. "I can walk by myself."

"If you insist."

By the time they got out to the sea of gaily dressed people on the wooden plank floor, her cheeks were bright red and her eyes were crackling. She was angry. No, she was hungry and frustrated, and anger was the easiest way of releasing the pressure.

Brandon Ferringer planted his hand on the small of her back, gripped her right hand and started whirling her in what should have been a Western two-step. It came out more as a tango, however, with her eyes burning into his gaze and the air growing so hot between them it sizzled.

"Why is Mom mad at Brandon?" Randy asked at the table.

His grandma patted his hand. "In a few years, dear. Everything will become clear in a few years."

Randy shrugged and went in search of tapioca pudding. On the other side of the table, Sarah sighed and dug in her purse for a chocolate bar. Wordlessly, her husband held out his hand for a piece.

"Four months, tops," she assured him.

"We'll buy more chocolate on the way home," he agreed, and wrapped his arm around her shoulder.

Victoria came up hard against Brandon's chest, released her breath in an outraged hiss and retaliated with a sharp rap of her heel on his toes. He promptly twisted her to the side, caught her arm behind her and moseyed forward four steps before twirling her against him.

"I thought you couldn't dance," she growled.

"I learn fast," he said mildly, but his blue eyes were much too dark and a light sheen of perspiration stained his cheeks.

"So now that you're officially a wildland firefighter, you think you can handle the heat?"

"Victoria, with you, I never make any assumptions."

He twirled her around, and she let him. And she knew as the sea of people whirled around them and the floor shook with the beat that she was losing the war. He brought her against his chest, his lips parted, his eyes raw. The guitar sang and the banjo twanged. She felt her defenses crumble. The music picked up. They moved faster. She told him with her gyrating steps where the music led, and he fiercely agreed.

* * *

"Thank you for dinner." She kissed her mother on the cheek, her voice low so she wouldn't wake Randy, sprawled out in the front seat. "Thanks, Dad." She embraced her father, who smelled comfortably of beer and spiced ribs, then gave Charlie a last congratulatory squeeze.

It was two in the morning and the Meese clan was finally pouring out of Moses's Honky Tonk—a late night for them all, which was setting Victoria's teeth on edge. She loved her family. She really did. She'd been ready to leave two hours ago, dammit. Her gaze went straight to Brandon.

He was still untangling himself from her sister-in-law. Then he climbed behind the wheel. They didn't say a word. She adjusted Randy's sleeping head on her lap. Brandon put the truck into gear.

It was a forty-five minute drive to the Lady Luck Ranch, a hop, skip and a jump for central Oregon. Still, she felt each mile keenly, as impatient as a two-year-old. Two weeks of foreplay was enough for anyone. She was ready to get down to business.

Is this the right thing?

She didn't want to have that thought. Brandon wasn't Ronald. He wasn't a thief or an addict or a liar. She'd chosen better this time around.

He still won't stay. Tonight will be sweet, tomorrow sweeter. But six months from now, when his term is up? How will you feel? How will Randy feel?

She looked out the window at the inky darkness racing by. Randy was old enough to understand about girlfriends and boyfriends. He'd met enough of Charlie's dates over the years. She didn't think he'd mind Victoria and Brandon dating. But could he understand the limitations? Would he understand Brandon's need to move on come fall?

Or would he take that personally? The way Victoria inevitably would?

She pushed the thought away again. She didn't want reality. She wasn't ready for reality. This was her Cinderella moment, and hell, she hadn't even gone to her own prom because Ronald had preferred to go off drinking. Surely every woman was entitled to one night from a fairy tale.

Brandon's fingers touched her cheek. She looked at him. His face was somber in the darkness, his jaw strong.

"I had a wonderful time tonight," he said, and she swore to herself that it would be all right.

He took Randy out of her arms when they finally pulled up at the ranch. She opened the front door and they crept through the blackened house like thieves, trying not to make any noise that would wake her son. His bedroom was next-door to hers. She pulled back the cowboy covers and Brandon laid him down.

"Tired," Randy groaned, smacked his lips sleepily, and rolled over. She pulled off his boots and jeans and left him in his shirt with the covers tucked around his neck.

Her hands were shaking. She hadn't planned on feeling so nervous. She was a twenty-seven-year-old woman, for God's sake. She'd given birth to a child. No blushing virgin here. But there had never been anyone but Ronald. Suddenly, that made her feel foolish.

She smoothed a hand over her shirt, inhaled a steadying breath and found Brandon waiting on the front porch. He turned as she approached. He studied her.

"Why don't we go to your cabin?" she said. "My room—" she licked her lips "—my room is next to Randy's."

"Are you sure?"

"Yeah. Yeah, I am. And you?"

"Yes," he said quietly. "Definitely, yes."

He held out his hand, and she took it. For one moment,

they stood apart, joined only by the grip of their fingers.
Then he tugged and she succumbed, coming into his embrace, opening her arms, arching her neck.

His lips met hers fiercely, his tongue already dueling
with hers, and the latent tension exploded, ripping through
her veins and leaving her dizzy. *Yes, yes, yes.*

"My cabin," he whispered urgently, nibbling the corner
of her mouth, tracing a path along her jaw, suckling her
earlobe. "Cabin."

"Argh, yeah, oh my," she said.

His lips returned. She clutched his cheeks, her body
pressed against his, his hardness stabbing her belly. God,
she was so damp and achy and hot.

"Cabin," he muttered thickly. "Cabin."

They sprang down the porch like teenagers and ran for
it. His porch loomed. She was tingling and tight with anticipation. In her mind, he was already naked and above
her.

Suddenly he yanked to a stop, jerking her hand.

"Oh, my God," Brandon said. *"The stables!"*

Chapter 8

Plumes of smoke rolled out of the stable's center aisle, thick and black. A nervous whinny erupted, then hoofbeats thundered as Doc plunged around the arena, enraged by the fumes and crackling blaze.

"The horses," Brandon shouted and raced into the heart of it. He had a last glimpse of Victoria running toward the closest stall, then he was struggling with his shirt, ripping off the cotton and holding it in front of his face as the acrid smoke seared his nostrils.

Up ahead, orange tongues of flames danced across the hay bales and licked the wooden stalls, heading for the rafters, seeking the rafters. If they caught...

The hose, the hose. He felt along the ground frantically, his eyes tearing, his throat closing up. Alfalfa burned densely. In his mind he could see the charts for fuel moisture to time of burning while his fingers scratched along the dirt floor trying to find the damn coiled hose.

He tripped over it, followed it to the end and flicked on the knob. Water streamed out, sweet and clear.

He turned and let the fire have it.

In the distance, Doc neighed wildly and careened toward the gate.

"Doc, no!" Victoria screamed. She bolted over the fence, waving her arms. Doc rolled his eyes in panic and just kept coming. The gate was too high. He'd break a leg.

"Down!" Brandon yelled.

She dove to the side. Suddenly water arched through the air, nailing the foaming horse between the eyes. Doc reared up, stopped cold. He screamed, a raw primal yell that hurt Victoria to hear. Then the horse twisted to the left, as desperate to escape the water as the flames, and took off running once more.

"I got him, I got him!" Victoria scrambled to her feet. "Open the gate, let him out!"

"He's too panicked, he'll break a leg."

She raced for the lunge rope. With a curse, Brandon hosed down the exposed rafters, then grabbed the hay hooks and ripped open the bales, exposing golden, burning embers and dousing them with water.

He could hear Doc whinnying again, long and furious. Then he heard Victoria's sharp yell.

"Dammit!" He dropped the hose and ran for the arena.

"Shhh," Victoria murmured. "Shhh."

Brandon burst through the smoke like a specter and Doc reared again, but she had him on the lunge line and brought him down. Brandon froze, almost as panicked as Doc. His torso was bare, the rippling lines of his chest clearly illuminated by sweat. Soot dusted the broad sweep of his collarbone, smearing through the small smattering of golden chest hair and drawing her gaze to a washboard stomach.

He was toned. Lord, he was toned, and sweat and water stained the waistband of his jeans, while his forearms tensed, sending ripples of tendons snaking beneath his skin. He was on edge, she was on edge. At the other end of the lunge line, the horse was on edge. The silence drew out, lengthened, then Doc's foreleg quivered and he rolled his eyes, ready for flight once more.

She jerked her attention to her horse and murmured soothing sounds she hoped would quiet them both. Adrenaline still buzzed in her ears.

"Do you want me to take him?" Brandon gestured toward Doc, his voice tight.

"I got him." Doc's nostrils flared, his coat dusty. "It's okay, boy," she whispered. "It's okay now. We're all okay."

The trick was to be calm. Horses responded to that more than anything. Of course, it was difficult to be calm when she was standing next to a half-naked man who only moments before had been prepared to sweep her into his cabin and strip her bare. She closed her eyes but still tasted his kiss on her lips.

"Are you all right?" Brandon asked. "I thought I heard a yell."

"Oh, we had a rough moment or two, but we're fine now." Doc's ears finally pivoted toward her at the sound of her voice, a good sign. She continued stroking his neck.

"The other horses?"

"Riches was the only one still in a stall—I turn Daisy and Specter out to pasture at night. Riches is fine. And Doc is calming down. The fear gets them in more trouble than the fire." She pointed at his foreleg, which was bleeding. "Probably hit it against a railing when he panicked."

"Anything permanent?"

"No, I just need to dress it. The fire's out, I assume."

"Yes, it hadn't spread from the hay bales."

She sighed and gritted her teeth. "Of all the lousy luck. The alfalfa must have spontaneously combusted. It happens around here. We get so much damn rain, everything's damp all the time, or maybe the alfalfa didn't dry out all the way before it was baled. Then it starts mildewing, generates heat and bam." She shook her head. "I thought we'd salted that batch, though. I do try to be careful."

She looked outside the arena gate. The feed area was blackened and charred. Two weeks of alfalfa were ruined, and alfalfa was expensive these days. The Oregon floods of 1996 had wiped out valuable pastureland, rocketing up prices across the board. Damn, damn, damn, damn. The joy of being a rancher was that if it wasn't one thing, it was always another.

Victoria wrapped her arms around Doc's neck. He stood quietly, big, enduring, reassuring. She hugged him closer. "It could've been worse," she murmured. "Much worse."

"I should check the rafters," Brandon said at last. His face was grim. He didn't meet her eye. "You can't be too careful about embers."

"Yeah. I need to treat Doc's leg."

He turned away and Victoria smiled wanly. The passion, so rampant earlier, was gone, and they both knew it. Moments came, moments went. Wordlessly, they got to work.

Brandon inspected the rafters thoroughly, determined every last spark was out, and finally turned the hose on himself to rinse off. The water was ice cold against his sweating chest. He barely noticed it. His shoulders were bunched. He could feel a tension headache rolling in and didn't bother to fight it. He was angry. So incredibly angry.

The chain saw, the falling tree, the burning hay. Accidents or not accidents? Related or coincidental? Chains did come loose, dead trees did fall, damp hay could combust.

And old ghosts could come back to haunt you when skeletons were rattled in the closet.

Dammit, he didn't know. Analytic whiz kid Brandon Ferringer just didn't know, and he hated that sensation most of all. He was frustrated. He was furious. And as he pictured the flames licking up the stable walls and heard the horses' frightened cries, he felt secretly guilty. What if it was all his fault? What if once more he was dragging an innocent woman into his problems? Max's problems!

Bloody hell.

He yanked on a fresh shirt and headed for the front porch. Victoria sat on the steps, her arms wrapped around her knees and her face exhausted. Her pretty lavender blouse was ruined, her good jeans ripped. He still remembered how she'd looked coming out of the house this evening—so beautiful it had hurt.

He sat. He plucked at imaginary lint on his jeans. "How's Doc?" he asked at last.

"A scratch. He'll be fine."

"Good. And you?"

"Just tired and frustrated."

"No kidding," he growled, and earned her startled glance.

They lapsed into silence. Victoria's features were tight, the worry corrugating her brow. He wanted to hold her and tell her it would be all right. He had no business making such promises. He wanted to comfort her. He might be the one to blame.

"I'll have to go into town tomorrow," Victoria murmured. She dragged a hand through her hair. The golden strands were dulled by the smoke. "Need to buy alfalfa.

Maybe find some raw lumber and patch up. That should do.''

"I'll buy it," he said abruptly.

"What?"

"The lumber, grain, alfalfa, whatever you need. I'll take care of it." She'd gone rigid beside him. He didn't take the hint. "You'll need new hay hooks and probably a hose. A fire extinguisher would be a good idea, as well. Wait— we'll get several. Stick one in each stall. Rebuild the feed area. I'll measure it in the morning."

"What the hell are you doing?" She was on her feet so fast she startled him. "How dare you, Ferringer? How dare you try to take over my life like that? I was just talking out loud, that's all. I was not asking for a handout! You oughtta know me better than that!"

"That's not what I meant—"

"You just said you would pay for everything. Hell, you just blurted out a shopping list for my ranch without so much as a by your leave!"

"I didn't mean—"

"Let's get this straight, Ferringer, because it's four in the damn morning and I don't plan on having this conversation again. I *do not* want your money. I am not looking for a Prince Charming for myself or Randy. I am perfectly capable of taking care of myself and my ranch. My alfalfa spontaneously combusted. Welcome to ranch life. In the morning, I'll go into town and take care of it. You get back to your hotshots and leave me and my ranch alone. And don't ever insult me like that again."

She was nearly shouting. Her temper sparked his own, and suddenly reserved, stoic Brandon Ferringer was on his feet.

"Bloody hell!" he said. "What do you want from me, woman? I offer to help and you bite off my head—"

"You didn't offer to help, you tried to buy my life!"

"And what is so damn wrong with that? I have money. I can buy you a new stables, I can buy you a truck and I can buy a damn horse. I can throw in a computer for Randy and a roof for the house. What is so bloody wrong with that?"

"Brandon Ferringer..." Her voice dropped to a low growl.

"What?" he demanded recklessly. "What, what, *what?*"

Her chest heaved. She looked one inch away from belting him and two inches away from making sure they never found his body. Abruptly, she thinned her lips. "I'm going to bed," she announced. "It's late, we're exhausted, and we're obviously not ourselves or you would know better than to suffocate me with dollars and I would know better than to want to kiss you anyway. Good night!"

She pivoted sharply, her eyes still ablaze, and stormed into her house. The screen door snapped shut. The front door slammed.

Brandon remained standing, his fists clenched at his sides, his blood on fire. She wanted to kiss him anyway?

He gave up, and in a storm of emotion, he kicked the ground, then pulverized a small sagebrush. Bloody hell.

He would never understand women! He would just never understand women! He bought his mother her damn estate back and still she called him just to tell him he was cold, unfeeling and remote. Julia said they never went out anymore. He took her to the best restaurant in New York. She said he no longer seemed to care, and he brought her a dozen roses. And even then, he could read her sadness from across the room when he came home at midnight. He was staying late for his *job,* for God's sake. It wasn't as if he went barhopping with the boys or flirted with other women.

He tried, dammit! He didn't want to be like his father, he knew he didn't. And he was a success—he'd made real money through good investments, not draining it from wealthy women. He'd taken care of his mother. He'd taken care of his wife. When his sister, Maggie, was kidnapped, he'd been the first to put up the six-digit reward. When C.J.'s fiancée had been arrested, he'd been the first to post the six-digit bail.

He was trying to be a team player. He was trying not to be *cold.*

He was trying to be a real *man.*

And ending up as Santa Claus.

The thought came out of nowhere and stunned him still. Santa Claus. God, it was true, When Maggie or C.J. or Lydia had problems, they called each other, not Brandon. They listened to each other, told each other about the petty concerns and little hopes that comprised everyday life. Brandon was the one on the fringe, the one they could never reach, the one who would arrive later with an exotic present or hopeful chunk of cash before he took off again.

He gave his family everything but himself.

Not even Julia had gotten all of him. And he knew, he understood deep down, that was how he'd failed her. He'd married her and then made her feel lonely.

He walked quietly to his cabin. He went to bed fully dressed without turning on the light, then lay there wide-awake, staring at the ceiling.

He kept seeing his wife, smiling at him in her pink waitress uniform the day they met.

"I'm trying to do better," he insisted. "I am."

He rolled onto his side, but his face remained grim and his blue eyes were stark.

Brandon woke up to the sound of a truck door slamming and an engine starting. He heard Randy's excited chatter, then the truck backed up and headed down the driveway. Victoria and Randy must be going into town.

To buy alfalfa and lumber and grain. So Victoria could take care of her ranch and he could try not to make an ass out of himself again. If he offered to hammer in a few boards would he be crossing the line?

He could have some money wired to a lawyer in her name. Say it was a freak inheritance. Or maybe lottery winnings or income tax withholdings that had been too high.

Let it go, Ferringer. Give her more credit and give her more respect.

He dragged himself out of bed and headed for the shower, his mood no better by morning than it had been at night. Half an hour later, he gulped down instant coffee and stirred more hot water into packets of instant oatmeal.

All right, Ferringer, time to focus.

He sat on the edge of the bed, turned on his cellular phone and dialed the Jacobses' number. Directory assistance hadn't had a listing for Ashley Jacobs, but it had had a Mr. John Jacobs. Perhaps a father or husband?

The phone rang once, twice, three times. They weren't in. No one was home. Should he leave a message—

"Hello?" A man answered, his voice deep but quivering, eroded by the years. According to the bronze plate beneath Ashley's picture, she was born in 1939, making her nearly sixty. This man sounded even older. Perhaps he was her father or an uncle.

"Hello?" the man rasped again.

"Ah, yes. I'm calling for Ashley Jacobs." Brandon was gripping the phone too tightly, his stomach fluttering as if he was a schoolboy asking a girl out on his first date.

The other end of the phone was quiet, too quiet. His nervousness increased.

"Of all the sick, cruel hoaxes!" The man suddenly exploded. "Why don't you kids get a job and leave decent folks alone!"

The phone was slammed down. Brandon sat back, stunned, his ears still burning.

What the hell was that all about? What had he done?

The cell phone remained silent. He finally turned it off. What to do now? He had only one option. He got into his rental car and drove to Bud Irving's place.

"Hello."

Victoria looked up from her hammering in the stables and discovered Brandon Ferringer staring at her. He had his hands thrust deeply into the front pockets of his jeans and wore his red Patagonia vest over a black turtleneck. He looked remote and he looked handsome.

She scowled and returned to the fresh two-by-four she was pounding into the charred gap.

Ferringer shifted from side to side, no longer so sure. She let him suffer. She was still angry with him, but also slightly ashamed. She resented that even more. Okay, so maybe she'd flown off the handle. Maybe she'd overreacted to his offer of help. It had been four in the morning, her evening had gone from wild passion to burning barns and frankly, she didn't switch gears that easily.

And she was unbearably self-conscious now. Dammit, she'd been ready to rip this man's shirt from his body, and he knew it. Her lips on his lips. Her hands gripping his cheeks. *Please, please, please.*

Her face turned bright red. She focused on the burned-out feed area and told her memory to shut up. She could have amnesia if she wanted to.

Ferringer finally hunkered down. Man couldn't take a hint.

"I know a chap," he said. "Not much of a diplomat but

he can pound a board. Maybe you'll get lucky and he'll give his thumb a smack or two.''

"I'm fine."

"He's just trying to assist. He did go a little overboard last night. He doesn't really like making an ass out of himself. Fortunately for him, you would never let him get away with such a thing. Victoria…"

"Oh, fine, fine, fine. See those boards? See that gaping black hole? The boards go there.''

"Wonderful.''

She gritted her teeth. She really did feel like a heel. She could be independent if she wanted to. Independence and pride were about all she had left. And if she'd learned anything from Ronald, it was the importance of taking care of herself. Men could just take, take, take, and a foolish woman could give, give, give.

She heard the distant shout of Randy playing with the foals in the pasture. She went back to hammering.

"How are you?" Ferringer asked. He'd selected a two-by-four and was measuring it for the slot next to hers.

"Fine."

"Throat burn? Any dizziness?"

"Just tired, Ferringer. Cavorting around until four in the morning isn't my style."

He nodded stiffly, her curtness registering but his stubbornness equal to hers. "And Doc?"

"Doc is fine! We're all fine! Soon we'll break into song."

"That would be something to see."

She turned toward him, her tongue poised to give him a clear dressing down solely because she was on edge, and dammit, he was destroying her peace of mind. But she took one look at his face and stopped cold.

He looked like hell. His jaw was clenched so tightly his

cheeks were hollow. His lips were thinned to the point of bloodlessness. He moved with short, deliberate motions, as if every muscle in his body was stretched to breaking point, and his eyes, his deep blue eyes, held a dark, feral gleam.

"Ferringer?" she whispered.

"Do you know who Ashley Jacobs is?" he asked shortly, selected one nail, lined it up and hammered it in.

"Yes. I mean no." She shrugged, genuinely confused. "I've heard stories, that's all."

"What stories?"

"There's not much to tell. It's been forty years since she disappeared, and that was well before my time—"

"Disappeared?" His raised arm stilled above the second nail. He gazed at her darkly, and she nearly shivered.

"It was a long, long time ago, Brandon. I don't know much. Every year John and Yvonne still hold the vigil for her in August, and every year they swear this will be the year Ashley will come back. Of course, she never has."

Brandon's lips twisted. He looked like he might be laughing, but no sound came out.

"She disappeared," he whispered. "She disappeared, she disappeared. And then Al Simmons disappeared in 1970, and Max disappeared in 1972. So all that's left is crazy Bud Irving. And he just shot at me."

His shoulders shook. She finally figured out that he was in shock.

"Ferringer," she said quietly, "maybe you'd better start at the beginning."

"We don't know much about my father. My grandmum—the one in Tillamook—has a glass bookcase with his life laid out like a banquet. There's a picture of four-year-old Max sitting on my grandpa's lap—Samuel died nine months later when his bomber went down over Ger-

many. Then we have a photo of Max in his football uniform. I gather the Tillamook Cheesemakers had quite a
team in 1955. Max was the captain and got to keep the
game ball from the state championship.

"He was a handsome fellow, the class president and
class valedictorian. Definitely, he was a hit with the ladies.
Lydia has a whole row of pictures of Maximillian with the
Tillamook Dairy Princess, the Homecoming Queen, the
Prom Queen, Miss Cheesemaker 1955. When he graduated
with Bud Irving and Al Simmons in 1955, he was voted
most likely to succeed."

"Uh-huh." They were in her kitchen, Ferringer sitting
at her table, his body rigid and tense. She poured two
glasses of iced tea and pushed one into his hand. His fingers
felt frozen. "Want something hot instead?"

"No, thank you."

"I'll heat up some stew." She bustled at the stove, giving her shaking hands something to do. Ashley Jacobs, Bud
Irving and his father? Bud had *shot* at Brandon? She felt
like she was suddenly in the Twilight Zone. "Keep talking,
Ferringer." She scooped the stew into a saucepan.

"We don't know what happened after high school. I
gather from records that Max formed a partnership with
Bud and Al—they were going to be importers and export-
ers. But everything changed. My father changed. Suddenly
he was jetting here and there and my grandmother never
knew what it was about. 'Business,' he'd say and wink. My
mum was the only child of a long-standing English family,
quite wealthy when she met Max in 1959. She thought he
was a self-made man, a successful American entrepreneur,
but it turned out he was just an entrepreneur. As soon as
they were married, he started borrowing against the estate.
I remember him traveling quite a lot, always on business.
There were women, too. Lots of women. He met Vivian, a

struggling actress, in California and fathered C.J. Max was still married to my mother at the time. Even when Caroline finally demanded a divorce, he didn't marry Vivian. She didn't have money.''

"Standards," Victoria muttered from the stove.

Ferringer's lips curved. "Quite, and he was just getting started. A year later he met Stephanie in Portland. She was a sculptor, the passionate artist type, quite beautiful. More important, she came from a rich family. They married in weeks and my sister, Maggie, was born. I remember getting the postcard. C.J. didn't even get that. Of course, Max kept his marriage and new daughter secret from Vivian for a while. She always thought she was the true love of his life, even as she lay dying.

"Max was still traveling all the time. He called it business and no one really understood what the business was. He had more women, I suppose. Stephanie kept pace with more men. I gather from Maggie that the marriage was quite bitter and passionate and the divorce was expensive."

"Lovely." Victoria stirred the stew vigorously. She was getting a vivid image of abandoned women and confused children. What kind of man fathered kids in three different ports, then left them to fend for themselves? She wanted to hurt Maximillian Ferringer. And then she wanted to hold Brandon close and tell him she was so sorry she got angry last night. Now she understood.

"Vivian died in L.A." Brandon said. "She passed away in a dingy, rent-controlled studio apartment with eleven-year-old C.J. promising her Max was on his way. It was a lie. Our father was always the person leaving, not arriving. 'Time to deal,' he'd say. 'Time to deal.'

"After Vivian's death, though, he had no choice. He took C.J. in, and suddenly C.J. was jetting all around the globe, as well. Max always traveled with a suitcase full of cash, but C.J. never saw him buy or sell anything. And Max never talked about work or his business partners. One morning they'd arrive and a week or two later, Max would announce that the deal was done, and suddenly they'd be on a plane.''

"You think he was doing something illegal, don't you?''

"C.J.'s one hundred percent convinced. Maggie is eighty percent of the way there. The rest of her secretly imagines him as James Bond. Maggie's a romantic.''

"And you?'' Victoria raised a brow. "I'm sorry Brandon, but Max doesn't exactly sound like an upstanding citizen.''

"But he was once,'' Brandon insisted. "Dammit, you can *see it* in the cabinet photos, Victoria. He was on the right track once. He had Boy Scout badges, he had honors. He was bright, he was talented. America had won the war, the economy was booming and young, talented men could do anything. I don't understand. Why the obsession with money? Lydia always got by. Why the travel, the secrets? He was once so all-American, and then...''

"People change, Brandon. Sometimes they change for the worse.''

"I know.'' He shook his head, his face furrowed and frustrated. Then he shrugged and said quietly, "In 1972, Max's plane went down in Indonesia. His body was never found, and a year later, he was declared legally dead. He was simply gone. How do they say it? Without a trace.''

The kitchen grew hushed. Victoria filled two bowls with stew, set them on the table and took a seat.

"Thank you,'' Brandon said absently. He didn't pick up the fork.

"I'm sorry I got so angry last night,'' she said abruptly.

"You were right. I was trying to take control of things, throw money at them. I have a tendency to do that.''

"It's not so bad to want to help people." She offered a smile as a peace treaty. "I have a tendency to bristle like a porcupine, myself. I'm good at it, too."

He finally smiled. "I like that about you, Victoria. I like your pride. Last night…" The memories and emotions rose up between them. Dancing together. His hand on her back, her body pressed against his. The drive home, feeling the heat, the anticipation, the longing. The sharp, spiking moment of thinking the time was finally at hand. His lips on hers. Running toward his cabin…

"Last night," she agreed weakly.

"I wouldn't ever want to hurt you, Victoria."

"I know. Maybe we should forget about last night for a moment. There's a lot of other stuff on the table. Brandon, you said Bud Irving shot at you. I'm a little concerned about that."

"I'm a tad concerned about it myself." He finally picked up his fork and stabbed his stew. "I just wanted to talk. Victoria, for most of his life, my father carried a locket containing Ashley Jacobs's portrait. Beaverville's Ashley Jacobs."

"Huh?"

"Precisely. Max's business partners were Al Simmons, who disappeared in 1970, and Bud Irving, who's bonkers in Beaverville. And Max is connected to Ashley Jacobs. Four people, joined by Max, and three of them have disappeared. Just disappeared."

"Maybe you shouldn't be asking too many questions, Brandon. People disappearing is not a good thing."

"Evidently. When I tried to ask my questions in Bud Irving's speaker box at his security gate, he opened fire and shot my bloody car."

"That's it! Let's call my dad. He can haul Bud's crazy

butt into jail once and for all. Someone should've locked him up years ago.''

"I don't want him locked up, I want him to speak to me.''

"Ferringer, the guy is paranoid. He's nuts, bats in the belfry, lights on and nobody home—''

"I don't know." Brandon's blue gaze was finally clear. "Think for a minute, Victoria. Four people, all connected through my father. Three are gone and presumed dead, the last is living in a fortress surrounded by barbed wire, feral dogs and security cameras. Maybe Bud isn't as paranoid as everyone things. Maybe Bud understands how much there is to fear.''

Victoria's jaw worked, but she couldn't think of anything to say. Sitting at her kitchen table, she suddenly felt a chill. "There must be someone else," she said, and chewed her bottom lip.

"I need to learn about Ashley Jacobs and what happened when she disappeared. Who can tell us about Ashley Jacobs?''

"I know," Victoria said promptly. "Tom Reynolds."

Chapter 9

"Don't tell him about my father. I don't want him to know about Max."

"Oh, for heaven's sake, it's Tom. I've known him most of my life." Victoria was striding across Main Street in total disregard for traffic, her face intent and her hands fisted for battle. Luckily, drivers in Beaverville were accustomed to Vic's style and swerved quickly.

Brandon caught her arm as she reached the door of the general store.

"Remember," he said seriously.

She rolled her eyes. "Scout's honor. Come on, Ferringer, let's get to the bottom of this!"

They found Tom at his soda fountain, washing down the Formica counter with his apron around his waist. His leathered face crinkled in a wide smile, and he gave her a hug.

"Vic. How're you doing?"

She assured him she was dandy while Brandon politely shook Tom's hand, still feeling wary.

"Two chocolate sodas?" Tom asked.

"Okay!" Victoria waved Brandon to the red vinyl bar stools. They had already decided she would take the lead in questioning to avoid rousing Tom's suspicions.

"How's business?" she asked conversationally.

"Same old, same old. I hear you had a little mishap at your stables last night."

"Alfalfa spontaneously combusted. Ferringer got most of it out before any damage was done."

"That's good to hear. That good old Oregon damp makes life a bitch, doesn't it?"

"And how," Victoria agreed. Tom served the sodas. He was looking at Victoria, but Brandon could tell Tom's attention was really on him.

"Tom, is that Ashley Jacobs's picture hanging in the library?"

"The big oil in the foyer? Yeah, that's her."

"Ferringer was wondering who it was, but I wasn't certain." Victoria turned toward Brandon guilelessly. "Ashley Jacobs is the daughter of John and Yvonne Jacobs. She disappeared...I don't know. What year, Tom?"

"Nineteen fifty-nine."

"That long ago? The town still holds a vigil every year—" she made a show of explaining to Brandon "—but she's never been seen since." She turned to Tom, still sucking her soda. "Do the police have any theories?"

"Oh, sure. You've never heard the whole story? I suppose that was before your daddy's time. Yeah, he was just starting out as a deputy when Bud Irving returned."

"Bud Irving is connected to Ashley Jacobs?" Victoria didn't have to fake her surprise.

Tom settled against the counter. "Yeah, 1959 was quite a year around here. Mind you, this is all before my day. I've just read about it in the old newspapers I archived.

According to them, John and Yvonne held a coming out party, so to speak, for Ashley in June. There was a big barbecue, and given that Ashley was quite beautiful and an heiress, a lot of young men turned out.

"At the time, we had three young men staying in town from Tillamook. They were hunting, maybe, something like that. Well, they went to the barbecue and were instantly smitten. More to the point, Ashley seemed quite taken with the three of them."

"What happened?" Victoria asked. Brandon was leaning forward. He had yet to take a sip of his chocolate soda.

"Well, all three young men pursued her. Flowers, picnics, sunset sonnets. The town spent the whole summer spinning rumors and living vicariously. Word got around that she was keen on one of the young men, but none of the three had the fortune her daddy required. Ashley Jacobs was a fragile young thing. Beautiful in that delicate sort of way, very sweet and totally governed by her parents. Frankly, the townspeople would've loved it if she would've eloped with the man of her dreams, but no one really expected her to have the courage.

"Then one night in August—I'd have to pull the paper to know the exact date—Ashley Jacobs disappeared. And so did all three young men. At sunset, they were around. By morning, all four of them were gone."

"And Bud Irving was one of those men," Brandon said. He could already guess who the other two men were, and he felt his stomach slowly sinking, leaving him shaky and hollow.

"Yes, he was," Tom replied. "The other two were buddies from high school. I forget their names."

Brandon looked away. *What were you doing here, Max? What did you get yourself into? Who did you hurt?*

"But Bud did return," Victoria said. "Didn't he tell people what happened that night?"

"Well, the sheriff—Sheriff Mulhaney back then—questioned Bud, of course. Bud was already not quite right in the head even then, so his answers weren't exactly clear. He implied that he'd seen Ashley that last evening. She showed up at the cabin the three of them were renting for the summer and told him she'd made her choice and he wasn't it.

"At that point, Bud packed up and left. He said he figured it had to be one of his buddies and he didn't want to stick around and find out. Ashley's decision had been made."

"And the sheriff believed this?" Brandon asked sharply.

Tom shrugged. "I can't tell you what a man does or doesn't believe. Bud was never arrested. John Jacobs personally paid him a visit and offered him cash, but Bud's story didn't change. He's always said he knows nothing, and it's never been proved otherwise. The other two young men were eventually tracked down. They each gave the exact same story. Ashley found them that night, told them she'd chosen another, so they packed their bags and left. You would think one of them is lying, but Ashley was never found with any of them. Most folks favor Bud Irving as the lead candidate. They think he did something to Ashley Jacobs, and that's why he's no longer right in the head."

"What do you think?" Brandon challenged. "Tell me what *you* think."

Tom was quiet, his face composed.

"There are those," he said at last, "who offer a different theory. Those who think the reason all three men tell the same story is because they were in it together. Maybe Ashley Jacobs *did* come to their cabin that night. Maybe she announced she wouldn't marry *any* of them because they were all too poor. And maybe they punished her for that. There are people who think Ashley Jacobs is still in Beaverville. And sometime when the river floods or when a hunter goes into virgin woods, we'll finally find her body.''

Tom leaned forward. He looked Brandon in the eye. "And do you know what John Jacobs does every year after the vigil? He goes to Bud Irving's house at midnight. He stands in front of the security cameras with a picture of his daughter lit by lanterns, and as the dogs bark and Bud fires warning shots, John demands his daughter's return. Forty years later, he prays for his daughter's safe return.''

Brandon remained silent on the drive home, his mind churning with visions of the summer of 1959 and all the things that could've happened. Three friends fell in love with the same woman—a story as old as time. She was a rich heiress needing a wealthy suitor, and they were just starting out. She could've chosen one or none of them.

Had Maximillian the Chameleon loved her? Was that why he carried her picture for so many years? By the end of 1959, Max was in England dating Brandon's mother. They married a year later, and Brandon was born a year after that. If Max had loved Ashley, he certainly hadn't wasted any time replacing her.

Or maybe he'd married Caroline for her money, thinking he would get a divorce and use his settlement to romance Ashley. Or maybe his interest in Ashley had been purely financial to begin with, and Ashley had avoided the trap Caroline fell into.

Or maybe Ashley was still alive and Max was still alive. Maybe it had been Ashley he'd loved all along, Ashley he'd been seeing on all those business trips, and his wives and children were a lie. He'd been supporting Ashley, who lived in secret, stockpiling money for them both from his marriages, and then when he had enough saved, he faked his own death to live with her forever.

Or Al Simmons had disappeared to be with Ashley.

Except why would rich, cultured Ashley Jacobs agree to be tucked away or hidden from her family? More likely Ashley Jacobs was dead.

And Brandon's father might be the murderer.

The muscle leapt in Brandon's jaw again. He wanted to run. Dammit, he *needed* to run, but he was afraid he'd reached a point where there was no place he could go to escape the demons. No speed fast enough to outrace the horrible thoughts searing into his brain.

Hey, C.J., hey, Maggie. Guess what I learned about Dad?

Victoria pulled into the driveway. Brandon jumped out of the truck.

"I'm leaving," he announced. "I'll get a hotel room in town."

"What?" Victoria slid down, completely bewildered.

"You heard me." He stalked toward his cabin.

"Oh, no, you don't, Ferringer! You don't announce something like that and then just walk away."

"Don't worry, Victoria. I'll still pay rent."

Her eyes flew open. Her breath hissed out in outrage, and she flew after him. "You stubborn SOB, if you think you can put me off that easily—"

Brandon strode into his cabin, yanked out his duffel bag and ripped it open on the bed. "It's not open for discussion."

He reached for the nearest shirt, and she slapped her hand around his wrist. He froze, looking at her clenched fingers for a long time. Then his gaze slowly lifted to her face. His blue eyes glittered dangerously. "My father might be a murderer."

"That's his problem, not yours."

"Let go of my hand."

"Like hell! You just announced you were leaving, insulted me, then turned your back. No way, Ferringer. That doesn't work for me." She stepped closer.

"I am doing what I think is best," he replied grimly. "Trust my judgment."

"Ha! You're running, Ferringer. When things get intense, you bolt, plain and simple. Well, not this time."

"I need to be closer to the hotshot base!"

"Don't lie to me!" Her nose settled an inch from his. "I won't give up on you, Ferringer. I'm not going to turn away because of something your father did. And I won't let you do it, either. You are Brandon Ferringer and you are not responsible for your father or your mother or anyone else in this world. You are responsible for yourself, and you are a very fine man."

"Dammit!" he said.

She smiled, a slow, challenging smile, and pressed her body against his. "Tell me to go away," she murmured. "Tell me you don't care."

The air heated up. He lost his train of thought. He felt her—solid, firm, loyal-to-the-core Victoria Meese. And she was right, he couldn't run from that, and maybe that's what scared him the most. He cared. He would fail, as his father had failed.

"This is ridiculous," he muttered thickly.

"Brandon Ferringer, you think too much."

She kissed him, and the tension exploded. His arms went around her immediately. He crushed her against his body, tasting chocolate soda and need, fizzy cola and desire.

Her fingers dug into his scalp, and her mouth opened

greedily, devouring him. It was urgent and passionate and perfect—Victoria, Victoria, Victoria. Solid, real, capable Victoria.

Victoria, who deserved so much more.

"This is wrong," he muttered against her throat.

"Shut up and kiss me."

It wasn't enough. They grappled with clothing, ripped at buttons. With a single swipe, Brandon cleared the bed, sending his duffel bag toppling to the floor, then falling on the mattress. He shouldn't. He didn't care. He wanted her. He needed her. She grounded him, dammit. She made him whole.

She climbed on top of him and grazed his chin with her teeth, her hands tugging at his button fly. He had his hands beneath her worn flannel shirt. He found the clasp of her bra, fumbled like an idiot and snapped it without grace. She gave up on his jeans, grabbed the hem of her shirt and pulled it over her head.

Then his hands were on her bared breasts and she was sighing and he was sighing. She had beautiful breasts, high, firm with deep brown nipples. He touched them reverently, then fiercely, and she shifted on top of him.

Her hands moved down. She found him through the denim, and they both gasped.

He wanted to be inside her. He wanted to bury himself in her damp, female folds and watch her eyes darken into slate gray pools of desire.

He wanted to lose himself in her. No more thoughts of Max and the sins of the fathers. With Victoria, he could simply be a man. Her man.

"Please," she murmured. "Oh, Ferringer, *please.*"

He reached for the waist of her jeans, and the sound of the beeper cut through the air.

They stilled. They looked at each other like two teenagers caught in the act, then glanced guiltily around the room for the intruder. Belatedly, Brandon realized it was coming from his waist. His hotshot beeper was going off.

Victoria closed her eyes and emitted an unladylike groan. She rolled to the side while Brandon unclipped the black box and glanced at the number.

"I have to call," he said quietly. "It could be a fire."

"There is a fire," she said tartly. "Right here. And I want you to extinguish it!"

She peered at him from beneath heavy-lidded eyes, wearing only blue jeans that followed every firm curve of her lithe, compact legs. His body was so damn hard he ought to burst at the seams.

"Damn, bloody damn," he muttered. He pawed viciously through the clothes on the floor for his cell phone, and she raised a brow as she reached for her shirt.

"Why, Ferringer, what happened to your British reserve?"

"Damn, bloody…"

His fingers finally latched onto the phone. Maybe it was just a drill. He'd call in, that would be that, and there would still be a chance to salvage things. How many times could two red-blooded people be interrupted by fire?

He wanted. Dammit, he *needed.…*

He turned off the cell phone a minute later. "Fire." He swore succinctly. "Idaho. I have twenty minutes."

Victoria shut her eyes. "That just figures."

She sighed, and her expression was miserable. Brandon took a deep breath. He hated to see her like this. He hated to think he'd hurt her, because God knows he'd hurt too many women in his life. And he really was trying to learn, to do better, to become something more.

He crossed to her and stood quietly. Her shirt was on but

unbuttoned. He touched her throat with his fingertips, feathering her collarbone.

"Would it be too shameless to request a quickie?" She smiled tremulously.

"I don't want it to be a quickie, Victoria. I want it to be special." He sat on the edge of the bed.

"I know. I...I know."

He pulled her against his chest. After a moment, she wrapped her arms around his waist. He rocked her, inhaling the scent of her apple shampoo.

"This isn't over yet," she whispered, her voice thick. "You're not just moving out when you return, you know. You're not doing that to me."

"We'll talk about it."

"No, we won't," she said and held him closer.

"Victoria," he whispered, "sweet Victoria," and rocked her against him.

Finally, he had no choice but to untangle her embrace and start to pack. She watched quietly. He could be gone as little as a few days and as long as three weeks. They wouldn't know until the fire decided the matter by giving up.

He was done packing in a matter of minutes—the single-duffel-bag man.

"Please be careful while I'm gone," he said. "I'm not sure the fire in the stables was accidental—"

"Damp hay combusts."

"And chain saws malfunction and trees fall, but I don't know if all three happen to one person in two weeks."

"What are you saying, Brandon?"

"My father may have been involved in some illegal activities, and I've been asking questions about them. Maybe someone doesn't want the past dug up. And maybe those accidents aren't accidents."

She didn't flinch. "And that's why you think you have to leave."

"I won't put you or Randy in danger."

"With all due respect, Brandon, that's my choice to make."

"Mention it to your father, will you?"

She scowled, but wasn't so stubborn she couldn't see his point. "Fine, fine, fine. Consider it done."

He nodded, more relieved than he could tell her. And then the moment grew awkward. His bag was packed. There was nothing more to say. This was it.

He brushed his lips over hers. Once. Twice. Three times. Then he suddenly wrapped his arms around her and held her tight. "I hate to leave you," he whispered fiercely. "I do, Victoria, I do."

She kissed him passionately, and they both pretended they didn't see the tears staining her cheeks.

No one could predict how he or she would handle anticipation. As rugged outdoorsmen, trained hotshots, they were all intimately familiar with adrenaline. They were the kind of people who *did,* while others thought. But in the hours before deployment, they sat in the small charter plane, homing in on their first fire of the year with nothing to do but wait.

Woody, the veteran member of the crew, sat calmly, chewing gum and shuffling a deck of cards over and over again. Charlie Meese cracked jokes—lots of them, loudly. It was easy to believe he was the relaxed, confident thrill seeker until you looked at his hands. They were shaking.

Beside Charlie, Barbara sat tightly, her knees pressed together, her shoulders hunched and her hands balled together on her lap. Her eyes had a tendency to dart back and forth. She was the only member of the crew who wouldn't be sent into the field—her ankle needed more time to heal, so she would observe from the command post— and it obviously bothered her.

Hank, Allison and Jerry played dominoes and made small talk. This was their third year as hotshots. They didn't seem concerned.

Brandon sat alone. His jaw was tight. Every now and then he would think to relax his muscles, and his ears would pop. This wasn't his first fire. He shouldn't be nervous.

But he would gaze at his seventeen crewmates, feel the enormity of that responsibility and start grinding his teeth again. He wished Victoria was here.

Four years ago, he hadn't been thinking when a bolt of lightning had struck a tree on the dry, brittle slope of Mount Washington and started a fire. He'd been hiking when the alarm had sounded, crews were deployed and volunteers requested. He'd been among the first to shuck his pack, pick up a Pulaski and listen to the crew boss's instructions. He'd worked a fire line with trained forestry personnel who managed the volunteers' efforts.

It had been hot, he remembered. Well over a hundred degrees, and the sweat had cut tracks through the soot staining his cheeks. Black, powdery smoke rose up in mushroom plumes that obscured the sun.

Then word had come down that Crew D couldn't be contacted by radio. They had been positioned to halt the fire by a natural stream, and the fire appeared to be picking up. Decisions were made. Fighting the fire took a back seat. Rescue of Crew D became the order of the day. Boss Hoggins rounded up his team, and they descended into the thick of it, fast and furious.

Brandon and the other volunteers were left behind to continue their efforts. And then another call came in. A pair of hikers was still unaccounted for, last seen in the vicinity of the fire.

Brandon hadn't thought. He'd picked up a hard hat, two water canteens and a first-aid kit, and he'd gone.

The landscape had been surreal. He remembered rocky slopes so hot they steamed as the water dripped from his canteens. The ground was painted black, shrubs and grass annihilated, hundred-year-old trees reduced to macabre, blackened scarecrows that seemed to howl as he passed. A deer bounded by him, running from flames that had already caught him. Later, Brandon saw the deer standing by a sooty stream, drinking ravenously, the condition that preceded death. The hair had been seared from its body. In places, flaps of skin curled back, charred.

The deer suffered, and Brandon had no gun to shoot it. He kept moving toward the fire as the air grew louder with the sounds of crackling twigs and roaring flames. He went into the fire, feeling his flesh beginning to bubble, and all he could think of was Julia and goddamn Max Ferringer, and how could anyone have taken his wife from him?

And then he'd been so angry, he hadn't noticed the flames or the heat or the acrid smoke that stung his throat. He'd plunged ahead like a madman, sparks flying, burning branches falling, and he'd run, run through the furnace, looking for the hikers. He would find the hikers. He would take on Mother Nature and snatch the hikers from her grasp. He would save two anonymous hikers because he'd failed the woman he'd loved.

He'd done it. He'd found the two hikers in the bewildering inferno and led them to camp. He'd tended their burns and given them water before passing out from smoke inhalation and exhaustion. It had taken three weeks to get his voice back. He'd assumed it was damage from the fumes. Later, Kyle, one of the teenagers, told him he'd

come bursting out of the flames screaming Julia's name like
a madman. That's how the teenagers had found him
through the smoke. His rage had roared above the flames.

The plane began to descend. For the first time, the hotshots could see the thick, black haze of the wildfire moving
across southern Idaho.

"Slow-moving creeper," Woody said, having been
briefed. "Good warm-up fire."

Everyone exchanged glances.

Brandon was thinking of that deer again, that poor
burned deer so desperately thirsty.

"What's wrong, rich Brit? Having second thoughts?"
Coleton peered from the front seat, his scarred face grinning, his dark eyes bright. The fire was coming, and like a
long-lost lover, Coleton was eager to resume the dance.

"I'm fine," Brandon said.

"Not nervous?"

"I can handle it."

"Don't forget your team. One fries, we all fry."

Brandon looked him in the eye. "I won't forget my
team."

Coleton grinned, his left cheek twisting "All right
gather up. I want us on the site first. Time to deal."

And Brandon turned toward Coleton as if in a dream
hearing the words again and again. Max standing at the
doorway in his black suit. *Gotta go, son. Time to deal. Time
to deal.*

He couldn't breathe. He couldn't think. He stared at that
scarred, misshapen face. *Time to deal, time to deal.*

No, it couldn't be. Eye color was wrong. And a son
ought to recognize his own father.

But the memory wouldn't get out of his head. He followed Charlie blankly off the plane, and his hands were
trembling.

In front of them, the fire beckoned.

* * *

"Have you heard anything?" Victoria asked her mother breathlessly.

"No, dear, I swear I haven't. It's only been three days."

"What about the status of the fire? Is it a big one, a small one?"

"I'm sorry, Vic, I just don't know. I'm sure they're all right."

"Yeah, of course. Of course." Victoria planted a bright smile on her face. "Oh, well, that's fine."

Randy shook his head behind her. "You're a bad liar, Mom."

"Hey, don't you have chores to do?"

Randy grinned. "I like Mr. Ferringer. I think you should marry him and then he can stay here forever."

Victoria shook her head hastily. "This has nothing to do with you, young man. Now go do your chores!"

The third day found them tired and exhausted. The first day they'd worked twenty hours straight, ringing the fire with a tight, quick fire line. Trapping a fire was what hotshots and Smokejumpers did best—no one could dig faster, and they took a great deal of pride in their speed. Once the fire was contained, however, adrenaline had dropped off and a different set of incentives kicked in. You wanted to dig a fire line quickly to contain the fire and preserve the woods. You wanted mop-up to go slowly because the real money came from hazard pay and overtime. And behind a deep appreciation for trees came a deep appreciation for dollars.

It was still hard, tedious work with few breaks. Time rolled together for Brandon, highlighted only by smoke and flames and thoughts of Victoria he couldn't get out of his mind.

Victoria smiling, Victoria grinning. Victoria driving a

truck like a maniac and Victoria, earthy and honest beneath him.

Victoria, Victoria, Victoria. After all the years of wanderlust, Brandon sat in the command post during a fifteen-minute break and wondered when he could get home.

The wind was dying. So was the fire. The job would end probably the next day. Not so long. Too long.

"Looking tired." Brandon glanced up to see Coleton Smith standing beside him. The superintendent had been as pleasant as a snarling hound dog for the past three days. Now, however, the older man pulled up another cheap metal chair and took a seat.

"We all are." Brandon offered him water. Coleton was too tough to take it.

"Fire's doing good," Coleton announced.

"It seems under control."

"Yeah, but it ain't over till it's over."

"Of course." Brandon emptied his canteen. In the distance, Charlie and Woody were playing soccer. Some of the crew were so wired, they were up and about even at night. They wouldn't sleep again until they were flying home. Then their bodies would crash and they'd sleep around the clock.

"Head bothering you?" Coleton asked gruffly.

"When did you come to Beaverville?" Brandon asked. He looked Coleton in the eyes, searching for signs of—of anything.

"Nineteen seventy-eight. Why?"

"Were you always a hotshot? Even before Beaverville?"

Coleton's eyes narrowed. "You want my damn résumé?"

"Just curious."

"You're pretty good, rich Brit. Cool. I like that. You

look me in the eye. Guys don't like to look a scarred man in the eyes. Too afraid they'll see their own reflection.''

"Did it hurt? The fire that caught you."

"Huh. No one's ever asked me that."

"I did."

Coleton shrugged. "It hurt. But I won. I got out, and I lived when they thought I would die. That's all that matters." He clambered to his feet. "Come on, you kids have had enough. Time to deal."

"I used to know someone who said that," Brandon whispered.

"Yeah? Well, lucky you."

At the end of the driveway, Deputy Eric James yawned. It was close to nine o'clock, and *Seinfeld* would be on soon. Deputy James liked *Seinfeld,* especially that loser George. George was a crack-up.

He glanced at his watch again, then made himself forget it. When Sheriff Meese asked you to watch his only daughter's house for signs of trouble, you didn't mess up your shift.

But James had sat out here for three nights without seeing a sign of anyone. If there had been someone prowling around the ranch causing trouble, he seemed long gone now.

Higher up the sloping hillside, Ray Bands watched the cop who watched the house. It always amused him to watch the guards watch their charges. Gave him a small thrill when, God knows, the job was boring enough.

This make-it-look-like-an-accident thing was a real pain. Ray missed the good old days of shooting through the temple with a pillow to muffle the sound. That was fast and efficient.

This was death by a thousand paper cuts. The fire in the stables had been a bad idea. He should've gone with the cabin. But the little boy came to the cabin often, and he couldn't harm a kid and then go home to Melissa. He just couldn't do it.

He was stuck thinking up more accidents that would hurt just Ferringer. And maybe the woman. Sooner or later, it would probably come to that. A woman was still better than a kid, and it would get the point across.

He needed to bide his time and be patient. He was chafing to get home. He missed Melissa. He sighed. Well, Ferringer would return to the ranch soon. And then Ray would set the next accident in motion and everything would be all right.

The phone didn't ring until Friday. Victoria and Randy were just finishing supper. Victoria bounced from the table and snatched the receiver off the hook.

"Yeah?"

"I heard," her mother said. "Fire's out, the team is coming home."

"Any problems?"

"Smooth as glass, your brother tells me. They'll be home by midnight. I don't suppose you'd want me to watch Randy tonight?"

"Oh, Mom, you are the greatest!"

She hung up the phone, her mind already whirling. "Randy, quick, gather your things. You're going to Grandma's tonight."

"Why am I going to Grandma's?" he obediently stacked his dishes.

"'Cause your Grandma loves us both very much!"

She'd just set down the phone when it rang again.

"Hi," Brandon said quietly.

Her heart stopped. It truly did. And by God, when she finally got her lips to form a word, she sounded breathless. "Ferringer."

"Fire's out. We're coming home."

She heard Coleton's voice in the background, yelling at the crew to board the plane.

"I know, I know," she said hastily. "My mother is taking Randy for the evening."

"Really?" Ferringer's voice missed a beat.

She smiled. "Really, Ferringer. Now hurry home. And I mean *hurry*."

She hung up the phone, dumped the dishes in the sink and declared it good enough.

She made a beeline for her closet.

Tonight, she was wearing her dress.

Chapter 10

Brandon got off the plane in Redmond's tiny airport at ten-fifteen. Charlie invited the singles to a local bar while the married crew members headed for home. Brandon went straight to his rental car and turned toward Beaverville.

He'd been in the field for five days. He was covered with soot, had ash in his hair and needed a shower. He drove faster.

Five days of heat and sweat. Five days of working next to his crewmates, digging the fire line, telling jokes and keeping each other sane. He'd done all right. Once, he'd taken off his pack to rest, left it a moment and returned only to find it twenty feet up in a tree. He'd gotten to climb up and retrieve it amid the chortling encouragement of the veterans, who'd explained they'd done it to teach him never to take off his pack. A hotshot's fire shield was in his pack, and you never knew when you would need your fire shield.

But he'd done it. He'd gone out there. He'd thought of

his team. He'd been a real player. And he'd been unbearably conscious of Coleton's gaze upon his back.

Time to deal. Time to deal.

It was just a phrase. Anyone could say it. Coleton Smith was not Maximillian Ferringer. Brandon would know his own father, dammit. And after all these years, wouldn't his father want to know him?

He hit the straight stretch of Route 26 and came close to doing a hundred. C.J. would be proud, but Brandon normally had no need for speed. This time, though, he wanted Victoria. *Badly.* So much, it should scare him. So much, it should hurt.

The Lady Luck Ranch drive loomed on the left, and he turned in fast enough to make the tires squeal. He sailed over bumps and rattled his bones on the landing. He roared into the yard in a plume of red dust and was out of the vehicle before the smoke cleared. The front door was flying open. Victoria appeared.

God, she was wearing a dress. A flirty, strapless swirling red dress.

Their gazes locked and the air burst into flames.

"I'm dirty and sweaty," he said matter-of-factly. "I stink to high heaven and need a shower."

"Well, then, Ferringer, I'll just have to scrub your back."

She came leaping off the porch, and he caught her in his arms.

"I missed you, Victoria. I *missed* you."

She covered his mouth with hers, and it was sweet. Her hands wove through his hair, scattering ash and raining pine needles. Her tongue tangled with his, long and slow. He could feel the curve of her breasts and the firm, muscled line of her body. Strong Victoria. Beautiful Victoria. Sexy in jeans, deadly in a dress.

"The shower," he murmured, taking a step toward the stables with his arm around her waist and his lips against her neck.

She tugged him toward the porch. "You can use the house now, Ferringer. And I got bubble bath."

"Oh, my, does your mother know about this?"

"Honey, where do you think I learned it from?"

She led him to the house, and he wasn't complaining.

They started stripping off his clothes in the foyer. His yellow flame-retardant coat fell somewhere in the corner while he was nibbling on her bared shoulder. His jersey knit shirt got left behind in the hallway—he'd discovered the inside of her elbow. The yellow fireproof pants were kicked off by the bathroom door. He brushed aside her hair and nuzzled the back of her neck while she took three tries to twist on the faucets. Goose bumps rippled up her arms and down her spine. He found every last one of them with his lips while she bent over the tub and closed her eyes.

Water lapped her arms. It splashed and made his hands wet as he went to work on the wide belt cinching her waist. The zipper rasped tantalizingly. The top of her dress fell forward into the water. They didn't notice.

"You're beautiful," he murmured, "so beautiful." Water neared the edge of the tub. She remembered to turn it off in time and added the bubble bath.

"Too late for suds," she whispered.

"Oh, I think we'll make some." He pushed her dress onto the floor, shed his briefs and led her into the water as the steam rose around their legs.

The tub was too small for two of them, but they squeezed together anyway, sucking in their stomachs as they sent torrents of water onto the floor. Her bottom nestled tightly against his groin. Her well-shaped legs pressed against his lean hiker's limbs. Steam curled her fine hair, sticking it to her cheeks and his chest. He drew blond strands together in a handful, then combed them to the side so he could run his finger down her jaw and chase a bead of moisture off the tip of her nose.

Her hips were restless against him. The churning was creating a white, floral-scented froth. He scooped up a handful and used it to decorate her breasts.

"How's Randy?" he whispered, finding a bar of soap and trailing it up her arm. He soaped the first layer of grime from his chest, then returned to tracing her long, white limbs.

"Fine."

"The ranch?" He slid the soap around her neck, down to her high, curved breast and over her hard, pebbled nipple.

"Just dandy," she gasped.

"Any trouble?"

"None at all. We're fine, everything is fine. Oh, yes...do that." Her eyes drifted shut.

His fingers had strayed down her torso, between her legs. Long, callused digits pressed against her, finding the nub of her desire and rubbing lightly. She squirmed and he picked up the tempo.

Her breathing became sporadic. He watched her chest rise and fall unevenly, memorized the soft, delicate sounds of her breath. His body was hard, so damn hard, and yet he made no move to turn her. He moved his hand lower, pressed the heal of his palm against her and slid the first finger inside.

She almost came out of the tub. Water sloshed and splashed. Bubbles bloomed to life. She exhaled in a shuddering moan, and he wrapped his free arm around her waist, holding her firmly against him while he plundered her folds.

"Victoria...sweet Victoria."

She came with a low cry and a snaking tremor. Her feet were braced against the head of the tub, and her strong legs pushed her back, rubbing her against him. He was almost undone.

He turned her and scooped her up in a spray of water. The floor was sopping and padded with clothing. He gave up on it and set her on the edge of the counter. Immediately her legs wrapped around his waist and her hand bracketed his collarbone.

She looked him in the eye, her cheeks flushed, her hair wild, her lips swollen.

"Now," she said. He entered her in a single plunge.

Her head fell back. His head fell forward. It had been so long and he was so close. Frantically his feet dug into the floor. Muscles, corded and defined by four years of hard living, leapt to life and levered him forward. He heard her ragged breath and he heard her low moan. He felt her teeth sink into his shoulder. He felt her body grasping him, pulling him in, claiming him.

And he gave himself over to the experience. He shut off his mind and trusted Victoria.

He thrust, the world shattered, she screamed and the water sloshed....

And it was perfect.

Sometime later, they found themselves curled up on her bed, the quilt on the floor, the sheets tangled around them. Her fingers stroked his chest, then lifted to trace his cheeks. In the shadows after midnight, she kissed him gently and he returned it. They made love slowly, the way lovers did on the brink of the precipice.

Afterward, he opened his mouth, but she lay a finger over it.

"Not tonight," she said. "Give us tonight."

He did.

"How do you like your eggs?"

Brandon opened his eyes slowly, slumber still weighting the lids. Sunlight streamed through the cracked blinds, illuminating a clear blue sky and a sun that had almost hit stride. Vaguely he became aware of the worn cotton sheet with little purple flowers tangled around his flanks. Most of the covers appeared to be on the floor. He was cradling a pillow against his stomach.

"Not that I'm so easily replaced," Victoria commented from the doorway.

His gaze finally found her. Her hair was disheveled, her cheeks rosy. Her clear blue-gray eyes held a special glow, and she wore nothing but a red-checkered apron. The morning after was a good look for her.

"It's eleven o'clock," she told him. "My mother won't keep Randy forever. How about some breakfast?"

He took the hint and rolled out of bed, standing with a long stretch of tired muscles and a sigh. Thirty-six was too old to be digging and hacking and hiking for five consecutive days. "Anything would be fine."

Victoria's eyes had locked on his bare chest. He looked around and realized belatedly that he had no clothes.

"They're in the dryer," she said. Her lips curved, and her cheeks flushed becomingly. "Everything was, uh, a little wet."

"A little?"

"Sopped beyond recognition and most likely ruined."

"I see."

She was still smiling. After a moment, a smile softened his face. He didn't know what to think. He didn't know how to feel. Last night he'd been obsessed with seeing her, with having her. Now…now she was leaning against the doorjamb in nothing but an apron, and he already wanted her again.

He pulled the sheet from the bed and tied it around his waist. She led the way to the kitchen, giving him an attractive view of her firm bottom.

She'd already cleaned up the bathroom. He was almost disappointed.

While she cracked eggs into a frying pan, he poured two cups of coffee and dug through the refrigerator for orange juice. Neither of them spoke. The kitchen was warm, companionable. As long as they didn't say too much, expect too much, want too much, they didn't have to break the tenuous, hazy glow.

They ate eggs over easy and home-fried potatoes with just a hint of onion. Brandon ate ravenously, the most he had in ages, but then he could afford the bulk. A bell dinged in the utility room. Victoria went to retrieve their clothes while Brandon stacked dishes in the sink.

Victoria didn't have a dishwasher. That was a shame. It would save her a lot of time, and she already worked much too hard. The kitchen could use fresh linoleum, too, and that refrigerator had to be from 1955. The ceiling had some cracks, and one corner was showing signs of water damage. The whole house was old. He could rip it down, build another with a modern washer and dryer and enough kitchen appliances to cook dinner and clean up the mess all on its own.

And the computer for Randy. A brand-new pickup truck.

He stood at the kitchen counter, and though he knew he shouldn't, he dreamed of fixing her life. He could make it better. He had the money.

He could give her anything she wanted.

Except all Victoria truly wanted was a man who would stay.

She came into the kitchen with the jeans he'd worn beneath his fire pants, his underwear and his jersey knit shirt. They were still hot to the touch. He took them from her without meeting her gaze and put them on in the kitchen. His feet were bare. He studied his toes for a long time. Two of his toenails were black—bruised from all the hiking. He had blisters. His feet didn't fit him anymore. They were the callused, scarred feet of an outdoorsman, not a Wharton finance major, not a Wall Street investor.

He couldn't imagine them in wing tips, only hiking boots. And he couldn't imagine slick Max Ferringer's son wearing hiking boots. Coleton Smith's son, on the other hand...

"You're a million miles away," Victoria said quietly.

He pulled his gaze to the refrigerator. His heart was still beating too hard in his chest. He felt outside himself and hated it.

"Randy will be home soon," he said. "I should unpack."

"That's not what you're thinking."

"It's been a long five days, Victoria, that's all."

"Brandon, I don't believe you."

Abruptly he was angry. Not at her, but she was around so she became the target. He turned toward her roughly, his face harsh, his eyes cornered.

"What do you want from me? What is it I'm supposed to be saying here?"

Her eyes warmed up. "Oh, I don't know. 'I had a nice night' would be a good start."

"Fine. I had a nice night."

"Hey, if you're scared, then talk about feeling scared,

because I'll understand it. I'm standing here feeling just a little bit terrified myself!''

"I can't. I can't!" He threw his hands in the air and turned away. The world was humming, closing in on him. There were too many thoughts in his head. He couldn't control them. He couldn't control how he felt. He needed distance, iron control and impenetrable walls. He stood in Victoria's kitchen and wanted to pull her into his arms and bury his face in her hair.

"I need space!" He headed for the front door.

And Victoria blazed to life, hightailing it after him. "No! No more walking away every time I get close. I hate this dance. You got something on your mind, then let's get it out. Let's get it all out on the table!"

Brandon opened the door.

"Damn you, Ferringer! What is going on here?"

He turned halfway, and the look on his face froze her. "This is what I do best," he said coldly. "This is it, Victoria. This is the real me."

He walked out the door and slammed it behind him.

She stood there, too stunned to move and too hurt to breathe. And then the rage and understanding galvanized her to life.

"That is not you, Brandon Ferringer. That is your father, and it is not your fault!"

She went running for her clothes, yanked them on savagely and gave pursuit.

She caught up with Brandon just as he reached the end of the bumpy driveway. He was walking fast, long, lean strides eating up the miles, but he'd had to stop and put on his boots, which had bought her some time. Besides, she was in good shape. She sprinted over the bumps, closed the gap between them and arrived with a heaving gasp.

"Go away!" He turned left and headed up the road.

"Like hell!"

The road headed up in a series of curves before it descended into town. His longer legs did better on the steep grades, but she wasn't letting him go.

"We need to talk about this."

"Victoria, there is nothing to talk about."

"Oh, bloody hell, Brandon! You are much too honest, much too good of a guy to suddenly be acting like such a jerk!"

He stopped abruptly, his eyes dangerously dark. "I never promised you anything."

"Nope."

"I never pretended any false emotions."

"Oh, yes, you did. You're pretending not to care, and that's false, Ferringer. We both know it's false."

His jaw was clenched, his hands knotted at his sides. His voice dropped to a guttural low. "I am *not* what you need! I am not the right man for you!"

"Why, Brandon, why?"

"I failed my wife!" cool, reserved Brandon Ferringer roared. "I loved her, she loved me, and I was a *horrible* husband. I put my job first. I put money first. I bought her everything and gave her nothing. I abandoned her, Victoria. I bloody well abandoned her even though I came home every night. I *was* my father!"

"Brandon Ferringer," Victoria said bluntly, "you are not your father, so get over it."

He clenched his teeth. A vein pounded dangerously in his forehead, and for a moment she thought it might explode. But beneath the raw, savage anger, she saw something else. A small, desperate flare of hope. The tiny kernel of strength inside Brandon Ferringer that kept him trying even though his mother had told him he was a failure and his wife had made him feel like a failure and it seemed that all road signs pointed toward his father as the only kind of man he'd ever become.

"I'm no good, Victoria," he said fiercely. "I look at your ranch, and I don't see me working next to you or me helping Randy. I see all the things I should buy you. I don't dream of us. I dream of giving you everything so you'll have to want me."

"Well, I won't let you buy me a new ranch, so you're safe."

"Why do I care so much about the damn money? I've been trying to lose it and yet all my investments turn to gold. I have millions and none of it does any good—"

"Money is security. Money is control. And you need security and control, Ferringer. It's everything you didn't have growing up."

He recoiled. She seized the upper hand.

"Don't you see? You could've gotten rid of the money, Brandon. You could've given it away to a charity, started a fund in your wife's name. But you kept it. Invested it, did whatever, then punished yourself with the success. Because you *don't* really want to give it away. You need the security. And yet you can't stand the thought of money because it makes you feel guilty, so you're caught in this horrible cycle where whatever you do is wrong. You're punishing yourself, over and over again. How many times are you going to punish yourself for your wife's being killed by a mugger?"

"I don't think it was a mugger, Victoria," he stated matter-of-factly. "My wife was researching my father right before she was shot. I think she asked too many questions. I don't think she was killed because she was in the wrong place at the wrong time. I think she was killed because she married Maximillian Ferringer's son.''

"Oh, my God!" Victoria closed her eyes, and it was so clear to her. Everything was so clear to her. "Brandon, let it go. Just *let it go*. Even if her death was connected to your father, it is *not your fault*. If you had been with her, if you had known she was in danger, you would've done anything for her. You would've thrown yourself in front of that bullet if anyone had given you the choice, because *that* is the kind of man you are. You are nothing like your father. Look at what you did for Barbara when she twisted her ankle. Look at what you did for me when my barn was on fire. Look at what you did for Randy when he needed help on his homework. Ferringer, you are one of the finest damn men I know, and everyone sees that but you.''

"I don't call my mother, I neglect my sister and C.J.—"

"Then change."

"I hate staying in one place. I have to hike, I have to move—"

"Then it's a good thing we have a lot of mountains around here.''

"Victoria." he shut his eyes and his voice was raw. "I am so damn *scared*.''

"I know," she whispered. "Me, too, Brandon, me, too.''

His eyes opened, and there was something in his gaze she'd never seen before. Need, gratitude, honest appreciation. No more stoic Brandon, no more impenetrable Brandon. This man was real.

And she loved him with all her heart.

The sound of a car engine cut through the still air behind her. She was too busy looking at him, too busy wanting to kiss him to pay attention. Abruptly the engine grew loud, as if the car was speeding up. She saw Brandon frown, looking puzzled, then his eyes widened.

"Look out!" he yelled and pushed her savagely.

She went tumbling to the side, looking up just in time to see Brandon leaping, as well. Everything was happening too fast, though. The big old Buick crested over the hill, clipped Brandon squarely and went sailing over the edge.

There was a loud crash and then the afternoon was silent once more.

Victoria scrambled to her feet. Her hands stung, but she barely noticed the gravel embedded in her palms. Brandon. She had to find Brandon. She ran to the edge of the road, where the grass had once bordered the fields, and found him sprawled on the ground.

"Ferringer!" She slid to a halt beside him, lost her footing on the trampled grass and fell hard on her butt. She snaked over to him, checking his pale face frantically.

He groaned, then his eyes fluttered open.

"Are you hurt? Where does it hurt? Brandon——"

"Quiet, quiet," he muttered and clutched his head.

Immediately she froze. He'd probably hit his head pretty hard on landing. He'd had a concussion not that long ago. Oh, God, what if he'd done serious damage?

Brandon struggled to sit up.

"Lie down," she ordered.

He sat up anyway and shook his head.

"Stubborn mule." She held up her hand. "How many fingers!"

"Two," he whispered.

She scowled. He was right. She tracked a finger in front of his gaze. He could follow it. So far so good.

"Name and date."

"Victoria, I'm just a little bruised and battered, not senile. You take as many tumbles as I have lately, you get to be good at it. Tuck and roll, every hotshot knows how."

She wasn't convinced and felt all his limbs anyway.

"Are you okay?" he demanded.

"Fine, fine. Nice shove." She reached his leg. He winced.

"A car hits pretty squarely," he murmured. "Help me stand."

Victoria didn't think that was a good idea, but having grown up with six brothers, she knew it was inevitable. She wrapped an arm around his waist and helped him up. He winced, took a few practice steps and shook his leg.

"Oh, yes, that'll get me in the morning," he muttered. "And the driver?"

Victoria's eyes widened. She'd forgotten about the driver. Immediately, they both glanced down the embankment. The car had sailed clear over, landing in a ridge of trees. They could see the front end, crumpled like an accordion. The windshield held a web of spidery cracks. Someone was slumped over the wheel.

"Stay here," Brandon said.

"No way—"

Brandon caught her arm with surprising strength for a man who'd just been tossed like a beanbag. "Victoria, that car didn't accidentally go over that embankment. It was aiming right at us."

"Why?"

But his gaze told her why. Because of him. Because he was Max's son and he'd been asking questions.

"Wait," she demanded fiercely. "Wait for the cops, dammit. Someone probably heard it, someone will phone it in."

A groan came from the car.

"He could be seriously hurt. I don't want him too injured. I want him to be able to answer questions!"

Brandon slid down the embankment. Victoria shook her head, gritted her teeth and slid after him.

The car door swung open as they reached the bottom. A hand appeared, groping for the door, and they both halted. Moments later, a large man staggered out. His face was weathered, his hair thinning. He wore a cheap gray suit Victoria associated with salespeople, and he was a good thirty pounds overweight.

He was waving a bag of fat-free pretzels as if it was a pom-pom. He shook his head once, then twice, then seemed to realize it was pretzels he was holding.

He scowled and threw the bag to the ground.

"Are you all right?" Brandon asked warily, edging in front of Victoria. The man wasn't what he'd expected. Maybe he'd been taking Maggie's secret agent theories too seriously. If someone was trying to kill him, he'd assumed it would be a professional.

This man looked like a used-up shoe salesman, one step away from a heart attack.

The man finally stopped swaying. His small, black eyes zeroed in on Brandon.

"There have been damn presidents easier to kill," the man muttered.

He pulled out a gun.

"Victoria, down," Brandon yelled. Gunfire cracked. He

could swear he heard the whistle of the bullet. As if in a horrible dream, he stared at his chest.

Nothing.

In front of him, the driver pitched forward. A red stain bloomed across his back.

"Oh, my God," Victoria whispered. "What is going on, Brandon? *What is going on?*"

Chapter 11

Brandon, Victoria and Sheriff Meese clustered in Brandon's cabin, their voices hushed. Randy was in the stables doing his chores, and though he would learn of the incident sooner or later, they didn't want him to overhear their discussion of all its frightening implications.

"Of course it has something to do with Max!" Brandon stated angrily. He wadded up another shirt and threw it in his duffel bag.

"But it's been twenty-five years," Victoria argued. She glanced at her father for support. He shook his head.

"He's right, Victoria. It's the only thing that makes sense."

"Where will you go?" Victoria asked. Brandon was leaving, and while she could understand why, she wasn't happy. After spending a night engaged in wild sex with a man, she preferred to have him hang around. Silly her.

"Hotel. In town. I can't go far. I have obligations."

"Are you putting your crew at risk?"

Brandon froze, a T-shirt suspended in midair. "I don't know."

"Too risky to go after you with your team," Sheriff Meese said. "Who wants to chase you into a fire?"

"They've tampered with my equipment. At this point, we must assume the chain saw and tree weren't accidents."

"But access to equipment is easy to come by. Just inspect yours regularly. At this point, they're being less subtle."

Brandon smiled grimly. "You know, that almost makes sense until you realize we have no idea who they are, what they want and why they are shooting each other." He shoved the T-shirt into his duffel bag and zipped it up sharply.

That quickly, that easily, he was ready to go. One bag, no hassles. He was that kind of man. He wouldn't meet Victoria's gaze, and the bag sat on the bed between them like an incriminating piece of evidence. Her eyes were beginning to burn. She swiped at them fiercely.

"I can't put you and Randy in danger," he stated forcefully.

"I know."

"Victoria, if I could handle it differently..."

"I know."

Sheriff Meese cleared his throat.

"Deputy James followed the tracks of the shooter to the road. The man came in on foot and apparently left that way. Weapon's a Remington twelve-gauge rifle, most common hunting gun around. We probably got more of them than people in Beaverville. It's gonna take some time."

"I see."

"Probably should have you under police protection until then, you know. I can have Deputy James monitor your hotel."

"I'd rather have him here," Brandon said. "Just in case."

"No need, son. I'll be staying here."

Victoria thinned her lips and looked away. She was frustrated. She wanted to help. She wanted to feel connected to this man and his challenges. Instead she was being shut out. It hurt. It scared her.

She was afraid that once Brandon walked out that door, he would never come back. He hadn't made any promises....

"None of this makes any sense," she muttered.

"Being shot at rarely does," Brandon said grimly. His eyes held a gleam, but it wasn't pleasant.

"Whatever your father did was twenty-five years ago! Ashley Jacobs's disappearance was even longer ago than that, nearly forty years ago. Why does it matter anymore?"

"What if Ashley Jacobs isn't dead and after all these years someone is trying to protect her?"

"Farfetched," Victoria snapped.

"What if my father isn't dead? What if he's been alive all these years and someone's trying to cover it up?"

"Far-fetched," Sheriff Meese intoned.

Brandon's gaze went from daughter to father to daughter. "One night forty years ago," he said quietly, "something happened. Three people have now disappeared and are presumed dead. There are a lot of loose ends. A lot of them. And I've been tugging at the bloody strings—"

"Brandon, there's no way to find out—"

"Oh, yes, there is."

And then Victoria knew where he was going. "No!"

"Yes." He swung his bag over his shoulder. She grabbed his hand, her fingers digging in fiercely.

"Dammit, Bud Irving shot at you last time. He's got dogs, he's got guns. Ferringer, please."

For one minute, he wavered. She could see the war in his eyes, the confusion, the frustration, even a glimmer of fear. Then his jaw tightened, and she knew she'd lost. He was going to handle this alone. He was going to retreat behind his stoic facade where she wouldn't be allowed to reach him.

"Don't do this," she whispered. "Brandon, please."

He covered her hand with his. He drew it away.

"I *have* to do this, Victoria. It's not about you, it's not about us. It's about me."

He headed for the door.

"For God's sake—" she turned to her father "—do something!"

"Let us handle it," Sheriff Meese said to Brandon, moving to intercept him. "I'll go speak to Bud. He's less likely to shoot me."

Brandon brushed by his shoulder. "But he's more likely to talk to me. I'm Max Ferringer's son."

"Bud might be the one shooting at you."

"Shooting at me, or shooting at the shooter to save my life?" Brandon's lips twisted. "You see the possibilities? Quite a puzzle, isn't it?"

He gave one last nod and disappeared out the door, his duffel bag over his shoulder.

Victoria closed her eyes. "Dad. Oh, Dad, he's going to do something rash."

"I know, sweetheart. I know." It had been a long time since Victoria had been hugged by her father, but he took her in his big burly arms as if she was a little girl and he could make the boo-boo go away. She rested her head against his shoulder.

She said, "I love him."

"I'll have Deputy James follow him."

"What if he never comes back?"

"He cares about you, too, Vic. Even if he can't admit to it yet."

But it was hard to believe that as she stood on the porch and watched Brandon Ferringer drive away. He didn't look back. He didn't say goodbye. She saw his lips moving in the rearview mirror, and she swore she heard him speak.

"Time to deal. Time to deal."

Brandon didn't think anymore. He didn't feel. He didn't listen to the rapid pounding of his heart or the low buzzing filling his ears. He drove, his hands tight on the wheel. Somewhere in the back of his mind, he was aware of the police car that caught up with him and dropped two car lengths back.

The sheriff didn't matter. The deputy didn't matter. This wasn't about professionals anymore. Everything was personal now. Maximillian the Chameleon's oldest son had had enough.

He yanked his car to the side of the road at the top of Bud's hill. He grabbed the 1955 Tillamook yearbook. And he grabbed Ashley Jacobs's locket.

The Dobermans started snarling the moment he approached the gate. One foaming, high-strung beast flung himself at the wrought-iron bars. Brandon kept his eyes on the security camera. He raised the yearbook and dangled the locket.

"Open up!" he yelled.

The dogs started to bay.

"I'm not going away, Bud Irving. You can fire your rifle, you can turn loose your dogs, but I'm going to stand here until bloody hell freezes over. I'm Maximillian Ferringer's son, and I want answers."

The gate didn't open. The security cameras didn't turn away. The dogs kept snarling, growling low in their throats and chomping at the bars. Behind Brandon, Deputy James climbed out of his car and unsnapped his holster.

"This isn't about you," Brandon said without turning around.

"All the same..."

The gate abruptly creaked open. The dogs shut up, backing up and appearing startled. They ran from side to side, never crossing in front of the gate, whimpering with confusion. One took a halfhearted lunge forward, then yelped and recoiled sharply. They slunk back.

Electric collars and underground wires, Brandon realized. Crazy Bud Irving had blocked off a narrow path leading to his house.

Brandon followed it.

The roofline was just visible from the gate. Rolls of barbed wire rimmed the gutters and kept anyone from making a roof assault. As he grew closer, Brandon could see that the yard had been gutted—all trees and shrubs removed until a fifty-foot bald perimeter surrounded the house while huge, three-hundred-watt searchlights were poised to banish all shadows and obliterate all secrets. No demons would be creeping up on Bud Irving in the middle of the night.

In the middle of the barbed wire, metal lights and rotating cameras, the house sat huddled on its foundation, a single-story, run-down rancher, clearly out of its league. The shutters hung crookedly. Shingles were loose on the roof. Bud might care about his security system, but he'd left the house alone, and it was worse for the wear.

Brandon knocked on the front door. When no one answered, he twisted the knob and walked in.

Bud Irving greeted him in the entry with a shotgun pointed at his chest.

"I hate you," Bud Irving said.

"I don't care," Brandon said and shut the door behind him.

"Tell me about her. Tell me about that night." Brandon paced in front of Bud Irving, dangling the locket. The older man's eyes followed it almost fanatically, his tongue wetting his lips.

Bud Irving didn't resemble his dashing high school portrait anymore. Tillamook's star running back had become a hunch-shouldered old man whose fears had twisted his features. Yellow-gray hair covered his scalp in clumps, obviously in need of a wash and comb. His shirt was stained, the red flannel frayed at the cuffs and buttoned incorrectly. His jeans hung on his bony frame and his feet were bare.

The whole room had the musty, rank odor of a cellar that hadn't been aired in a long, long time. The ceiling was cracked. The hardwood floor was stained. The few pieces of Salvation Army furniture were covered in inches of dust.

Brandon ignored all of it. He kept his gaze on Bud's trembling form and watched the man's finger caress the trigger of the rifle.

"I could shoot you." Bud stared harder at the picture. "She wouldn't like it, though. She never liked violence. Guns scared her. They never understood that, but I did. Too much violence. My baby, my baby, my baby."

"What happened that night?"

"I can't tell you. I swore, and I keep my word. I was never big, never smart like them, but I was loyal. You tell Al that, see what he says."

"Do you know where Al is?"

"Gone, I think. Kaboom, but they never found his body so you can't be sure. Tough son of a bitch. You gotta watch out. I check the cameras every night. No Al, no Al. Thank God, no Al.''

"Did you leave the house today? Did you shoot the man trying to kill me?''

"Trying to kill you?'' Bud recoiled sharply and his face turned ashen. "They're back, they're back! I knew they would come back. It never ends. I resigned. I kept my word and never went back, but no one cares. They always remember what you did. So many ghosts in the closet. So many ghosts. You can hear them whispering at night and the searchlights can't find them. Nope, they slide right on through.''

Brandon hunkered down. "Bud, is my father dead?''

"Never found the body,'' Bud whispered. "Never found the body.''

"Is Coleton Smith Maximillian?''

"Who is Coleton Smith?''

Brandon closed his eyes. This wasn't going to be easy. He held the locket closer, swung the picture in front of Bud's rheumy blue eyes.

"Tell me, Bud. I need to know.''

Bud shook his head.

"I am his son. I have the right! Why was my father carrying Ashley Jacobs's picture?''

Bud's face crumpled. He held out his hand for the locket, and his fingers were trembling.

"Please,'' he whimpered in a quavering voice, "please. Give me back my wife.''

And then Brandon began to understand.

First Brandon traded the locket in exchange for the loaded rifle, which Brandon set on the floor. Unarmed, the man seemed to shrink into himself. He clutched the locket against his chest, rocked back and forth and expelled the happenings of that night in fits.

Ashley had been pursued by Bud, Al and Max that summer. She was sweet, beautiful and easy to talk to. She didn't flirt, didn't play games like other girls did. Ashley was sheltered, almost a complete innocent. You looked at her and you wanted to take care of her. You wanted to be her hero because she was the kind of delicate, sweet woman who made you feel like a man.

They were all smitten, though none of them had the requisite fortune. They were, however, young and handsome and much more fun than the stuffy suitable men clambering for her attention. They also made lots of cash in their line of work and they didn't mind spending it. In the summer of 1959, they knew how to have fun.

Max led the chase, as he'd led in everything all their lives. The star quarterback and class president was always the one who got the prom queen, while Bud and Al settled for the prom queen's two friends.

But not this time. Al wanted Ashley. Smaller, rough around the edges, he was tough and sometimes mean. His father had used him as a punching bag a lot, and Al had inherited his temper. But in a good mood, he came up with the best ideas and he could be counted on in a scrape. If Max couldn't talk their way out it, Al could blast their way out with a pugilist's skill.

And then there was Bud, quick, small, quiet Bud, who was always tagging along for the ride. He caught Max's perfect tosses and plodded to the end of the field while Al made the strategic blocks. They were showmen and he was the audience.

Except in Ashley Jacobs's eyes. She saw a quiet man. She saw a sensitive man. She saw a man who would never hurt her the way her father did.

And gradually, over the course of that summer, she came to tell Bud all the things she never told anyone else about what went on in John Jacobs's big fancy mansion at night. She danced with Max. She laughed with Al. She gave her heart and plotted her escape with Bud.

August fifteenth. Such a night. You could hear the crickets, and it was warm and balmy. Not too hot, like it could get in August. Not too dry. A perfect night. She came to their cabin on a social call, perfectly on the up-and-up. For the last month, she'd been arriving wearing one set of clothes beneath another. She would take off the inner garment and leave it behind with the bits of jewelry and cash she'd spirited out. Finally, she was ready.

When she showed up August fifteenth, Bud had all their things packed. They would drive to Idaho, then head into Canada. There, they would start over under new names. Bud had already gotten them the new ID. Her father would never be able to find them.

They had no illusions about what would happen if he did.

Bud had accounted for everything—except Al.

Al had returned early that night. He'd been playing poker at the lodge, losing heavily and drinking even more. He spotted Bud, Ashley and the suitcase and became immediately belligerent. Bud could tell simply by the look in his eye that Al was in one of *those* moods.

Slowly but surely, Bud edged Ashley toward the door. Ashley loved him, Al kept crying. She was just using Bud. No one could love Bud. Bud wasn't much of a man.

It was gonna get ugly.

Bud got Ashley into the car. She curled up in the back seat, trembling. Right before he shut the door, Bud looked at her face. She was terrified. His sweet Ashley, whom he'd sworn to protect, was scared to death.

Bud found his strength. All his life he'd played second fiddle. Not tonight. Bud quietly took off his jacket and prepared to fight.

Just then, Max arrived.

It took him just a moment to apprise the situation, but then Max had always been the bright one. His jaw was set. He looked at Ashley hunched in the back seat, he looked at the packed bag, and he looked hurt. Generally, it was hard to tell what Max thought about a woman, he'd had so many. But maybe he had thought Ashley was special. Maybe he'd thought she was the one. Who knew?

Max turned to Al and quietly told him to stand down. Ashley had made her choice, and they should respect it.

Al, however, turned on Max with fury. He charged his best friend and they went down in the dirt. Bud sprang forward, then heard Ashley's cry.

"Come on," she whispered frantically. "Please come on."

Bud looked at his wrestling friends and he looked at his soon-to-be wife. He made his decision. As he drove away, he saw Max and Al rise out of the dirt.

They were standing, and each of them had a gun.

"But they didn't shoot each other," Brandon interrupted. "They both lived after that night."

Bud nodded against the locket. "Yes, but Al didn't give up. He went a little crazy after that night, you know. And I should know." For a moment, his lips curved.

"We made it to Canada, Ashley and I. I quit the business. We settled in with our new identities. I didn't tell anyone but Max where we were. He was the only one— our parents, our friends, everyone else we let go. That's hard, people don't know how hard that is. So hard. But we had to keep Ashley safe. Max came by. Good friend Max, all we had left. He told us about Al. Crazy Al. Turncoat Al. Who would've known? I swear we were careful.''

Bud became earnest. ''It wasn't a great life, but Ashley understood. I gave up the business for her and she liked that, she did. Max and Al, they never understood that. Ashley didn't want money or diamonds or pearls. She needed to feel safe, my sweet baby. She needed someone to hold her and keep her together. Poor, sweet, scared, baby. I love you.''

His voice warbled. ''She loved me, too. She did. Oh, Lord.''

''What happened?'' Brandon asked gently.

''Ashley disappeared,'' Bud whispered. ''My baby disappeared,'' and his lower lip began to tremble.

''Ten years, not such a bad life, I swear not such a bad life, and I never let my guard down. Never, never, never. We heard stories of Al and John Jacobs. Mr. Jacobs had money, but Al had contacts, Al had *skills*. I know those skills, I helped him develop them, I didn't forget, I swear I didn't forget. I'd promised I would protect her. I promised, I promised, I promised.''

''I know,'' Brandon said, ''I'm sure you did. I'm sure Ashley knows that you did your best.''

Bud Irving was rocking back and forth rapidly. He chewed on his thumbnail.

''I let him get her.''

''Who, Bud? Who?''

''Al liked to hide bodies,'' Bud whispered. ''That was his signature. He thought it gave him style. He didn't just pop people, he orchestrated it, you know.''

''What?''

''Found her car parked on the side of the road, August fifteenth, 1969. She was going to the beauty parlor to have her hair done for our anniversary dinner. No signs of a struggle, they say. I bet she begged. I bet she pleaded. My poor baby, my poor baby.''

"Oh, my God," Brandon said.

"They never found a trace. Gone, poof. Ten years was all we had, and she deserved so much better. She was just starting to walk around without trench coats and sunglasses. Starting to feel strong enough to do things alone. I told her I would protect her from her father, and then I let my best friend kill her. I failed. I failed. I failed...."

Bud began to cry silently. The love of his life had disappeared, and he'd returned to Beaverville, the place where he had found her, the place where maybe she'd return. But he knew in his heart she was dead—Al got her, and Al never left things undone. Bud lived out his days alone and terrified, and every year John Jacobs showed up with his picture and lanterns and prayers. The hypocritical bastard pretended he loved and missed Ashley, too, while Bud called upon her spirit to keep him from killing the man.

John Jacobs would never learn where his daughter had gone on August fifteenth, 1959. Bud had kept his word. The promise was the only thing of his wife's he had left.

Brandon took his hand. "Did you kill Al?" he asked gently. "Is that why Al Simmons disappeared the next year?"

Bud shook his hand. "I couldn't. I quit the business. I promised Ashley no more. Max did it, I think. It was overdue. You gotta kill the rabid dog. Everyone knows, you gotta kill the rabid dog.''

"My father killed Al? Did he tell you this?"

"I never saw Max again. Didn't even come to the funeral. But maybe he couldn't. The business was like that. Orders came first. By then, he probably had his."

"Orders to do what?"

"Orders to kill Al, of course. He'd gone Commie."

"Bud, what was it you guys did?"

Bud looked at him blankly. "We were fix-it men, of course. We killed people."

When Brandon emerged from the house, the sun was gone. Bud turned on the searchlights, and the light was too bright, burning Brandon's eyes. He staggered down the narrow path, the Dobermans growling and snarling at his heels, and headed for his car.

Deputy James was still at the side of the road. Brandon didn't look at him, didn't speak to him. He got into his car and drove.

His father was an assassin. His father may have killed his best friend.

Kaboom, Bud Irving whispered in his mind.

The truth was too raw and bitter to be borne. His father had been some kind of government agent. He'd followed orders. He'd done as he was told. He'd been working for the good guys, but doing the kinds of things that even after all these years no one wanted exposed.

It made so much sense. The job he never spoke about. The vague travel itineraries. The need to always have cash.

The phone call C.J. had received six months ago. *You're almost as good as your father. You're just a little too straight.*

Brandon Ferringer, you just learned your father didn't leave you all those times to make money—he was killing people. Your father was a spook. How does that make you feel?

Brandon drove faster. Beaverville whizzed by and the pine trees rose dark and thick along the road. His eyes were burning. He didn't know why. It was so long ago. Why should he care about what happened so long ago?

Except Julia died just four years ago, shot down after

asking questions about Max. And then there was the fire in
Victoria's stables, the car that had aimed for them both.
The man who had pulled out a gun and the person who'd
shot him.

So much violence. Julia. Victoria. Julia. Victoria.

He pulled to the side of the road savagely. He was out
the door while it was still rolling to a stop.

And then he was running. Thundering through the black,
inky woods, tree limbs whipping at his face and snatching
his skin. He ran hard through the darkness, the pine needles
soft, the lava rocks tricky.

He finally burst into a clearing. The moon was full and
waxy overhead. An owl hooted mournfully.

Brandon fell to his knees. In the middle of nowhere,
surrounded by fifty-foot pine trees and a midnight sky, he
raised his head and he screamed.

"Damn you, Max! Damn Max Ferringer!"

Victoria woke with a jolt. She sat abruptly and froze. He
stood at the foot of her bed, swathed in shadows.

"I walked here," he said hoarsely. "I wasn't followed."

"Brandon, what's wrong?"

He remained perfectly still. She could see the tension
tightening his shoulders, the arms pulled against his torso,
the hands balled into fists. Brandon Ferringer was walking
the edge of some razor-sharp precipice, and at any moment,
he could tumble over.

She threw back the sheets. She swung her bare legs over
the edge of the mattress and approached.

His eyes glittered in the darkness. She could feel his gaze
raking her exposed white limbs and her tangled blond hair.

"It's all right," she whispered. "It's all right now."

She placed her hands on his shoulders gently and settled

her body against him. He was rock hard, and the rage that emanated from him startled her.

"My father was an assassin."

She kneaded his arms, trying to soothe him.

"He probably killed Al Simmons."

She cupped his cheek and felt him tremble.

"My *wife* probably died because of what he did!"

She wrapped her arms around his waist and held him tight.

"You, your barn, your ranch. It's all his bloody fault. It's all his damn, bloody fault!"

"Brandon, I love you."

He put his arms around her harshly. She thought he would kiss her savagely, and she was prepared. But he buried his face against her neck, and she felt his shoulders begin to shake.

"Come to bed, Ferringer. Come to bed."

She stripped his clothes slowly in the moonlight. Then he was gripping her face, angling her head. He kissed her fiercely. This was Brandon Ferringer, raw, live and in person.

This was the man she loved.

They fell onto the bed, his clothes hastily pulled from his frame, her legs curving around his waist, her hands guiding him inside her.

The first penetration was like silk. They stopped, they gasped, they enjoyed the pure, exquisite beauty. Then slowly, he began to move inside her, and she held his face in her hands, staring into his eyes while he filled her, stretched her and consumed her.

His body bowed. She dug her teeth into her lower lip, wanting to prolong it, but the climax slapped her hard. She expelled her breath in a rush, and he bit back his gasping release in the silence. He fell on her heavily, and she stroked his sweat-streaked back.

"It's okay. It's okay," she whispered.

"I won't let anything happen to you," he said. "I'll protect you."

"Of course, Ferringer. Of course."

She held him until he fell asleep, but the night was long. He woke up four times, jerking in the throes of some nightmare and calling various names. Sometimes it was Julia. Sometimes it was Victoria. And once it was Ashley Jacobs.

At six, she woke up to the sound of beeping. Brandon was already struggling out of bed. He found the beeper in the pile of clothes, glanced at the number and began pulling on his clothes. A hotshot saw thirty to fifty fires a season.

He stood, and their gazes met.

"I have to," he said simply.

"I know."

"My team."

"I know."

"Victoria, I love you, too."

He strode out the door.

Chapter 12

"**C.J.**'s taxidermy. You snuff 'em, we stuff 'em."

"C.J.!" Brandon yelled into his cell phone above the roar of the plane engine.

"Brandon? Where the hell are you calling from, a Laundromat?"

"An airplane."

"Oh. Of course. Back to Indonesia?"

"Colorado."

"Hmm. Looking for real estate investments?"

"Putting out wildland fires."

"Well, that was going to be my next guess."

"I'm a hotshot, remember?"

"You mean you actually did that?" C.J. sounded impressed, not a feeling he bestowed upon Brandon often. "Congrats, man. That's serious stuff. So wait a minute—you're on the way to a fire *now?*"

"Yes." Brandon twisted away from his team and cupped his hand over the phone. What he was going to say next he didn't want overheard. But he hadn't had time to make the call from the ground. "C.J., someone's trying to kill me."

"You mean Lydia finally figured out that social security windfall was from you?"

"No, C.J. I mean someone is trying to kill me. I've found out about Max."

At the other end, through the static there was stunned silence.

Brandon spoke as calmly as possible. "Our father was a government agent of some kind, an assassin. He came to Beaverville in 1959 with his two best friends, Al Simmons and Bud Irving. They fell in love with the same woman, the woman from the locket. Bud married her and retired from the business. Al went berserk. Bud thinks Max killed him."

"God," C.J. said.

"I need to learn more, C.J. Do you have any military contacts, anyone who can ask around?"

"I don't know, Brandon. Government agents are serious suits. I'm just a former Marine. We don't exactly do lunch."

"C.J., I'm in trouble. Someone's been tampering with my equipment. Then a man shot at me, but someone shot him in the back and killed him. I thought maybe Bud Irving was the shooter, but he's not. In short, there's someone else out there I haven't identified yet, and whoever he is, he's playing for keeps."

"That's it. I'll be on the next plane."

"No. Listen to me. Find out what you can from your end. If I can figure out who we're dealing with, maybe I can get them to call off the dogs. Someone killed my wife to keep Max's secret. I want to know who that is. Do you understand?"

C.J. understood too well. Someone had gone after Tamara once. He had paid.

"I need you to do something else," Brandon said quietly.

C.J. was still. Two requests for help in a single phone call. Send your brother to Oregon, and he comes back a whole new man. "I'm listening."

"There's another woman."

"Really?"

Brandon ignored C.J.'s shock. "Her name is Victoria Meese. She lives in Beaverville with her son, Randy. If anything happens to me, I want you to make sure she's taken care of. And my estate… I love her, C.J. Make sure."

"God, Brandon, you have been busy."

"Promise—"

"Brandon, nothing will happen to her. You have my word. Now, let me come out there—"

"Her father's the sheriff. He's taking care of her for now. I could be in Colorado for who knows how long. Make the phone calls, C.J. That's what I need. Names."

"Then I'll start at the bottom end of the Pentagon's food chain and work my way up. Something will fall down."

"Give my regards to Tamara. And, if anything happens, tell Maggie I'm sorry I traveled so much. She was right. I shouldn't have shut you all out."

"It's okay. We understood."

"Yes, but you shouldn't have had to."

Brandon hung up. For some reason, his hands were shaking. He folded up the cell phone. Business was attended to. Victoria would be taken care of. C.J. would push the investigation forward. Everything was under control.

He turned to find Coleton staring at him. "Getting your affairs in order, rich Brit? It's just a measly fire."

He grinned, and the scars on his face twisted. The plane began to descend.

"Time to deal," Brandon said, straight-faced.

Coleton's grin spread. "That's right. Time to deal."

The crew was strangely quiet when they deplaned. Already they could smell acrid smoke and burning pine. A low, dense smog hung in the air, and embers of burned grass floated around their cheeks. This area contained lots of dense timber, which created intense heat. If the wind picked up, the fire might crown or create fire whirls or both. Then the air temperature would reach two thousand degrees, devouring all the oxygen and burning out a man's lungs without ever touching a hair on his head.

They shouldered their twenty-five-pound packs and got moving.

Even Woody looked nervous.

Victoria picked up the phone on the third ring. Randy was enthusiastically devouring his oatmeal at the kitchen table. She'd merely been toying with hers. She missed Brandon.

"Hello?"

"Vic, honey, is Brandon there?"

She relaxed at the sound of her father's voice. "Ferringer got called to a fire. The team just flew out."

Her father was silent for a minute.

"Anything wrong?"

"Well," he said slowly, "it turns out we got a witness."

"To the shooting?" She was honestly surprised. Randy perked up, looking startled.

"Is there a break in the case?" Randy asked in a perfect stage whisper. She nodded vigorously.

"Turns out some kid was out bird shooting. Saw a man

ahead, carrying a Remington and trying to cover his tracks. The kid thought that was a little strange, reported to his father, and his father called me this morning. It's the right time and area for your incident.''

"Who'd he see?'' she asked breathlessly.

"Tom Reynolds.''

"Okay, hotshots, here's the drill.'' At twelve hundred, Superintendent Coleton Smith paced in front of his team armed with a topography map of the area and their undivided attention. Everyone was in full gear and wearing their packs. In fifteen minutes, they would join two other hotshot crews and one Smokejumper team. Already, a hundred acres burned.

"This fire is slow and hot. It was started by lightning just twenty-four hours ago, so there could be more sleepers and spot fires waiting to happen.''

The crew nodded. When lightning struck a dead tree surrounded by light brush, the falling embers immediately caught the bush and burst into flame. But sometimes the tree was surrounded by rocky terrain or pine needles—more stubborn fuel materials. In that case, the burning embers from the tree would fall upon the pine needles and slowly cook, building up heat and fuel over time until suddenly, a fresh whiff of air hit the embers and the pine needles burst into flame. A new ground fire was born—sometimes three hours after the initial lightning storm, sometimes three weeks.

Sleepers didn't start big, but they could become big if not spotted and handled. Then multiple fires burned in multiple places, calling to one another. The heat of the fire built a vacuum and sucked more fire toward it. Hotshot crews became boxed in. Team members got cut off. Life became tricky.

"The terrain is tough," Coleton announced. He didn't like this fire. It was obvious from his expression, and he wasn't about to sugarcoat it. "It started in a canyon with dense timber. It's damn hot, moving half a mile an hour and running three hundred degrees. We got the river on the west for a natural fire line. Now it's already crested one ridge to the north and is moving down that side of the canyon." He illustrated the progress of the fire on the map, then halted at a point by the river. He tapped it twice. "You will hike in from a river landing. The gulch rises up to five thousand feet and bottoms out at three thousand. That is steep."

They all nodded. That was *steep*.

"The good news is that that side of the gulch is rocky and has only sporadic coverage of pine and fir—smaller trees only six to eight inches in diameter. The bad news is that the whole damn area is covered with cheatgrass and bunchgrass." He smiled grimly. "At least it's not August."

The crew didn't return his smile. People were exchanging glances. Grass fires made a hotshot nervous.

In the beginning, timber fires were what people feared—the heat and the intensity of a thick patch of Douglas fir catching flame. Those fires grew so hot they devoured everything in their paths, making trees pop and boulders tumble. But like a big dumb jock, a timber fire lumbered along slowly and awkwardly, giving crews plenty of time to plan, dig fire lines, lay hoses and trap the beast.

Grass fires, on the other hand... In the forestry service's history, more men had died in grass fires than timber. Grass fires didn't produce much heat, but fed by light, dry fuel, they wicked over the terrain faster than the speed of sound, sometimes brushing over houses so quickly the roofs smoked but never caught.

A grass fire could fry, however, and moving at phenomenal speeds, it easily gained on fire crews running for their lives, tapping them on the shoulder and consuming them whole.

Timber and grass. Heat and speed. No, the hotshot team was not happy.

"Close to the top of the ridge is rocky terrain," Coleton continued, stabbing a spot on the topography map. "Stick toward the top. If the fire gets out of hand, it's as good a safety zone as you're going to get."

He picked up four handheld radios and tossed them. Woody caught one. Brandon got one, and Larry and Trish took the other two.

"That's all the communication equipment we got," Coleton said, and the team groaned. "Hey," he snapped. "Be happy we got four. Budget cuts aren't designed to make our lives easier. Woody, Brandon, Larry, Trish, stand up. Woody, you're crew boss. Ferringer, you serve as second. Okay, folks, make sure one of these people is in your sight at all times. We got the national forecaster monitoring this situation every second. A warm front is currently sitting tight over the area, building up the heat. If a cold front moves in…"

People nodded. If a cold front moved in, the wind would kick up, hit the crown fire and turn it into a blowout. Wonderful.

"If the wind even hiccups," Coleton vowed, "we'll send out the call and get your butts outta there. Is that clear?"

That was clear.

"This fire is high risk," Coleton added. "Make sure you got your fire shields. And if things get out of hand, remember, you have four choices. Get to the safety zone. Start a backfire. Start an escape fire. And if all that fails, turn and hit the fire on your terms. Find the thinnest wall of flames, trust your fire suits, and run through the flames to the black.

Do not let the fire pick the time and place it meets you. Because if you let it catch you, it's gonna hit you with the hottest, fastest, fiercest section, and you cannot wade through a three-hundred-foot front.

"Okay, folks. One fries, we all fry."

They stood. Brandon clipped the radio to his belt and they assumed formation. Woody, as crew boss, took the front. It was his job to size up the fire and spot threats. The most veteran member of the crew and a permanent employee, he would formulate the strategy for the fire line and give orders.

Brandon brought up the rear. As second, his job was to make sure that all seventeen crew members were following orders and that no one was left behind.

It was eleven in the morning. Most likely, they would work straight through the night.

Charlie fell in beside Brandon along with Larry. Both carried chain saws, which meant they walked toward the rear where no one could trip and fall onto the vicious equipment.

Brandon carried a Pulaski and a first-aid kit and his pack. Twenty-five pounds of gear.

"No laughs today," Charlie muttered as they moved toward launch point.

No one disagreed.

"Vic, meet Tom Reynolds. Retired Agent Reynolds, CIA."

"Huh?" Victoria looked at her favorite chocolate soda vendor blankly, then turned to her father. He'd asked her to come down to his small two-room sheriff's office to hear Tom's story. Apparently, it was some story. "You're kidding, right?"

Her father held up a fax. "Got the verification right here."

The fax from the Central Intelligence Agency stated that Tom Reynolds was recently reactivated and not to be bothered. They'd included his fingerprints to confirm his identity.

Tom smiled pleasantly. "Kind of shocking, isn't it?"

Victoria took a seat. "What the hell is going on? This is Beaverville, for God's sake. You own the general store!"

"I do," Tom said. "That isn't a lie. I retired from the CIA fifteen years ago and moved here to live quietly. Admittedly, I was given an extra retirement stipend to monitor Bud Irving while I was at it."

"Bud Irving is CIA?"

"Former. He retired in 1959. But he had contact with Agent Maximillian Ferringer and Agent Al Simmons. Given the mystery surrounding both men's disappearance, we figured Bud was our best chance of learning more."

"Oh, boy," Victoria said.

Her father added, "Better start at the beginning, Tom. Er, Agent Reynolds."

"Tom is fine." Tom got comfortable on the hard wooden seat. He looked from the sheriff to Victoria to the sheriff. "You have to understand, this doesn't leave this room. I'm only telling you because I've seen you with Brandon Ferringer, and I think you can help."

"We can help," Victoria said forcefully.

"Then here we go. As I told you, Vic, 1959 was a big year. Not because three of our agents fought over the same woman, but because of the results. Bud Irving married her, resigned his post and ran away with Ashley Jacobs to live under an assumed identity in Canada. Maximillian went to England. Al seemed to be continuing his job, but then we started to hear some nasty rumors.

"We began to tail Agent Simmons, and by 1965 it was clear he'd become a KGB mole. Furthermore, he was actively trying to locate Bud Irving and Ashley Jacobs.

"We did what we could, of course, assigning Agent Ferringer to the case, since he knew Al best and could anticipate him. He followed Simmons for many years, trying to pinpoint who he was working with and if there were additional CIA turncoats. We don't like to admit to such things, of course."

"Of course," Victoria said dryly.

"In 1968, Simmons disappeared. Max lost him cold. Then, just eight months later, Ashley Jacobs disappeared, and we knew it must be Al. Ferringer took it personally. He'd failed his watch. But the organization had had enough at that point, too. It was decided that Simmons was too dangerous to be left alive and the assignment went to code red—kill on sight. In 1970, two agents tracked down Al Simmons and planted a car bomb. The car went up, but Simmons's body was never found. We suspected he might be still alive. When Maximillian Ferringer disappeared in 1972, we knew the truth—Al Simmons was very much alive and still one step ahead."

"Sounds like you guys are just brilliant," Victoria muttered.

"The loss of Agent Ferringer was taken very seriously in the organization," Tom said levelly. "Al Simmons is good, though, very good. We'd given up on ever finding him when Brandon Ferringer suddenly started asking questions. Then, a month ago, we learned a hit had been placed on his head and he was coming here. I was reactivated, given that I already lived here and knew the situation. My assignment has been to monitor Brandon Ferringer, protect him and see if Al Simmons emerges to take the bait."

"You're using Brandon Ferringer as bait?" Victoria scowled.

Tom shrugged. "He stepped into the fray voluntarily. We would be fools not to take advantage of the situation."

"Get to the shooting," Sheriff Meese interrupted.

"The man I shot was Ray Bands, a longtime hit man. I think he was responsible for the accidents, as well. It took me a bit to catch on to his presence." He added a trifle defensively, "I have been retired for fifteen years."

"What about Al Simmons?" Victoria prodded. "Have you seen any sign of him? Is he around?"

For the first time, Tom appeared troubled. "I have a new theory," he said quietly. "But it shames me to admit it."

"Spit it out, Tom!"

"I think Al Simmons has been living here all along. I think I've spent the last fifteen years with Agent Simmons right beneath my nose."

"*Who?*"

"I don't have any proof," Tom said levelly, "but I've been doing some checking in Montana. Coleton Smith exists, all right, and has a stellar record as a forestry service employee. He's also, however, known as a bit of a loner. No family, no relatives. The man I spoke to said he was committed to the forest one hundred percent. That man also described the Coleton Smith he'd known in 1977 as five foot six and blue-eyed. So why is our Coleton Smith five foot ten and brown-eyed?"

"Oh, my God," Victoria whispered. "The hotshot crew!"

Tom called for transportation. Victoria got her mother to watch Randy. At eleven-fifteen, Victoria, her father and Tom Reynolds boarded a chartered plane for Colorado.

"I'm sure Brandon's all right," Tom kept saying. "Why would Al Simmons jeopardize his whole team? I'm sure Brandon's just fine."

Victoria and Sheriff Meese didn't reply.

Deployment took longer than anyone expected. The river currents were fast, or the guide was slow, or maybe he just hadn't been planning on the extra weight of their gear. At any rate, he pushed their chain of three rafts into the river and almost immediately lost control. It took Brandon, Larry and former white-water guide Trish to get the crafts together.

They fought the wayward current all the way down. By the time they finally landed at their destination, they were forty-five minutes late and exhausted.

They assumed formation once again, checked in with command central where Coleton and Barbara were monitoring the situation and set out again. Several gulches and canyons sprouted from the river. They headed straight into the middle one, climbing up to four thousand feet as instructed and following the natural curve into the heart of the gulch. Below them, they could see a thicket of dark trees. To their right, across the gulch, they could see smoke. Up ahead and to the right, the real fire burned, having crested from the other side and now working its way down.

The Smokejumpers had landed somewhere way ahead four hours ago. They were taking the advance line to the east. The Beaverville crew was in charge of flanking any movement to the north. The wide river would serve as a natural fire line to the west. The fire had already burned out to the south.

In theory, a second crew would be joining them shortly. Then again, if they got the same river pilot...

They'd hiked about a mile when the first sleeper flared

up. Brandon heard Woody shout, "Holy smokes!" Flames were suddenly shooting into the air. Smoke billowed from another four patches of damp, knee-high bunchgrass.

Then, to the left, a second spot of fire suddenly erupted. For a moment they froze. It was an eerie sight, two blooms of fire in the middle of the rocky, craggy surface. The fires seemed to dance with an unknown partner, then suddenly spotted each other and reached out snaking tendrils to hold hands. They wrapped together quickly, gobbling up the grass and seeking fresh fuel.

Woody belatedly shouted orders, and they sprang to life. Pulaskis and shovels walloped the fire cold. They hacked down the grass and covered it with shallow layers of silt. Charlie gave a cry. Another fire had broken out. Other smokers seemed to be sprouting around their feet. Brandon had never seen anything like it. Suddenly they were prancing around like nervous horses, batting at thin tendrils of smoke and chasing ghosts. The whole mountainside was lousy with sparks.

Then Brandon began to realize how much he was sweating for how little he was working. The air was too hot. He looked up and saw a bloodred sun, shimmering with heat.

The timber fire had crowned. It was cooking the mountaintop, sending out a front wave of thick, cloying heat, drying the damp grass and live trees for the eruption about to come.

The fire was building, getting ready, becoming prepared.

Brandon glanced at Woody.

He was holding up a finger, testing for wind.

"Still nothing," he said to their unasked questions.

But at that moment, Brandon could have sworn he felt a breeze tickle his chin.

Barbara was slumped in the chair, staring out the window of the watchtower glumly. With her wrapped ankle, she still wasn't fit for field duty, so she was stuck with Coleton. Clearly, she was not happy.

Coleton watched her from across the tiny room. He was standing in front of the fax machine, waiting for the latest news to come in. He wore a smile.

It always amazed him, the small twists of fate that could determine who lived and who died, the seemingly insignificant decisions and choices that suddenly meant so much. In Mann Gulch, the fire claimed an out-of-shape forest ranger who'd once been a lean, mean Smokejumper but quit because his mother thought the job was too dangerous. In Storm King Mountain, there was the man who'd promised this would be his last fire, and indeed it had been.

In Colorado, there would be the woman who twisted her ankle on the qualifying run but made the crew thanks to the efforts of her teammates. She would be frustrated that she couldn't join her team at the fire.

She would be the only one left alive by the end of the day.

The fax machine finally chirped to life. Coleton Smith, superintendent of the Beaverville crew, received the national forecaster's update. Cold front moving in. Evacuate now.

And Al Simmons, whose hatred of Maximillian Ferringer had never died, crumpled the paper and threw it away.

"No news," he told Barbara blandly.

She resumed staring out the window, where the sun had gone crimson.

The twin-engine plane was making its descent when it hit the first wave of incoming air and jerked up. The pilot corrected gamely, but the wind currents were strong, and for several sickening moments, the plane was battered by conflicting winds.

Victoria grabbed the edge of her seat. Her father turned pale. Tom looked a little green around the edges.

The plane went into a dive, then at the last minute bottomed out.

"Sorry," the CIA pilot called back to them. "Bad front, had to get underneath it. Hope you're not planning on staying for long, because once that kicks up, this plane is grounded. That's gonna be one hell of a windstorm."

They were still hiking to their destination point, where they would start digging the fire line. Their steps were faster now, an unspoken urgency moving through the group. The air was hot, much, much hotter than any of them expected, and even the veterans were antsy. It hurt to breathe too deep, the air searing fragile lung sacs. They learned to use shallow puffs, moving over the ridges and curves of the rocky, churning land.

They crested the small hump, and Woody stopped cold.

The shimmering air seemed to contract on itself, and then in the next moment it exploded. Burning pinecones burst through the air, and two team members ducked. Rocks flew like bullets, driven by an unimaginable force, while ten-foot-thick trees abruptly combusted from the heat of their own resin.

And through the smoke, through the wavy, tearing heat, the wall of fire rose up like a beast, six hundred feet tall and mad as hell. It turned toward them and blasted its first blow.

Woody moved his lips, but the sound was lost in the ensuing roar. Brandon's hair was swept from his face. He felt his clothes suddenly compress against his skin, and he staggered from the gust.

Woody's lips moved again.

This time, Brandon understood him. The veteran wildland firefighter said, "God help us. God help us. God help us."

Tom pulled out a nine-millimeter. Sheriff Meese had a .357 Magnum. Victoria was ordered behind a van and told not to move.

Al Simmons, aka Coleton Smith, might be old and he might be scarred, but he was still a man who'd once been the best in the field. They wanted to take him out fast and quick, before he had a chance to take any hostages for wheeling and dealing.

Tom gave the nod to go ahead.

As Victoria watched through the van's windows, her father opened the door at the bottom of the watchtower and pivoted in, gun first. After a moment, Tom followed.

Both men disappeared from sight.

Barbara had reached down to pick up a paper clip when the door behind her burst open.

"Sheriff!" one man cried.

"Don't move," a second man screamed.

She turned slowly to find two old men pointing guns at her and Coleton Smith. "Sheriff Meese," she said stupidly. "What are you doing here?"

Her words were drowned out by the sound of a man laughing. Coleton Smith doubled over, clutching his side with glee.

"You're too late," he gasped. "Look!"

Barbara followed his pointing finger. Far to the right of the window, a small windmill jutted from the watchtower, designed to help determine velocity and strength of wind. High winds were deadly to a fire crew.

The windmill was churning furiously.

Barbara's face went pale. "My God, what have you done?"

"Run!" Woody roared. "Drop gear *now*."

Pulaskis and chain saws clattered to the ground. Water canteens and emergency kits followed. As a unit, they burst forward.

One fries, we all fry.

Stay behind! Stay behind! Brandon's legs wanted to leap. His lungs burned from the heat, and he felt an unbearable pressure in his chest. But he stayed. He stood his ground. He was second in command. It was his job to bring up the rear, his job to make sure everyone was following formation.

He would not lose his head. He would not succumb to panic. He would not fail his team.

I am better than Max. I am Brandon Ferringer.

Woody sprinted by, hard-muscled legs pumping. He still held his radio in his hand. He was screaming, but the words were hard to hear. Brandon's radio crackled to life. Barbara. She was crying about Coleton. Then, suddenly, Victoria's voice cut in, cool and strong and urgent.

"Run," she said. "Get out, get out, get out!"

Larry raced by, Trish, Winston, April and Charlie. Brandon waited and waited. His eyes teared from the smoke. Another pinecone fired by his head. He smelled his mucus membranes beginning to burn.

"Marsha," he screamed, and urged the stumbling hot-shot forward. "Go, go, go."

Victoria was still speaking through the radio at his waist. "Get out, get out, get out."

He looked one last time to make sure everyone had gone, and he saw the most ethereal sight. The fire was dancing. The six-hundred-foot wall of flame was ripped and joined,

torn and married by the fickle, buffeting wind. Until the
fire collapsed on itself, then rose up. Until it died and was
reborn, carried by a warring, traitorous wind, half-cold,
half-hot, slamming against itself.

And then, as he stood transfixed, the wind resolved its
differences. The cool shoved the hot, the hot twisted back,
and a wind tunnel was formed. The fire suddenly balled
into a tornado and took off like a cyclone, spitting eighty-
pound boulders.

Brandon ran.

"Helicopters!" Victoria screamed. She held Coleton by
the lapels. She was so angry, so terrified she was spitting
in his face. Barbara stood right behind her, looking ready
to tear the man from limb to limb. "Call rescue helicopters!"

"Can't get in," Coleton said gleefully. "Wind's too
strong now. It's a full-scale blowout, updrafts, downdrafts,
vacuums and funnels. Ain't nothing going in. Ain't no one
coming out."

Victoria wanted to kill him. In that instant, she truly did.
And the rage rose up in her, and the terror rose up in her,
and she knew Brandon was going to die. And Charlie,
sweet twenty-two-year-old Charlie. Dear Lord.

"Don't worry," Coleton whispered innocently, "Ferringer's got good legs and much better lungs than the others.
He's got altitude training they don't, and much more stam-
ina. All he's got to do is leave them behind and maybe
he'll make it. Not your brother, he's too rash. He'll push
too hard, breathe too deeply and pass out from the fumes.
If it's any consolation, he'll be unconscious when the fire
hits."

Victoria's father stepped forward with a growl. Tom
barely caught his arm.

Coleton smiled, his gaze on Victoria. "But Ferringer might make it. If he leaves the others. If he focuses on himself, he can do it."

And then Victoria knew that Brandon was lost, that Coleton had outmaneuvered them all. Because Brandon would never leave his team. He would never be like his father.

Coleton had taught him well.

Woody was running up the slope, angling for the ridge. They stumbled after him, running flat out but disoriented by the smoke and dazed by the heat. The air didn't hold enough oxygen. It had all been burned away and replaced by carbon monoxide. The fire whirls were filled with poisonous gases, twirling around them, flicking fire at their hair and cheeks, showering them with burning tree limbs and fresh embers.

They ran faster, gasping and heaving. They shouldn't be heading up, Brandon thought, but could no longer remember why. In this churning inferno, the lessons of the classroom seemed far away. The lack of oxygen and the noxious fumes made it hard to think. One by one, they fell back on instinct and did what their young bodies and well-conditioned muscles were trained to do—they ran. They sprinted over rocky terrain, angled hard and made a beeline for the craggy promise of the ridge where the fire would finally be thwarted by lack of fuel.

Running uphill is no good. The thought whispered through Brandon's mind again. He wanted to be able to grab it and turn it over clearly, but he was having trouble thinking. He chest and throat burned. Dots spotted his vision.

Somewhere in the back of his mind, the cool, rational part of him told him he was losing consciousness. He wasn't getting enough oxygen. His three-layer flame-retardant gear, formulated to withstand seventeen hundred degrees for up to five seconds, was beginning to melt and shrink-wrap his skin.

It felt as if a burning poker was pressed along his spine, and he was running faster and faster to escape the heat without it making a shred of difference.

It sounded as if he was standing in the middle of a jet engine.

Trish stumbled on a rock and went down. Charlie tripped over her and stumbled. Larry went running by, his hair singed and covering his scalp in white. April sprinted behind Larry, looking like a ghostly deer while embers burned through her coat. Their eyes were wide and panicked, their faces lined and grim.

Run, run, run, he could almost hear them cry.

Brandon scooped an arm around Trish's waist. He staggered and almost fell. No damn oxygen. Couldn't breathe, couldn't think. The others were running up the hill, the fire giving wings to their feet.

Damn, they shouldn't be running uphill. Uphill was bad, but he couldn't remember why. Bloody hell. His stomach rolled.

He was going to vomit.

Poisonous gases, the rational part of his mind supplied. *Cover your mouth.*

He found a handkerchief, wetted it and tied it around his mouth. Trish was sitting, dazed, disoriented and confused. He covered her mouth. He could hear a roar behind them.

The fire was coming.

Don't let the fire meet you on its terms. Stop reacting, keep control, formulate a strategy. Cool, cool rich Brit. Think, think, think. Fast.

Up ahead, Charlie picked himself up. The glow of the fire made his eyes look red.

His lips were moving. "One fries, we all fry."

He joined Brandon, and they wrapped their arms around Trish's waist. And then, ungainly and slow but developing a rhythm, they took off once more.

Behind them, the fire roared. Coming uphill from the left, a new fire burst to life.

Think, Brandon, think.

The smoke closed in on them and the world became a tiny, desperate place.

"Brandon," Victoria yelled into the radio. "Brandon, please!"

There was no answer.

In the corner of the watchtower, Barbara began to cry. Coleton, handcuffed to a chair, smiled.

Victoria determinedly pressed the relay button again. "Keep moving, Brandon," she commanded. "Don't give up, please, I need you, Brandon. Watch out for yourself, watch out for Charlie. *You are my hero.*"

Victoria was talking to them. Brandon thought it was odd, but he didn't think it was odd. In this crazy, smoky-heated world, anything was possible. A figure appeared ahead. It was Larry, sitting on the hot ground. His hair was gone, his scalp bright red.

He had a dazed look in his eyes, as if he was a child lost in the mall.

Victoria spoke to him, too. "Run, run, please run. Don't give up, you can't give up."

Brandon leapt up and turned wildly, as if expecting to see ghosts. He suddenly wanted to laugh. So did Trish. The world was all helter skelter and filled with pretty colors. His vision was blurring. He almost didn't mind.

Breathe slower. Don't hyperventilate, don't give in to the gases.

"One fries, we all fry," Charlie gasped.

"Come home to me, Brandon, come home to me," Victoria commanded.

All of a sudden, a dozen forms burst in front of them. It was the rest of their crew, disoriented and turned around. Woody was in the lead. His eyes were wild. He clutched his throat. He saw the fire, came to a startled halt and seemed to realize what he'd done—he'd led the team into the flames.

They would never make the ridge. This was it, and they were thinking of the crosses that remained scattered across Mann Gulch, and the rows of bodies in silver fire shields recovered from Storm King Mountain.

The fire wall thundered down upon them. They were young, they were exhausted, and they still couldn't believe they were losing this war.

"Fire shields, fire shields," the crew boss croaked.

He fumbled with the matches at his waist. And then Woody's back suddenly arched, he gave a great, heaving gasp of noxious fumes, and the veteran firefighter pitched forward and passed out cold.

"Run," someone yelled. "Head down. Run through it!"

"No!" Brandon cried. His head was spinning. He saw lights and thought he might pass out, too.

"Fire shields now," he heard someone yell in a raw, hoarse voice. It was his voice. Brandon Ferringer was screaming above the flames.

And then he was lighting a match and tossing it into the grass. "Into the black," he roared. "Beaverville crew, into the black!"

Behind them, the blowout approached with fury. In front of them, the low-heat grass fire scoured through the fuel while skimming harmlessly over their fire suits.

"Beaverville crew," he screamed again, "into the black! Into the black!"

They crossed into the black.

They dove down one by one, the wall of flames boring down on them. They fumbled with fire shields in a last desperate bid that would determine who won and who lost.

Charlie had his face pressed in the black ashes, where oxygen remained. He yanked his fire shield up and was lost beneath the blanket of silver. And then Larry and then Trish and April...

"Go, go, go," Brandon was screaming, trying to find his fire shield, trying to position Woody.

The fire was almost upon him. He couldn't hear his voice anymore. He couldn't breathe in. He held his breath as the tears evaporated in his eyes. He fumbled with the fire shield as the fire hit the home straight and made a beeline for him.

His hair was singed off. The back of his hand was burned. He fought to seal the edges. Had to get it down or the wind would rip it off and expose him and Woody to the flames.

A fire shield wasn't meant to hold two people, anyway. He couldn't get the edges down far enough over the extra bulk. It wasn't going to work. He should let Woody go, save himself.

I am Brandon Ferringer.

He smashed the edges down.

The fire arrived with a whoosh.

The world blew up, and then it blew away.

They emerged slowly, one by one, hours later, when the air had finally cooled enough to breathe and the horizon was filled with an eerie calm generally associated with death.

Trish emerged first. She shook ash out of her hair. Charlie crawled out next. He had new lines permanently carved into his young face. Larry rolled over, breathing shallowly. He couldn't stand. His windpipe was seared and swelling up. He needed medical attention.

Person by person, they crawled from their narrow silver shells and stared at a world that had become black, alien and surreal. Finally, they turned toward the unnatural hump of two people crammed into one fire shield.

They glanced at one another. Woody and Brandon were the only two unaccounted for.

Charlie stepped forward and somberly did the deed—he pulled back the fire shield.

"Oh, my God," he said.

Victoria ran outside as the first National Guard chopper landed. It was followed by another, then another. Three helicopters to haul out seventeen people. Ambulances were on the scene, lights flashing, people yelling.

She ran from chopper to chopper, seeking.

"Brandon?" she cried. "Brandon?"

He heard his name from a long way away. The world seemed to be in a fog. His arms didn't want to move. His legs didn't want to move. The world had become small. He remembered that clearly. The flames had eaten everything. He remembered that, too.

And yet he still functioned, because the cool enclave of his brain made him function. The cool little spot in his mind wouldn't let him give up. He was Brandon Ferringer. Hotshot. Team member. Maximillian Ferringer's son.

Victoria Meese's hero.

He heard his name again. He turned. And then there she was, running toward him, her strong face earnest.

He clamored through the throng of people. He fought to

get off the chopper. He had to stop to let a stretcher pass. Woody looked up from the bed, holding an oxygen mask to his face. With his other hand, he gave Brandon a thumbs-up sign, and Brandon took his hand.

Then the medics passed, and Brandon glanced frantically for Victoria once more.

"Victoria! Victoria!"

She burst through the crowd and landed against him hard, snapping her arms around his bruised and battered body. He held her tight and inhaled deeply. Apple shampoo and the scent of horses. Spring days and summer rain.

She was here. Everyone was safe, everyone was all right. Victoria was in his arms. Suddenly, his whole body was shaking.

"I dreamed your voice," he said hoarsely.

"You didn't dream."

"I didn't leave them, Victoria. I didn't leave. I proved myself. I can be your hero now. I love you. I love you. God…"

"I know, I know. Shh, it's all right. It's all right."

He was on his knees. He buried his face against her stomach as his shoulders began to move and finally he started to sob.

"I love you," she whispered. "I love you."

He cried harder, and behind him, his teammates were suddenly doing the same.

Victoria knelt on the ground beside him. They held each other together and rocked back and forth until the worst of the storm was spent.

Charlie came over. They welcomed him, too.

"Come home," Victoria whispered.

"I will," Brandon promised. "I will."

Epilogue

They stood in front of the grave silently, three heads bowed—one red, one blond, one sun-bleached brown. Behind them, the warm September sun glinted off the vast sloping roof of Tillamook's historic blimp-hangar museum. In front of them, a gentle coastal breeze blew across the waist-high grass, bringing earthy scents of salt water and cow manure.

It was a beautiful day in Tillamook, the weather surprisingly balmy, the sky incredibly blue, the mountains unbearably green. It was a perfect day for revisiting the past.

Maggie, C.J. and Brandon had spent a week in D.C., where Tom Reynolds's lobbying had finally yielded them an interview with the CIA. The information had been good and bad, redeeming and yet unchanging. They had flown back together, each lost in their separate silence.

They had come here, to Maximillian's final resting place in the small dairy community he'd grown up in and been too hasty to leave. Lydia had buried him here, where she could come out often and speak to her only child, whom she'd never understood.

Lydia had stayed home today, wanting to give Maggie, C.J. and Brandon time alone to make their peace. Downtown, in the Shilo Inn, their respective loves also waited. Cain, Tamara and Victoria had taken an instant shine to each other and were currently waging a friendly war over blackjack. Cain felt it was all a matter of statistical tables. Tamara and Victoria had their own ideas.

No one was sure who would lose the most money, but it was bound to be interesting.

In the graveyard, Maggie finally moved. Her gait was slightly rolling. She was seven months pregnant, and her face was full and radiant. Motherhood suited her, and Brandon saw a peace and contentment in his sister's face he'd never found.

She might have been an awkward child once. She might have been the hunch-shouldered, skin-and-bones waif who had followed him and C.J. with longing. But these days, Maggie was gorgeous.

She placed two lilies on their father's grave and stepped aside.

C.J. took his turn. His face was relaxed, his eyes crinkled from the sun and natural good humor. The man was comfortable with his own skin in a way the angry, rebellious boy had never been. Street rat, wiseass C.J. was solid to the core.

He placed ivy on the grave, not a choice Brandon would have made.

Then C.J. stepped back, and it was Brandon's turn.

He stepped forward, feeling his heart beat hard in his chest. What did his siblings see when they looked at him? Was his face still too grim, his cheeks too hollow? Did they see the reserved, stoic English boy who'd sworn never to cry in front of them, the boy who grew too old and too cold trying to hold everyone's life together? Or did they see the man he was becoming—the loyal, generous, caring man who was learning to give as well as receive and who looked at Victoria Meese every morning and saw his hero?

Brandon placed the Tillamook High School yearbook on top of his father's grave. Those were the times to be remembered.

He stepped back, and Maggie broke the silence.

"Well, now we know. Does it make it a difference?"

"Yes," C.J. said.

"Maybe," Brandon replied.

Maggie's lips curved into a smile. "It wasn't about the money," she said at last.

"But it was," Brandon argued. "He married my mom for money, he married your mom for money. Granted, his travel and crazy hours were due to government orders, but Max was still obsessed with the dollar."

"It's not cheap to be James Bond," C.J. said with a shrug. "I mean the movies show spies driving sports cars and wearing tuxedos in Monte Carlo, but frankly, even CIA agents are merely government employees, earning an average wage. So he was enamored with the glamour. So he thirsted for the full spy experience. He was doing the work."

"Assassin," Brandon muttered.

Maggie shook her head. "You heard what the man said—"

"'CIA agents are trained to handle a variety of situations,'" Brandon intoned wryly. Even C.J. was grinning.

"Well, he wasn't an assassin," Maggie insisted. "He was a government agent. He followed orders. Granted, he did things they never will tell us about, but he was an agent and he did lots of…of agent stuff."

C.J. laughed. "Agent stuff." He chortled. "Oh, my, oh, my. How official. Kind of like house-chore stuff except on a global scale."

Maggie scowled and poked him in the arm. "You ought to understand, Marine."

C.J. did his best to appear somber. "Yeah, yeah, I suppose so. He was one of the good guys, you can't knock that, Brandon. We may not have understood him, he may not have been the best father, but at least he was doing something a little bit more meaningful than importing hand-carved wooden figurines."

Brandon still wasn't sure what he thought about that. He went back to staring at the tombstone, and they lapsed into silence.

The CIA had tried to tell them the bits and pieces that it could. Maximillian Ferringer had been one of their top agents. His marriages and children had been of his own volition, and they'd been as surprised as anyone that he'd started families, given his occupation.

He had pursued his best friend, Al Simmons, during the late 1960s, when it was discovered that Al had become a KGB mole. And by Al's admission two months ago, Al had caught him first. Al had killed Ashley Jacobs. Al had killed Maximillian Ferringer. Al had let Bud Irving live because it amused him to watch crazy Bud suffer.

Al swore he had not killed Julia Ferringer. As far as anyone could tell, Brandon's first wife had indeed been shot by a mugger.

Sometimes, that thought gave him comfort. Most of the time, he realized it didn't mean a thing. C.J. and Maggie had been right in the end—discovering the truth hadn't miraculously changed his life. Julia was still dead, and her murder remained tragic. Max was still gone, and still enigmatic.

He'd been a loyal friend and a good patriot. He'd served his country, and according to the CIA, he'd been among their best. Max had grown up without his father, having lost Samuel to Nazi fighter pilots. Apparently, Maximillian had felt that loss much deeper than anyone had realized. And when he'd graduated from high school, he'd convinced his two best friends to join him in pledging their lives to defend their country.

He hadn't been a great father, and he'd been a lousy husband. But then the secrecy and shadows one learned to sustain as an agent probably didn't do well at home. And he'd never had an example of what a father or husband should be.

So there it was. Maximillian the Chameleon. Take him or leave him.

"You know what I think about the most?" Maggie asked abruptly. She looked at them, her sapphire eyes calm, her face tranquil. "I think about that first summer we met. Do you remember that?"

C.J. and Brandon nodded. Maggie smiled.

"I remember C.J. telling Brandon to go to hell. I remember how shocked you looked, Brandon, and how quickly you covered it up." She grinned. "I have lots and lots of memories of C.J. washing his mouth out with soap. You got that down to a science."

"It's all a matter of technique," C.J. said blithely.

"I remember the first time you cried, C.J., and I cried, too. We cried silently and I thought—that's what Max taught us. To cry quietly, so we wouldn't disturb him, so we wouldn't need anything from him." She turned to Brandon and her gaze was somber. "I don't remember you ever crying, Brandon. It's taken me years to realize what an injustice we did to you. We let you play the strong one without ever questioning it, without ever realizing it. Without ever giving you a chance to grieve, as well.''

"That's okay," Brandon said stiffly, feeling suddenly awkward with C.J. and Maggie staring at him. He looked at the tombstone. He shrugged. "I…I was the oldest. I was supposed to be strong."

"Because if you'd been a better child, Max wouldn't have left or hurt us," Maggie filled in softly.

He nodded. Her lips curved sadly.

"Oh, Brandon," she said, "that's exactly how I felt."

"Me, too," C.J. said quietly. "Me, too."

Brandon's throat closed up. He nodded. The tombstone was beginning to blur in front of his eyes.

"It doesn't matter," he said abruptly, and as he said the words, they brought him strength. "I remember the first summer, too, Maggie. I remember the three of us, you so sad, C.J. so angry, and me as frozen as a Popsicle. But look at us now. You have Cain, Maggie. A beautiful house, a gorgeous daughter and a second child on the way. You are a great mother and a happy wife. And you, C.J. If you and Tamara exchange any more of those looks across the room, the bloody carpet will catch on fire. I can already picture you and Tamara dragging two point two tots to the race-tracks.

"And then there is me," Brandon said. "I met Julia, who brought me so much. And now I have Victoria. I'm twice blessed. I'm…*happy*."

Maggie smiled, and it spread across her face. "Then we did it. We grew up perfectly."

"In spite of Max or because of Max?" C.J. asked.

"Both," Brandon said at last. "That's the only answer."

"Both," Maggie agreed.

Brandon drove to the Shilo Inn alone. He stopped along the way, picked a ridiculously huge bouquet of wildflowers and continued.

He found Victoria in their room, just hanging up from talking to Randy. He stood for a moment, looking at her, and thought of how lucky he was.

She sat on the edge of the bed with a smile. Her face had darkened from a summer outdoors. Her eyes were a clear, tranquil blue-gray. She never wore makeup, her hands were a mess of broken fingernails and yellow calluses, and she was still the most beautiful woman Brandon knew.

His heart swelled in his chest.

Belatedly, he thrust out the flowers, a tangled bouquet of honeysuckle, poppies and wild roses. "For you. Picked them myself."

"Oh, my." Victoria inhaled deeply, then coughed violently. "Ah, yes, that Tillamook eau de toilette. Guess what? Randy showed Libby. We may have a buyer."

"Victoria, that's great." He crossed to her and decided the occasion was worthy of a hug, then a kiss, then a deeper kiss. It was several moments before either of them drew back. He tucked her hair behind her ear, his arm still around her waist. "Randy must be thrilled."

"Ready to take full credit, of course," she assured him. "He deserves it, though. He worked hard."

Randy had spent most of his summer training Libby with Victoria. When Brandon wasn't fighting fires, he would spend his morning watching mother and son together and doing odd jobs around the ranch. Randy had inherited Victoria's touch with horses. Someday, he would be a great trainer, too, if his major league baseball career didn't get in the way.

"I've been thinking," Brandon said quietly.

"Uh-oh."

"Exactly. Fire season is over now. I'm too old to be a permanent employee. I need something to do."

"I see." Victoria's voice was hesitant. By mutual agreement, they rarely spoke of life after September. Though there had been times lately when Brandon would catch Victoria staring at him with those questions in her eyes. And sometimes, right after they made love, she would drift into a silence he couldn't penetrate, and he could feel her pain and love hovering beneath the surface.

"I've been thinking that an old geezer like me should settle down."

"Really?"

"Yes. City life is no good, you know. And I don't think I could do Everest again. I'm thinking I need a warm, cozy house. Maybe a ranch where I could work hard to earn my keep, dabble in investments on the side. Of course, I'm going to need a woman to keep me in line—we both know I'm incorrigible on my own."

"Absolutely."

"And I've been wanting to work on my pitching. My math skills, as well. It's very easy to get rusty, and there's nothing so tragic as forgetting how to multiply mixed numerals."

"It would be a shame."

"So I was thinking. Where could I find a nice ranch in need of some assistance, a beautiful woman willing to keep me straight and a sports-happy eight-year-old with an incredible pitching arm?"

"I have an idea," Victoria said.

"Really? How perfect!"

Her fingers were sliding up his shirt. "For the right price, I might even tell you." She found the top button and slid it open.

"Yes, well, I understand that. Someone told me once that

ranch owners and single mothers can't be bought with any
old trinket, either, so I've given this some thought.''

Suddenly, he was down on one knee. Victoria gasped,
grew flustered, then went soft all over. He thought he would
be nervous, but he discovered he'd never felt steadier as he
looked into her blue-gray eyes.

He took her hand. He withdrew the ring box he'd been
carrying for two weeks. He opened it to show the finest
opal he could buy. It was brilliant with red and green fire,
sparkling and hissing with a life of its own. It reminded
him of Victoria and suited her better than any diamond
would've done.

''Victoria,'' he asked somberly, ''will you take on an
unemployed federal employee, fire-scarred and rough
around the edges? Will you love me forever and share your
home and son with me? Will you make me breakfast again
wearing only your apron?''

''Okay.''

He slipped the ring onto her finger. He folded his hand
over hers. ''And I will love you forever, Victoria. I will
give you all of me, my heart, my soul, my hopes and my
despair. I will share myself one hundred percent, giving
you my time and attention, and if I ever shut you out, I
hope you kick my butt to here and back so I will know to
do better. I love you, Victoria, and I want to make you
happy.

''I want to be the kind of husband and father who stays
forever.''

''Okay,'' she said again, and she was crying.

He rose and pulled her into his arms. And it was right
and it was sweet and the fierceness that gripped his chest
made him strong. He saw Julia and he saw Max. He saw
his bitter mother who'd never learned how to move on. And

he knew he'd learned enough. He'd become the man he wanted to be.

"You make me whole," he whispered to Victoria. "You make me whole."

* * * * *

Alicia Scott knows how to win fans!
As a special treat, the first of
THE GUINESS GANG, *AT THE MIDNIGHT HOUR,*
will be available next month in our
BESTSELLING AUTHORS IN THE SPOTLIGHT
promotion. So check the stores this March and snap
up Alicia Scott's wonderful novel at a terrific price!

Silhouette Romance is proud to present
Virgin Brides, a brand-new monthly
promotional series by some of the bestselling
and most beloved authors in the romance genre.

In March '98, look for the very first
Virgin Brides novel,

THE PRINCESS BRIDE by Diana Palmer.

Just turn the page for an exciting preview of
Diana Palmer's thrilling new tale...

Chapter One

Tiffany saw him in the distance, riding the big black stallion. It was spring, and that meant roundup. It was not unusual to see the owner of the Lariat ranch in the saddle at dawn lending a hand to rope a stray calf or help work the branding. Kingman Marshall kept fit with ranch work, and despite the fact that he shared an office and a business partnership with Tiffany's father in land and cattle, his staff didn't see a lot of him.

This year, they were using helicopters to mass the farflung cattle, and they had a corral set up on a wide, flat stretch of land where they could dip the cattle, check them, cut out the calves for branding and separate them from their mothers. It was physically demanding work, and no job for a tenderfoot. King wouldn't let Tiffany near it, but it wasn't a front row seat at the corral that she wanted. If she could just get his attention away from the milling cattle on the wide, rolling plain that led to the Guadalupe River, if he'd just look her way...

Tiffany stood up on a rickety lower rung of the gray

wood fence, avoiding the sticky barbed wire, and waved her Stetson at him. She was a picture of young elegance in her tan jodhpurs and sexy pink silk blouse and high black boots. She was a debutante. Her father, Harrison Blair, was King's business partner and friend, and if she chased King, her father encouraged her. It would be a marriage made in heaven. That is, if she could find some way to convince King of it. He was elusive and quite abrasively masculine. It might take more than a young lady of almost twenty-one with a sheltered, monied background to land him. But, then, Tiffany had confidence in herself; she was beautiful and intelligent.

Her long black hair hung to her waist in back, and she refused to have it cut. It suited her tall, slender figure and made an elegant frame for her soft, oval face and wide green eyes and creamy complexion. She had a sunny smile, and it never faded. Tiffany was always full of fire, burning with a love of life that her father often said had been reflected in her long-dead mother.

"King!" she called, her voice clear, and it carried in the early-morning air.

He looked toward her. Even at that distance, she could see that cold expression in his pale blue eyes, on his lean, hard face with its finely chiseled features. He was a rich man. He worked hard, and he played hard. He had women, Tiffany knew so, but he was nothing if not discreet. He was a man's man, and he lived like one. There was no playful boy in that tall, fit body. He'd grown up years ago, the boyishness driven out of him by a rich, alcoholic father who demanded blind obedience from the only child of his shallow, runaway wife.

She watched him ride toward her, easy elegance in the saddle. He reined in at the fence, smiling down at her with faint arrogance.

"You're out early, tidbit," he remarked in a deep, velvety voice with just a hint of Texas drawl.

"I'm going to be twenty-one tomorrow," she said pertly. "I'm having a big bash to celebrate, and you have to come. Black tie, and don't you dare bring anyone. You're mine, for the whole evening. It's my birthday and on my birthday I want presents—and you're it. My big present."

His dark eyebrows lifted with amused indulgence. "You might have told me sooner that I was going to be a birthday present," he said. "I have to be in Omaha early Saturday."

"You have your own plane," she reminded him. "You can fly."

"I have to sleep sometimes," he murmured.

"I wouldn't touch that line with a ten-foot pole," she drawled, peeking at him behind her long lashes. "Will you come?"

He lit a cigarette, took a long draw and blew it out with slight impatience. "Little girls and their little whims," he mused. "All right, I'll whirl you around the floor and toast your coming-of-age, but I won't stay. I can't spare the time."

"You'll work yourself to death," she complained, and then became solemn. "You're only thirty-four and you look forty."

"Times are hard, honey," he mused, smiling at the intensity in that glowering young face. "We've had low prices and drought. It's all I can do to keep my financial head above water."

"You could take the occasional break," she advised. "And I don't mean a night on the town. You could get away from it all and just rest."

"They're full up at the Home," he murmured, grinning at her exasperated look. "Honey, I can't afford vacations, not with times so hard. What are you wearing for this coming-of-age party?'' he asked to divert her.

"A dream of a dress. White silk, very low in front, with diamanté straps and a white gardenia in my hair.'' She laughed.

He pursed his lips. He might as well humor her. "That sounds dangerous," he said softly.

"It will be," she promised, teasing him with her eyes. "You might even notice that I've grown up.''

He frowned a little. That flirting wasn't new, but it was disturbing lately. He found himself avoiding little Miss Blair, without really understanding why. His body stirred even as he looked at her, and he moved restlessly in the saddle. She was years too young for him, and a virgin to boot, according to her doting, sheltering father. All those years of obsessive parental protection had led to a very immature and unavailable girl. It wouldn't do to let her too close. Not that anyone ever got close to Kingman Marshall, not even his infrequent lovers. He had good reason to keep women at a distance. His upbringing had taught him too well that women were untrustworthy and treacherous.

"What time?" he asked on a resigned note.

"About seven?"

He paused thoughtfully for a minute. "Okay." He tilted his wide-brimmed hat over his eyes. "But only for an hour or so.''

"Great!"

He didn't say goodbye. Of course, he never did. He wheeled the stallion and rode off, man and horse so damn arrogant that she felt like flinging something at his tall head. He was delicious, she thought, and her body felt hot all over just looking at him. On the ground he towered over her, lean and hard-muscled and sexy as all hell. She loved watching him.

With a long, unsteady sigh, she finally turned away and remounted her mare. She wondered sometimes why she bothered hero-worshiping such a man. One of these days he'd get married and she'd just die. God forbid that he'd marry anybody but her!

That was when the first shock of reality hit her squarely between the eyes. Why, she had to ask herself, would a man like that, a mature man with all the worldly advantages, want a young and inexperienced woman like herself at his side? The question worried her so badly that she almost lost control of her mount.

The truth of her situation was unpalatable and a little frightening. She'd never even considered a life without King. What if she had to?

She rode home slowly, a little depressed because she'd had to work so hard just to get King to agree to come to her party. And still haunting her was that unpleasant speculation about a future without King…

But she perked up when she thought of the evening ahead. King didn't come to the house often, only when her father wanted to talk business away from work, or occasionally for drinks with some of her father's acquaintances. To have him come to a party was new and stimulating. Especially if it ended the way she planned. She had her sights well and truly set on the big rancher. Now all she had to do was take aim!

* * * * *

Return to the Towers!

In March
New York Times bestselling author

NORA ROBERTS

brings us to the Calhouns' fabulous
Maine coast mansion and reveals the
tragic secrets hidden there for generations.

For all his degrees, Professor Max Quartermain has a
lot to learn about love—and luscious Lilah Calhoun is
just the woman to teach him. Ex-cop Holt Bradford is
as prickly as a thornbush—until Suzanna Calhoun's
special touch makes love blossom in his heart.
And all of them are caught in the race to solve
the generations-old mystery of a priceless
lost necklace...and a timeless love.

Lilah and Suzanna
THE
Calhoun Women

A special 2-in-1 edition containing
FOR THE LOVE OF LILAH and
SUZANNA'S SURRENDER

Available at your favorite retail outlet.

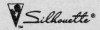

Take 4 bestselling love stories FREE

Plus get a FREE surprise gift!

Special Limited-time Offer

Mail to Silhouette Reader Service™

3010 Walden Avenue
P.O. Box 1867
Buffalo, N.Y. 14240-1867

YES! Please send me 4 free Silhouette Intimate Moments® novels and my free surprise gift. Then send me 6 brand-new novels every month, which I will receive months before they appear in bookstores. Bill me at the low price of $3.57 each plus 25¢ delivery and applicable sales tax, if any.* That's the complete price and a savings of over 10% off the cover prices—quite a bargain! I understand that accepting the books and gift places me under no obligation ever to buy any books. I can always return a shipment and cancel at any time. Even if I never buy another book from Silhouette, the 4 free books and the surprise gift are mine to keep forever.

245 SEN CF2V

Name	(PLEASE PRINT)	
Address	Apt. No.	
City	State	Zip

This offer is limited to one order per household and not valid to present Silhouette Intimate Moments® subscribers. *Terms and prices are subject to change without notice. Sales tax applicable in N.Y.

UMOM-696   ©1990 Harlequin Enterprises Limited

BESTSELLING AUTHORS
IN THE SPOTLIGHT

WE'RE SHINING THE SPOTLIGHT ON SIX OF OUR STARS!

Harlequin and Silhouette have selected stories from several of their bestselling authors to give you six sensational reads. These star-powered romances are bound to please!

THERE'S A PRICE TO PAY FOR STARDOM... AND IT'S LOW

$1.99 U.S.
$2.50 CAN.
Special Offer

As a special offer, these six outstanding books are available from Harlequin and Silhouette for only $1.99 in the U.S. and $2.50 in Canada. Watch for these titles:

At the Midnight Hour—**Alicia Scott**
Joshua and the Cowgirl—**Sherryl Woods**
Another Whirlwind Courtship—**Barbara Boswell**
Madeleine's Cowboy—**Kristine Rolofson**
Her Sister's Baby—**Janice Kay Johnson**
One and One Makes Three—**Muriel Jensen**

Available in March 1998
at your favorite retail outlet.

PBAIS

SANDRA STEFFEN

**Continues the
twelve-book series—
36 Hours—in February 1998
with Book Eight**

MARRIAGE BY CONTRACT

Nurse Bethany Kent could think of only one man who could make her dream come true: Dr. Tony Petrocelli, the man who had helped her save the life of the infant she desperately wanted to adopt. As husband and wife, they could provide the abandoned baby with a loving home. But could they provide each other with more than just a convenient marriage?

For Tony and Bethany and *all* the residents of Grand Springs, Colorado, the storm-induced blackout was just the beginning of 36 Hours that changed *everything!* You won't want to miss a single book.

Available at your favorite retail outlet.

**Make a Valentine's date
for the premiere of**

◆ HARLEQUIN® **Movies**

starting February 14, 1998 with

Debbie Macomber's

This Matter of

Marriage

on  **the movie channel** ᵗᵐᶜ

Just tune in to **The Movie Channel** the **second Saturday night** of every month at 9:00 p.m. EST to join us, and be swept away by the sheer thrill of romance brought to life. Watch for details of upcoming movies—in books, in your television viewing guide and in stores.

If you are not currently a subscriber to The Movie Channel, simply call your local cable or satellite provider for more details. Call today, and don't miss out on the romance!

the movie channel ᵗᵐᶜ   ◆ HARLEQUIN™
100% pure movies.   ᵀᴹ 𝓜akes any time special.™
100% pure fun.